774

SASHA'S SECRET (SPECIAL FORCES: OPERATION ALPHA)

SPECTRUM SECURITY INC #2

CHRISTIE ADAMS

Dear Readers,

Welcome to the Special Forces: Operation Alpha Fan-Fiction world!

If you are new to this amazing world, in a nutshell the author wrote a story using one or more of my characters in it. Sometimes that character has a major role in the story, and other times they are only mentioned briefly. This is perfectly legal and allowable because they are going through Aces Press to publish the story.

This book is entirely the work of the author who wrote it. While I might have assisted with brainstorming and other ideas about which of my characters to use, I didn't have any part in the process or writing or editing the story.

I'm proud and excited that so many authors loved my characters enough that they wanted to write them into their own story. Thank you for supporting them, and me!

READ ON!

Xoxo

Susan Stoker

For Helen.

Thank you for giving Rocco both his name and his nonna.

CHAPTER 1

When Rocco Equizi stepped out of the air-conditioned terminal of the small regional airport, several months' worth of ever-increasing tension finally dropped away, leaving him with the sense that this transfer to the US arm of Spectrum Security truly was the fresh start he craved.

The jury, however, was still out on whether staying with Spectrum for the long term was the right decision for him. Although his last assignment had gone well, Rocco had come out of it feeling restless and wondering if it was time to move on. With a generous bonus burning a hole in his pocket—his reward for keeping his somewhat notorious, headstrong principal alive during her visit to London—he'd been tempted to use it on getting lost in some obscure corner of the world. Possibly permanently.

Before he could do anything about it, though, his boss had hauled his ass into her office for a friendly chat. The last thing he'd expected was the offer of a close protection position in the States.

"Don't get me wrong, Rocco," Ros Northwood had said. "I have plenty of work for you and I'd be happy to give you your choice of assignments, but I suspect there's more going on here than another bodyguard gig can cure. You're a great asset to the business, and I don't want to lose you to the competition, so what can I do to help?"

He hadn't known how to answer, given he wasn't sure what the problem was, unless it was the same problem that had dogged him for years, but he doubted it was solely responsible for his current disquiet. So Ros had carried on talking, and when she'd mentioned the operation they were launching in Texas, a spark of interest had come to life inside him.

"You probably wouldn't have had much to do with our long-distance CFO, but he was the one who came up with a radical solution to the issue of where to site our US base. I happen to know he's looking for a close protection expert for a high-profile client. Do you think an equally radical change of scenery might help?"

"Would it be a permanent move?" Interested though he was, Rocco hadn't been sure he was ready for that level of commitment.

"Leaving aside the formalities, from a company point of view, it's as permanent as you want it to be. If you don't want to stay on after your first assignment over there, there's nothing to prevent you from coming straight back, if that's what you want. Take a few days to think about it, Rocco. There's no pressure on you to go—the decision's entirely yours."

So he'd made that decision, and here he was, ready to take on whatever his new boss was going to throw at him. Or rather, whoever. "High-profile" could mean anything. He'd find out soon enough.

Rocco flexed his shoulders. Business class for the transatlantic flight had enabled him to stretch out, but cramming his six-foot-one-inch frame into the economy-class seat for the flight to the regional airport had been a challenge. Fortunately, the drive from there to his ultimate destination wouldn't take too long.

Although Nick Blackmore had offered to meet him at the airport, Rocco had declined, in favor of making his own way out to the ranch. They'd Skyped a couple of times since Rocco had made his decision to head across the Atlantic, but at the end of a very long day, he hadn't relished the prospect of making small talk on the final leg of the journey. All he wanted to do was throw his bags into the trunk of the rental SUV, program his destination into the GPS, and concentrate on the road.

On the flight over, he'd used some of the time to review his schedule for the first few days. One particular item on the agenda had attracted his attention, and that was gaining his license to carry a concealed weapon. Good. He could have done with that a couple of times on his last assignment, but… different country, different laws.

They'd allowed a few days for orientation, dealing with the formalities, and generally acclimatizing to the change of surroundings. Rocco didn't expect it to take too long—thanks to his training and experience, he was nothing if not adaptable.

Although the drive wasn't long and the GPS made navigation easy, Rocco was still relieved when his vehicle's headlights swung off the road and lit up the wide gateway to Honey Fields Ranch, a name that still seemed at odds with its function as the headquarters for a security organization. When he'd checked the itinerary for his journey, he'd even asked if it was a joke.

Now, he was about to find out for himself.

There was a certain surreal quality to driving up the approach road to Honey Fields Ranch, especially in the dark, with the lights picking out fence posts and tree trunks on the way. When he'd realized he needed a change of scenery, he'd never imagined the notion would lead to adding another few thousand miles to the distance between him and his father. Given the way their last conversation had ended, that was no bad thing.

At the end of the approach road, he found his destination. Illuminated by powerful floodlights, the ranch house was a sprawling structure, all wood, stone and glass, and an impressive centerpiece for the assorted buildings whose outlines lurked in the shadows beyond the circle of light.

Rocco pulled up close to the main house, alongside a pair of black Cadillac Escalades and a midnight-blue Dodge Ram pickup. All three looked near enough brand new. As he exited the vehicle, footsteps on the wooden porch alerted him to the presence of another.

"You found us, then. How was your journey?"

His new boss strode toward him, hand outstretched in greeting. In person, Nick Blackmore was more relaxed and approachable than Rocco had expected, and judging by the gray, open-necked shirt, work-worn jeans, and dusty cowboy boots, had pretty much gone native in a matter of months. The only thing missing was the Stetson.

The man's grasp was firm, cool and dry, projecting an image of relaxed confidence. Maybe making small talk with his new CO wouldn't have been such a hardship after all. "It was good, thank you, sir. Better than the average troop transport."

The CEO of Spectrum Security Inc. raised an eyebrow and chuckled. "Glad to hear it. And you can forget the 'sir'. It's Nick. We're very informal around here. No, leave your bags where they are. I'll take you in and introduce you, then show you where you'll be staying—for the next few days, anyway, while we take care of your induction. Dinner'll be ready in about an hour. It'll give you time to freshen up, and then afterwards, we'll leave you in peace until the morning. You okay with that?"

Rocco gave a mental shrug. It was all the same to him—if the boss wanted him to start his assignment right now or a week from now, then he'd run with it. "Sounds fine to me."

He followed Nick into the ranch house, into a great, sprawling, open-plan space that incorporated several functions in one. The décor reflected the rustic exterior, but Rocco didn't have a chance to take much more in, due to the approach of a petite woman with short blonde hair and a warm, vibrant smile. She too held out her hand as she neared him.

"You must be Rocco. I'm Charity Blackmore. Welcome to Honey Fields."

Nick coughed. "I was about to introduce you properly."

She shook her head, gave her husband a long-suffering look, and stood on her toes to kiss his cheek. "Don't be such a stuffed shirt, hon. You're not guarding the Queen of England now."

Rocco pressed his lips together to quell the urge to smile. When he'd been informed who he'd be working for, he'd done some research. As an officer in the Household Cavalry, Nick Blackmore had done exactly that during his career in the British Army—along with having an exemplary service record in theater—whereas Rocco's former role in the SAS had been rather more clandestine and a hell of a lot less ceremonial. "It's a pleasure to meet you, ma'am."

"Charity, please. Can I get you something to drink?"

He could use a glass of water, but Rocco was reluctant to indulge in anything that might extend his time in Nick and Charity's home. They might run the business from here, but it was still the place where they lived, and that made him a tad uncomfortable. "No, I'm good, thank you."

She nodded. "Okay then. You should find everything you

need in the cabin, but if there's anything else, please let me know, and we'll see you at dinner."

"Thank you."

"Okay. Let's get you settled in." Nick picked up a key fob and a small envelope from the top of the nearest cabinet. "We'll drive over. You can follow me in your rental."

Nick took one of the Escalades, and Rocco drove behind him. The distance wasn't that far—he could jog it in a few minutes and not break into a sweat. He was also pretty damn sure Nick could too, which begged the question, why had he chosen to drive?

On arriving at the cabin, Nick waited at the door, while Rocco retrieved his luggage from the SUV.

"We've started to implement a security upgrade around here." Nick extracted a key card from the envelope and held it up. He inserted it in a slot in the reader unit, then tapped a code on the numeric panel on the display screen. "This one's been programmed for you. The code's on the envelope. You'll find a similar unit inside, but on that one, you can change your access code."

"You didn't go with biometrics?"

"We evaluated that option, but concluded we'd be using a sledgehammer to crack a walnut, at least for the time being. Right, I'll let you settle in, and we'll see you in an hour, but one more thing before I go." He held out the key fob for the Escalade. "Your company car. Let me have the key for the rental, and we can make arrangements to return it."

Rocco could have sworn there hadn't been anything about a company vehicle in his contract but he wasn't about to argue. "Thanks. Is there anything else I need to be aware of?"

Nick shook his head. "Not right now. We'll make a start on the details in your orientation tomorrow. I'm glad you decided to join us here, Rocco. I hope you'll find the work interesting and worth the upheaval."

And with that, he drove off in the SUV, leaving Rocco to silence, his new home... and old thoughts. One thing was for sure—his new billet was a damn sight better than the accommodation at the likes of Camp Bastion. Once he started his assignment, though, he'd be spending little time, if any, around here. He'd be wherever his principal was, until he was no longer required.

And then what? Hopefully another assignment, and then another and another, anything to maintain the extra distance from his old man. London was only three hours from Sicily, and that put him too damn close to his father's disapproval of his life choices. Dario's passionate, headache-inducing defense of the vineyard and winery that had been in the Equizi family for generations still reverberated through Rocco's memory, as did his tenacious expectation that Rocco would take over the business one day.

No fucking way was that ever going to happen. Hell would freeze over before he'd willingly choose a dead-end existence working the land the way his father did.

Rocco stifled a yawn. A demand for sleep was gnawing at the edges of his consciousness but he wasn't about to give in to it. He'd get through dinner with his boss and his wife, and then he'd crash.

After changing the code on his key card, Rocco headed for the kitchen. A quick look around confirmed his initial impression of the standard to which it had been fitted out. The huge refrigerator was stocked with the basics, and the water from the dispenser in the door was chilled to perfection.

Boots off, Rocco sprawled on the brown leather couch. He glanced at the bags, still sitting where he'd dropped them. There was little point in making himself too much at home here. If all went according to plan, a week from now he'd be far from the cabin and fully focused on protecting his principal.

All he had to do was get through that week, starting with dinner with his new boss. Then he'd unpack his clothes and deal with any creases. No matter what, his personal standards wouldn't allow him to turn up for a new assignment looking like an unmade bed.

Around three hours later, as he made his way back to his accommodation, Rocco was considerably more at ease than he'd been before dinner. With food as the icebreaker, conversation had flowed freely, and he'd even joined in with the laughter as Nick and Charity entertained him with the trials and tribulations of trying to set up a multi-million dollar business and get married—and in Nick's case, acclimating to Texas as well.

However, the major success of the evening was the file Nick had reluctantly handed over, in advance of providing Rocco with access to a company laptop and cell phone. He'd tried to insist Rocco wasn't on the clock yet, but as far as Rocco was concerned, he'd been on company time since he'd boarded the plane back in London. When he went to meet his principal, he wanted to hit the ground running, and the sooner he made a start on what would enable him to do that, the better.

The physical file was mostly a hard copy of what was held on the electronic case file on the company database, prepared by Charity in case Rocco wasn't able to connect to their private network at any time. She was some sort of IT specialist, although when she and Nick had first met, she'd been running her own coffee shop. Rocco had a feeling there was a lot more to that story than met the eye.

After grabbing a tall glass of chilled water, he stretched out on the couch and started on the file. His top-level brief was to review the security arrangements at his principal's home in the light of recent threats, and provide personal protection when she left the property, so every piece of background information he could get his hands on would be useful.

The information pack consisted of various sections, including dozens of examples of the social media posts that had caused alarm in the first place. He skimmed through some of them, noting the vicious nature of the increasingly menacing threats. They weren't really his area of expertise, but for now, Rocco was more interested in the people anyway.

His client was Linzi Suto. The name seemed vaguely familiar, and as he continued to read, he soon discovered why. She was the latest pop sensation, a talented but undeniably egocentric diva, if the majority of the news clippings were to be believed.

He sighed. That was all he needed—another temperamental principal. Nothing he could do about it now, but that was it—no more impulsive, willful women. He didn't need them in his life. Not for work, and hell, not for play. His last relationship had ended with an explosive argument where he'd been accused of sleeping with the woman for whom he'd been providing close protection services.

Oh, the irony. Had his girlfriend but known. His principal in that case would much rather have slept with his now-ex than him.

He leafed through the handful of photographs of Linzi. There were a couple of publicity shots, all posed and perfect, not a hair out of place and with her face plastered with makeup, and some paparazzi images, taken against a crush of fans when she was arriving at some gig or other. Granted, she was pretty enough, and clearly talented enough to make a significant impact in the fickle world of show business. Age twenty-two, a Texas native, five-two, around a hundred pounds—maybe—with platinum blonde hair and blue eyes. Both parents still alive. On the negative side, there were reports of her throwing a few public tantrums too many for Rocco's peace of mind. That kind of behavior attracted attention, and in spite of what those who lived their lives in the public eye might think, not all attention was good.

He continued through the file. It appeared he was going to be plying his trade at an estate situated near the state capital, Austin. He grimaced when he came to a description of the riverside location. Although it was characterized as a private compound comprising three residential properties with several ancillary structures, with that much riverfront open to any passing shithead in a boat, securing it effectively would be... problematic. Rocco filed the details away for further investigation once he was on site.

The file also contained information about those closest to Linzi. Gerry Brookes was her manager. He'd been around the business a few years, handled quite a few stars in that time, but was now a one-trick pony—the pony being Linzi. Fifty-something, twice divorced and currently single, he had the look of a man who'd partied hard in his time. Rocco didn't see anything that made him particularly uneasy, but again, he'd check the man out thoroughly once he was on site.

Rocco yawned. He checked the time—add on the time difference between his current location and London, and he'd gone well over twenty-four hours without sleep. Bed was beckoning, and getting some decent rest before dealing with the bureaucracy that was on his agenda for tomorrow was probably a good idea. Sometimes it was too easy to slip into the routines they'd followed in Afghanistan and forget that that life, with all its risks and deprivations, was a million miles away. He didn't have to call on his inner reserves for days on end anymore.

On the other hand, he didn't like leaving things unfinished. He quickly scanned the pages relating to the individuals Linzi had on staff at the estate, until he came to the last—Sasha Morgan, Linzi's assistant for the last two years, and probably the most significant of all. To make things interesting, before he turned the page, he had a small bet with himself about what she'd be like—Linzi Mk. II, a small-town girl from the Midwest who had aspirations of stardom but didn't have the talent to make it big. Probably a similar age, probably blonde, probably a virtual carbon copy of Linzi. Maybe they'd even attended school together at some point.

What the hell. He was going to have to deal with the woman, so he might as well get a feel for what he could expect. Sure it would be the worst, he turned the page.

The image in front of him was stunning. Sasha Morgan was not what he'd expected at all. Her hair was blonde all right, but it was frosted in half a dozen subtly different shades—as subtle as her make up. Her lips, a perfect shade of pink, summoned him to her, filling him with a volcanic urge to kiss her not only until there was no trace of her lipstick left, but until the last breath left his body.

What mesmerized him most, though, were her eyes. Hazel flecked with green wasn't an unusual combination, but the longer he studied the image, the more he surrendered to the hypnotic depths of her gaze. The confidence she radiated blew him away.

One thing was for sure—she wasn't the scatterbrained ingénue he'd anticipated. This was a sophisticated, cultured woman, mature enough to have seen enough of the world to regard it with a healthy dose of realism—someone who knew life wasn't all roses and rainbows.

The more Rocco studied the photo of Sasha Morgan, the more his curiosity—and more—about her was aroused. A man would have to be dead not to be affected by such intense beauty. She was flawless. For a man who'd so recently sworn off relationships, he was finding it all too easy to imagine her beneath him as he made love to her.

He wanted her. The visceral reaction ripped through the veneer of civilization and connected with every primal instinct he possessed. And while his head tried to remind him of his assignment and pound some sense into him, those instincts roared and raged, threatening to tear apart anything and everything that stood between Rocco and making this woman his.

The mission would come first, as it always did, but life was too short and there was something about Sasha he couldn't ignore. It might be a cliché, but he truly was drawn to her like a moth to a flame. If there was half a chance there could be something between them, he'd seize it with both hands, and then they could be consumed in the blaze together.

CHAPTER 2

"The new guy'll be there Monday."

Sasha Morgan frowned. In another life, she'd have told the asshole that wasn't acceptable and ripped him a new one. Why the hell wasn't he taking this seriously?

Why the hell wasn't he taking *her* seriously?

Because you're a personal assistant now, and the Agency is history. Suck it up.

"Monday? Can't they send someone sooner, Gerry?"

Gerry Brookes was Linzi's manager, and Sasha was not his biggest fan. She never had been. There was something about the man that made her antsy, and it bothered her that, even now, she couldn't put her finger on what it was. His flippant attitude to this possible threat to his client's safety bothered her even more, especially since he hadn't Skyped her this time. She could usually tell a lot from reading his expression, but all she had to go on was his voice.

"They don't have anyone else available, and this Equizi guy's supposed to be the best."

"Equizi, huh? I thought you said we were getting a Brit."

Sasha didn't just think it—she knew it. She remembered exactly what Gerry had said during their previous conversation on the matter.

"We are. Half of him, anyway. Not sure which half, though."

Gerry laughed as if he'd cracked the funniest joke in the history of stand-up comedy. Sasha rolled her eyes. The man gave her hives at the best of times, and this was not the best of times. "What's that supposed to mean?"

"His passport says he's a Brit, but with a name like that, he must be half-Italian or something. Only just arrived in the country yesterday. I guess there are formalities they have to observe."

Which they wouldn't if Gerry had taken her advice and contacted a local company. And by local, Sasha meant anywhere in the continental United States. "So what made you hire a start-up staffed by non-US citizens?"

That made her even more antsy. Texas was awash with hundreds of private security contractors with a proven track record in the field of VIP and celebrity protection. Gerry could have gotten a recommendation from any of his dozens of contacts in the entertainment business, yet he'd gone for Spectrum Security Inc., an off-shoot of a similarly named outfit in the United Kingdom. As soon as he'd dropped the name, Sasha had picked it up and run with it, to carry out her own research. Though what little she'd been able to find made interesting reading, the very fact there was so little had done nothing to improve her peace of mind. The damn company might as well be a start-up.

"Staffed by *Brits*. You know… all that *God Save The Queen*, cups of hot tea—why the hell would anyone drink hot tea?—and calling soccer 'football' shit. They add that touch of class."

Sasha doubted Gerry would know class if it kicked him in his well-padded ass. And *class*? Really? What the hell good would *that* do in the face of a deadly weapon?

Which reminded her. "If he's a Brit, he won't know one end of a firearm from the other. How's he supposed to protect Linzi? Throw a cup of hot tea over a potential kidnapper?"

"Ah, that's where you're wrong. He's ex-military."

Sasha resisted the opportunity to roll her eyes. British ex-military probably meant he was one of those toy soldiers in the pretty red uniforms who stood guard outside Buckingham Palace. If they wanted someone who was ex-military, why in the name of all that was chocolate didn't they get a SEAL, or a former member of Delta Force, or a US Marine? Someone with some real military skills. She sighed. "Okay, but is he any good?"

"I told you—he's the best. Look, Linzi's not going anywhere for the next couple weeks, and nothing's gonna happen there. He'll have a chance to check everything out. It'll be fine."

Sure—she'd heard that one before, usually just before the shit hit the fan. "If you don't mind, I'll reserve judgment until I find out more about him." If what she'd found out about the company was minimal, what she could uncover about the man was likely to be non-existent.

At the other end of the phone, there was an indistinct sound of mild irritation. "Sash, that ain't your job any more, honey. You're a secretary now."

Now she had two more reasons to punch his ever-loving lights out. *No one* called her "Sash", and as for *honey*... Actually, it was three reasons, because she was nobody's secretary, either, no matter what her job description said.

As she ended the call, Sasha's mind drifted back almost

two years, to the meeting that had set her on her present course.

"I know she's a brat—hell, the whole world's seen it on social media—but she's..." Her supervisor shrugged.

"Family. I get it. I'll watch out for her."

He nodded, relief all over his face. "Her manager's in on this, too—or will be when I call him. You ever find anything that doesn't seem right, talk to him, and we'll take it from there. You okay with all of this?"

"Sure. It's a win-win, right? You have someone to keep an eye on your goddaughter, and I don't have to prep a résumé and attend a bunch of interviews to get a job."

Logically, it had made sense. The time had come for her to leave the Agency, but letting go hadn't been so easy, in spite of her emotional state at the time. A decade and a half had given her a lot of memories, not all bad, and for all that time, her job had been her life. Taking on the role as Linzi Suto's assistant had seemed like a good way to ease herself into civilian life—just as well she had, since they were now going to have a British ex-soldier prowling around.

Whatever the reasoning behind his recruitment, the guy was going to need a room in the staff wing. As she added a note to her growing to-do list, every professional instinct was telling Sasha to make sure the suite allocated to him was close to hers. She might have left the Agency behind, but she hadn't forgotten her training. For all any of them knew, they could be letting a hit man take up residence, and Sasha had no intention of breaking the news to her former supervisor that some harm had come to Linzi on her watch.

Because like it or not, if the worst-case scenario became reality, Sasha would call on all her skills and expertise to ensure Linzi remained safe, no matter what—if anything—the Brit was bringing to the table.

And if necessary, if the Brit failed, and if even her skills and experience came up short, she still had some contacts she could call on who'd be more than happy to lend a helping hand.

Remembering the circumstances under which they'd first met, Sasha allowed herself a small smile. It was about time she caught up with those guys…

Every day since he'd arrived in Texas, Rocco's preconceptions about the state had been challenged, but never more so than when he saw the sheer opulence of the mansion at the end of the winding, access-controlled road that led to the center of the twenty-acre riverside property. The place screamed wealth, and at a guess, was probably worth the kind of money he wouldn't even see in a hundred lifetimes.

Rocco parked the Escalade in one of the marked spaces, alongside a handful of vehicles that included some premier European marques, including a Bugatti and a Lamborghini. They suited the Italianate appearance of the mansion, with its light, honey-cream walls and red-tiled roof. The irony wasn't lost on him—he'd come all this way to escape his roots, only to be confronted by an environment drenched in their influence.

He'd been around too many wealthy clients to be impressed by ostentatious displays, but what did bring him up short was the sight of the woman with long, blonde hair emerging from the mansion's portico. Every sense went on alert as she strolled in his direction, a stunning beauty in an ice-blue, button-up shirt and ivory slacks, and the living embodiment of his dreams from the first moment he'd seen her image.

In the flesh, Sasha Morgan was even more striking than the woman in his fantasies, from her hair glinting in the sunlight, to the graceful sway of her hips and the stylish heels that adorned her feet. His body responded on a primal level to each confident step that brought her closer to him, letting him know in no uncertain terms that it had no intention of giving up the fight for dominance. He exited the vehicle's luxurious, air-conditioned interior, pulled on his jacket and rounded the front of the Escalade to meet her.

"Ms. Morgan. It's a pleasure to meet you." Rocco offered his hand in greeting.

Sasha took it in a cool, firm grip that echoed the confidence in her approach. "Mr. Equizi. Welcome to Casa Millefiori. Won't you come in?"

He followed her inside. Impressions of space and light bombarded him, along with stone and wood, and the intrinsic coolness of marble. The interior was designed to a standard to match the exterior, a fact that was even easier to appreciate when they reached a plush office. By the way Sasha took up a position by the ivory leather executive chair behind the sleek desk with its state-of-the-art computer and invited him to take a seat, this was her territory.

"Can I offer you something to drink? Coffee? Something cold, maybe?"

Although the drive hadn't been too long and he'd made it in the comfort of the Escalade, Rocco wasn't averse to the idea of "something cold", given the American propensity for chilling cold drinks to absolute zero. "Water would be fine, thank you—if it's not too much trouble."

"No trouble at all. Still or sparkling?"

"Still. Thank you."

She crossed the room to retrieve two bottles of water from a well-stocked, glass-fronted undercounter refrigerator. She handed one to Rocco, took her place behind the desk, and promptly cracked open the bottle she'd retained, to take a sip straight from it. Rocco followed suit, welcoming the flow of icy liquid.

"Texas is too damn hot, even in winter." Sasha replaced the bottle top.

"You're not a native?" That item of data had been missing from the sparse information in her file.

She shook her head. "Army brat. I've moved around a lot all my life. Last place I lived was Virginia. I'm still more used to seeing snow in winter."

Which could explain why he was having some difficulty pinning down her accent. He was no expert on all the variations, but some were easier to identify than others. "You weren't tempted by a military career?"

"No. I was… drawn in another direction."

Rocco wondered exactly what that direction was, and if it was the reason there was so little background information about her. And Virginia? Putting the pieces together, the obvious answer was the CIA, but if that were true, how did she end up here?

Whatever the truth about Sasha was, she was the one who'd first noticed the problem that had brought him here. Having seen some of the social media posts she'd provided as evidence there was an issue, Rocco had initially assumed a trained analyst was responsible for the alert. Then, on discovering Linzi Suto's assistant was responsible, he'd switched to thinking it was natural talent and attention to detail. In light of what he'd just learned, he was inclined to believe his original opinion was correct.

"We're not here to talk about me, Mr. Equizi. I've arranged for you to meet Linzi in," Sasha consulted her watch, "about thirty minutes. She's in the studio rehearsing right now, and after she's seen you, she has an interview with a music magazine."

"She's traveling to the interview?" If so, he'd have to hit the ground sprinting, not merely running.

"Not this time. It's taking place online here, in the media suite. I'll provide you with full access to Linzi's schedule, although I can tell you now, she's not due to venture into the outside world any time soon."

"Good, thank you." Assuming that continued to be the case, he'd have an ideal opportunity to familiarize himself with both the environment and the people who lived and worked within it. "Is Mr. Brookes around?"

Now there was an interesting reaction. Sasha didn't appear to be too impressed by his principal's manager, judging by the shadow of disapproval that briefly passed over her face.

"He's in New York for the next few days." She glanced toward the computer screen to her left and pressed a couple of keys on the keyboard. "Is that a problem?"

"Not at all."

Head tilted to one side, she raised an eyebrow. Whatever it was about, Rocco could almost hear the debate taking place in her mind. Then her hazel gaze pinned him to the spot as if he were an insect imprisoned on the board of a collector.

"Tell me, Mr. Equizi. Why did Gerry hire your company to protect Linzi? Spectrum has no track record over here—at least, none that I've been able to find. It's not as if we have a shortage of US companies like yours."

So, she wasn't one to beat around the bush, and she'd done her research. He liked that. "Ms. Morgan, I can't answer the first question, because I don't know why Mr. Brookes engaged Spectrum. What I can tell you is that, while we may not have a track record over here yet, back home, the company is highly thought of. We operate in multiple environments, and when it comes to close protection, we have experience at the highest level."

Her gaze locked with his in a silent battle of wills. She was a cool one, all right, but it would take a great deal more than that to deter Rocco. Nick, his boss, might have gotten to dress up in the flashy breastplate and plumed helmet of a member of the Household Cavalry during his service in the British Army, but the man knew what he was talking about when it came to Spectrum. He'd anticipated these questions might arise and primed Rocco with a heap of background information. Rocco was already aware of a lot of it, but it didn't hurt to add more knowledge to the arsenal.

"Sasha," she said at length. "We're not formal around here. After all, it's you Brits who are known for having a stick up your ass."

Rocco blinked. Then his lips twitched as he fought to keep a straight face. "Rocco, and I'm only half a Brit," he corrected her. "In my case, it's a toothpick."

At first, he thought his attempt at ice-breaking humor had fallen on stony ground, but then he caught it, the little twitch of her cheek that betrayed her true reaction.

However, this was a business meeting, not a social one. "Sasha, my brief here is to review current security arrangements, provide personal protection for Linzi, and facilitate an in-depth investigation of the threats you've identified in her social media. I'll also need to speak to her security team. Can that be arranged?"

"Already on it. You have a meeting with Frank Schofield tomorrow morning. I figured speaking to the head of on-site security would be high on your agenda."

It was, but Rocco had another question on his mind. "Thank you. I take it he's aware that threats have been made?"

Sasha's reaction was interesting. She didn't immediately

respond. Instead, she appeared to be engaged in another internal debate before replying.

"I've only told him you're here as a consultant here to evaluate the security systems for potential upgrade and advise on best practice, so unless he's taken the initiative to monitor her social media of his own accord, no, he's not aware. Also..."

"Yes?"

"The possibility can't be discounted that... someone inside Linzi's inner circle is responsible."

A possibility that hadn't escaped Rocco, either. And if it was an inside job, then Sasha and Gerry Brookes could be as guilty as anyone who worked there, in spite of the part they'd played in discovering the threats and hiring him. That said, his gut was leaning toward discounting Sasha as a threat. There was something about her that made the idea absurd, but he was also wary of reaching that conclusion too quickly.

"I know you're Linzi's assistant, but do you have anything to do with managing any aspects of the estate as well?"

Sasha laughed, but not unkindly. "I'm good at what I do... but not that good. There are not enough hours in the day, and that is one more headache I do not need. Alilah Corday manages the domestic staff and everything connected with the accommodation on the estate, and before you ask, Leah Bennett takes care of the contracts and schedules for maintenance of the grounds and external facilities. Both Alilah and Leah nominally report to me, but unless there are any major issues that require my input to resolve them, they have a free hand."

"Would either of them have cause to threaten Linzi?"

Sasha shook her head. "I can't see they would, but I wouldn't dismiss it either, even though it's unlikely. They have a pretty easy ride here, so I doubt they'd do anything to disrupt that."

Which Sasha didn't approve of, that was obvious. Rocco added the two names to his list of people to speak to, if only to discount them as suspects. "Is there anyone else who might bear a grudge against Linzi?"

"No one who comes to mind right now. Look, I know this is your job, but may I tag along when you make your inquiries? In case I can contribute something."

Pride warred with desire—the former protested against what could be interpreted as a slur against his ability, while the latter was greedy for any excuse to keep her close. "Are you sure you'll have time?"

"I'll make time."

Rocco's inner caveman roared in triumph. "In that case, you're welcome. We also need to schedule a meeting so you can take me through what you've found that triggered your suspicions, and why. I've had a look at some of the messages and posts, but I'd appreciate your insight."

"No problem. We can fit that in whenever it's convenient for you. As I said, my role here is twenty-four seven."

"Some of the staff live on site in one of the other homes on the estate, while the third is used for guest accommodation. Linzi lives here in the main house, of course, and there's a wing set aside for core members of her domestic and administrative staff."

Sasha remained as professional as she'd ever been during her career, but inwardly, she was still reeling from the initial impression Rocco Equizi had made on her as he emerged from behind his SUV.

Truthfully, she'd been expecting bulging muscles and an IQ that was too small to be allowed out unaccompanied, but what she'd gotten was the hottest man she'd laid eyes on in a long time and a primal force to be reckoned with. Even his smooth stride suggested the feline power and grace of a panther. Giving a guided tour of the multi-million-dollar mansion while fighting a losing battle against the onslaught of visceral attraction was proving every bit as difficult as infiltrating the cartel in Colombia.

Before the tour started properly, Sasha had suggested they take a swift detour to Rocco's on-site accommodation. Although he was due to meet Linzi in less than thirty minutes, there was still enough time for him to take a preliminary look around. The meeting itself was likely to be short and not necessarily sweet, and Rocco was unlikely to gain much from it. Linzi lived in her own little world, where she was the queen, living her life with the carefree abandon of an overindulged child, doing what she wanted, when she wanted. When performing, she relied on Sasha to ensure she was where she was supposed to be when she was supposed to be there; at all other times, Sasha's role was to organize her day-to-day life and cater to her whims.

"Including you?" Rocco asked.

Maybe this was going to be *more* difficult than the cartel. Rocco would be one hell of a distraction—if she allowed it. Sasha risked a sideways glance. "And you, now. As I said, my role theoretically means being on call twenty-four hours a day, so it makes sense for me to be close by. Your role is to protect her, so it makes sense for you to stay here, rather than in the guest house."

"Do you often get a summons at zero two hundred, then?"

"Not really, at least not in the way you mean. If she's on a high after a late-night show, she might take a while to come back down, in which case none of us hit the sack much before zero four hundred."

"Sounds as if you don't get much sleep when that happens."

Sasha shrugged. "The day kind of just moves to the right for a few hours. You get used to it, and it's not as if I haven't worked crazy hours or gone without sleep before."

"Oh? What did you do before this?"

Although the question sounded casual enough, the interest behind it was clearly anything but. "I guess you could call it crisis management. Crises rarely keep office hours. Anyway, in addition to keeping you close to Linzi, I thought it might be useful for you to have a suite along the hall from mine. I figured we might need to liaise on various aspects of your investigation. Here we are."

She'd made the decision for practical reasons when Gerry had first talked about hiring a security consultant. It was for those same reasons she'd also decided to make room for him to work alongside her in her spacious office. Would she have made the same decisions if she'd known her hormones were going to go crazy at the sight of some of the finest eye candy she'd seen in a long time? Her head wanted to say no, but she didn't believe it for one minute.

In common with the place Sasha called home—at least while she worked for Linzi—Rocco's suite was an entirely self-contained apartment, and no expense had been spared in furnishing it. Even the kitchen had been equipped with state-of-the-art appliances, although in Sasha's case, they were used infrequently. She had little incentive to cook for herself when Linzi employed a Cordon Bleu chef from Europe. Even his assistant could work miracles with even the most basic of ingredients. Between them, they kept the main kitchen well stocked with works of culinary art. So long as she kept up with her exercise regime, Sasha didn't have a problem.

She watched Rocco keenly as he circled the sitting room that formed the heart of the suite. Senses honed in a previous life alerted her to the cool assessment he was making of his accommodation and the particular attention he paid to the sliding doors and private terrace beyond.

"The grounds are monitored twenty-four seven by closed circuit cameras, and there's always two guards on duty in the control room to raise the alarm if any intruders succeed in infiltrating the estate."

"That's good to know." Rocco slid open one of the doors and leaned out. "In addition to Frank Schofield, I'll need to speak to all the members of his team. Were they background-checked before being taken on?"

Sasha told herself he didn't know her or her previous history, so there was no way he could know she'd not only asked the question herself but had called in a few favors to double-check when her suspicions had first been aroused. "They were. I can pull the reports for you."

He turned away from his examination of the outside space. "Thanks. I'd appreciate it."

"No problem." Sasha paused, watching Rocco as he continued to assess his surroundings. She'd do exactly the same thing in his position. "Look, we have fifteen, twenty minutes until we go see Linzi. We can either finish looking around the house, or you can unpack and settle in, and meet me in my office when you're ready for me to take you to the studio block."

His dark gaze fixed on her. A woman could melt into eyes that brown and never be seen again. "I don't want to disrupt your day any more than I have already."

"You haven't. I pretty much cleared my diary for today—I'm at your disposal."

Why did the thought of being at his disposal stir up a whole load of impulses she hadn't felt in a long time? Why did she want to read more into the subtle change in his expression that she'd probably imagined anyway? She was more professional than this.

"Thank you. Even so, I'll try not to take up too much of your time. Shall we continue? I can unpack later."

"That's fine. I thought we'd start with the places where Linzi spends most of her time when she's here. It's probably safe to say there's a good sixty-five, seventy percent of the grounds that she never sees or uses."

"Really? Then why live in such a—"

"Such an ostentatious display of wealth?" Sasha shrugged. "Because she can, I guess. And for privacy. The only area where she might be seen by the paparazzi or members of the public is the riverside, and she never goes down there. Why would she, when she has three outdoor pools to choose from?"

"Three outdoor pools? Then there's an indoor one, too?"

Sasha sighed. "Two of them."

Rocco nodded. "Understood. I'll still need to take a look down by the river. It provides open access and a gift of an opportunity for attack. Securing that area may be... problematic."

As Sasha had tried to point out when Linzi had first shown an interest in the property. Linzi, however, had set her heart on the place and Sasha had lost the argument. Especially when Gerry Brookes had weighed in on Linzi's side, no doubt motivated by all the prospective opportunities to enjoy the facilities.

"I'll have the plans and blueprints for the whole property retrieved from the archive, but as soon as I return to my office, I'll contact the architects for the electronic versions."

To Sasha's surprise, Rocco chuckled. She almost wished he hadn't, because her body responded with a squirming feeling that reminded her how long she'd been without a lover.

"Tell me," he said, "are you always this good at anticipating people's needs?"

"I get a lot of practice with Linzi. Her focus is on her songs, her dance moves, and her fan base. I have to take care of the practicalities of life for her. Besides, if I were looking at security, it's what I'd want to see."

A string of colorful curses that would have done her father proud zipped through her mind. *Rookie error.* Her last statement was a throwback to her former life—the key word being *former.*

Not to mention the fact that she'd prefer to keep that part of her past from Rocco.

His eyes narrowed—she definitely wasn't imagining that. *Time for diversionary tactics.*

"That's what they'd do in the movies, right?" She gave Rocco her brightest smile and flicked her hair back. Okay, so it was a stereotype—she was winging it and hadn't had time to prep her cover.

For a split second, he had the look of a man hovering between believing her and calling her on it, then the corner of his not-unattractive mouth turned up in a half-smile. "Something like that. I'm ready to move on when you are."

"Okay. We might as well make our way through the house, then take Linzi's usual route to the studios, which should get us there in time for your meeting. The studios are housed in a block away from the main house and the other accommodation," Sasha explained. "As well as the recording studio, there's a general rehearsal studio, a dance studio—Linzi has a choreographer who comes to teach her the moves for her official videos—the media suite, restrooms, and a relaxation area."

Rocco collected his jacket from the back of the long, brown leather couch, where he'd dropped it just a few moments earlier. "Are the videos made here?"

"Not so far, and I doubt that'll ever change. It's a privacy thing. And I guess a security thing, too," she added, still trying to ignore the perfect fit of the white dress shirt that had been concealed by the jacket. What she couldn't ignore was the reassuring sight of the Glock 19 nestling comfortably in the shoulder holster he wore. It was good to know the Brit—half-Brit—wasn't a wuss when it came to bearing arms.

"I assume she has dancers who accompany her on the videos—do they ever come here?"

"Sometimes, but they always travel with the choreographer, and don't stay long enough to need to stay over. Also, it's probably only for one or two sessions, just before the video is filmed. There is one exception, though—her boyfriend, Ram. He's one of her dancers, and he sometimes stays for a few days."

"He doesn't live here?"

Sasha shook her head. "They haven't been together long."

"I see. Does Linzi have any dance sessions confirmed for the next couple of weeks?"

"No. She's busy rehearsing for a new album, so her focus is on her songs right now. The recording sessions are booked at a professional studio in Austin about a month from now."

Rocco opened the door and stood back to allow Sasha through first. "She can't record the album here?"

"She could, but the equipment at the Austin studio is state-of-the-art, and it's where the backing tracks were put together. That's what she's using to rehearse, although perhaps rehearse isn't quite the right word."

"It isn't?"

"The music business, in some respects, is as much about technology as talent. With the equipment here, they can get a good idea of how they'll need to set everything up for the master recording." Sasha's mouth curved into a wry smile. "At this point, I'd be really grateful if you didn't ask me to go into any more technical detail, because... let's just say, I'm not looking for a career change in that direction right now."

"How about if I ask you to take me to the studio instead?"

His wry smile had probably charmed a lot of women in far more intimate locations than this. She stomped down hard on the embryonic fantasy that she wouldn't mind being one of them. *Keep your mind on the mission at all times.*

Her lips curved in response, but she didn't quite allow the smile to reach her eyes. "That, I can do. Come this way."

CHAPTER 3

In person, Sasha Morgan was everything Rocco had pictured and more—poised, elegant, and a model of efficiency when it came to her job.

However, the impact she'd had on him as an image on a sheet of paper was nothing compared to that of finally seeing her in the flesh. Everything he'd experienced then was intensified in her presence, and so far, he'd seen nothing that would diminish his reaction to her.

For now, though, he had to keep his mind on the job, so he turned his attention to his surroundings. Noting the placement of the closed circuit cameras reminded him of something she'd said while discussing the staffing of the control room—specifically, her use of the word *infiltrating*. In his experience, it wasn't a word that ranked highly in the everyday vocabulary of civilians, yet Sasha hadn't even hesitated.

"So, does Linzi own the estate, or is it rented?"

Sasha shot him a look that almost made him wish he hadn't asked. "You'd have to take that up with her slew of financial advisers, but I believe the property is owned by some sort of trust. Why? Is it important?"

"Yes. No. Maybe."

On its own, probably not, but Rocco was trained to look beyond the surface of any situation. Connections were just as important—in some cases, even more so—and the most esoteric factors could often be connected to a perpetrator's motives. Or the most straightforward, like good old-fashioned envy and greed.

"Thanks for the clarification. That makes perfect sense."

For a split second, he thought she was being sarcastic, but then he caught the grin. *Equizi, you're going to have to lighten up.* "Okay then—maybe, if the motivation for the threats is greed, it could be a significant element. People see a place like this, make certain assumptions, and decide they want a piece of it, or what it represents. And sometimes, they'll do anything to get it."

"I know."

Sasha stopped walking—so did Rocco, a couple of steps ahead of her. He turned to face her and waited.

"I know it's not a laughing matter, either," she continued. "I shouldn't have been so flippant."

Rocco shook his head. "You think that was flippant? Some of the guys I've worked with? Their version of 'flippant' would make your blood run cold."

Her gaze seemed to see all the way through him, to the darkest shadows of some of the more horrifying sights he'd witnessed during his service. "I don't doubt it. We'd better get moving. Linzi will be finishing in the studio soon—as well as meeting her, I'll introduce you to her producer."

Someone else he needed to look into, although his gut was telling him he was unlikely to be a suspect. "Does he spend much time here?"

"No. He comes in for sessions like this and leaves at the

end. He's not much interested in anything going on outside the studio."

A couple of minutes later, a bend in the path revealed their destination. The gleaming, white, single-story annex, set against a backdrop of tall trees, was separate from the main house, and accessed by a path that took them past one of the swimming pools.

Rocco also caught a glimpse of a bright-red SUV parked beyond the building, partially obscured by the trees. That meant only one thing—the path from the house wasn't the only way to access the building. "Sasha?"

"Yes?"

"The vehicle parked over there—who does it belong to?"

She leaned slightly to one side to get a better view. "Ah. The man we were just talking about—Linzi's producer, Trent Birling."

Rocco turned his scowl back to the vehicle. "It looks as if he knows his way around the compound."

Sasha punched in a security code on the numeric pad by the door. "I doubt it, unless he's going someplace on the route between the main gate and the studio block. I don't think I've met anyone quite as single-minded as Trent. Come on in."

Once inside the annex, Rocco found himself standing at the end of a corridor that stretched the length of the building. Eight windows on the left hand side looked out on the gardens, while a glaring red light drew attention to the last of half a dozen doors on the right hand side.

"The recording studio's at the far end. Standing orders are not to enter when the light's on, but I warned Linzi you'd be here for the end of her session."

"Which is?"

Sasha checked her watch. "In about ten minutes—or it should be. Would you like to see her at work?"

"Please." If nothing else, it would give him the opportunity to gain an impression of his principal from real life rather than a dossier.

Sasha led the way into the studio. The building must have covered more ground than Rocco imagined, for it to accommodate the spacious live area—large enough for several musicians—and a separate area with a mixing desk that looked like the flight deck of a spaceship from some science fiction movie.

And it appeared they'd arrived in the middle of an artistic meltdown. Linzi's raised voice came through loud and clear on the speakers in the control room. Rocco had a feeling they'd have heard her through the huge glass window even without the benefit of the sound system.

"So how was that, Trent?"

Impatience and more than a touch of aggressive sarcasm, unless Rocco was mistaken. He turned his attention to the man seated at the desk. Birling's lips were pressed together, and the set of his shoulders radiated tension. Those same shoulders rose and fell as he took a deep, centering breath before speaking into the microphone.

"Linzi, you're almost there." He looked briefly at Sasha and raised his hand in acknowledgment, sparing only a fleeting glance for Rocco. "I need it one more time, to make sure."

"Trent, I'm tired. I've already done it, like, forty-six times today."

Rocco waited. A whine like that really deserved the accompaniment of a petulant stamp of the foot.

"Linzi, one more time. Then I'll be out of your hair." Trent's hands moved over the desk as he manipulated the controls. "From the top, when you're ready. You know what to do."

The light touch of a hand on his forearm drew Rocco's

attention back to Sasha. When she took a seat on the long couch at the back of the booth, Rocco sat down beside her.

"It won't be long now," she whispered.

Rocco didn't mind. His job often involved waiting around, so this was no different. Besides, this gave him the opportunity to size up Linzi's producer.

The man was somewhere in his thirties, casually dressed in high-end designer labels, and probably as successful as those labels implied. His intense concentration was characteristic of someone who was consumed by their work to the point of obsession, so it was doubtful he'd do anything to jeopardize that. On balance, he was an unlikely candidate, but Rocco would still run a check on him.

The producer wasn't the only subject of Rocco's attention. As the music continued, he checked out the high-tech control room. Speakers, mounted flush in the walls, shared the space with large, ultra-high definition monitors. The displays were an incomprehensible representation of the sliders and dials on the desk, and each movement of Birling's hands changed the configuration on the screens.

For all that she had the reputation of being a brat, Linzi was a good singer—not the kind Rocco preferred to listen to when the opportunity presented itself, but he could understand her appeal to her target audience, which was definitely not someone like him.

When it came to what he found appealing, Sasha Morgan took it to a whole other level. He stole another glance in her direction. She was stunning. Her profile was classical and elegant, and he could only too easily picture himself moving that heavy curtain of honey-blonde waves to one side, so he could kiss the delicate column of her neck. Her shirt would have to go, so he could kiss his way to her shoulder. Then he'd hook his finger under the narrow strap of her—

"That was great, Linzi. You've nailed it. Time to call it a day."

Birling's voice lobbed a grenade into the fantasy playing out in Rocco's imagination. On the other side of the glass, Linzi signaled her agreement and removed her headphones. She tossed her hair back, and then bounded towards the door, bursting into the control room seconds later. Rocco automatically stood, as did Sasha, who sent a totally inscrutable look in his direction.

Linzi headed straight for the man at the desk. She opened her mouth to speak, but Birling headed her off before she could say a word.

"Great work, Linzi. Replicate that at the recording session, and you've got another hit on your hands."

"Thank God, because I am so over that song."

Birling laughed. "You'd better not be over it, because you're going to be singing it everywhere."

Linzi rolled her eyes and gave a melodramatic sigh as her shoulders plummeted downward. "Gross."

"With the right mix, it'll make a fortune, trust me." Birling started gathering his belongings and putting them inside his aluminum attaché case.

"Linzi?"

"Oh. Hi, Sasha." As if someone had flicked a switch, the demanding diva adopted an almost childlike persona. At the same time, she finally realized a stranger was in their midst and directed her next question at Rocco. "Who are you?"

"Linzi, this is Rocco Equizi. I told you he was coming to conduct a review of security?"

Interesting how Sasha referred to only one of the reasons for his presence. "Good afternoon, Ms. Suto." He extended his hand in greeting, only for it to be ignored.

"Hey, you're a Brit. Weird accent, but you're kinda cute."

She looked him up and down as if he were a prime cut of meat.

Rocco's internal alarm gave a warning peal. All of a sudden, he was very, very glad Linzi wasn't due to go anywhere for the next few days. It meant he wouldn't have to spend too much time in her company, and in the meantime, he could work on a strategy to keep her safe when the time came for her to venture beyond the estate boundaries.

And the sooner they got to the bottom of the threats the better, because the last thing he needed was to have his principal crushing on him. Sasha, on the other hand...

He glanced in her direction, and though her expression didn't reveal anything of what she was thinking, he got the impression she was less than comfortable with her employer's behavior. Her next words seemed to bear that out.

"Linzi, don't you think that's a little impolite—"

"No, it's all right, Ms. Morgan. Think nothing of it. After all, I am the stranger here."

Sasha seemed to weigh up what he'd said and made the right decision. "How about if we finish the introductions, then I'll carry on showing Rocco—Mr. Equizi—around the estate. Trent Birling, Linzi's producer."

"It's a pleasure to meet you." This time, Rocco's gesture of greeting met with a more positive response. Birling's handshake was smooth and practiced—hardly surprising, given his profession.

"Likewise, Mr. Birling."

Judging by his frequent glances at the wall clock, Birling wasn't eager to make small talk or delay his departure. Not that it mattered to Rocco—the full background check would fill in the blanks. Birling might be a maestro when it came to the high-tech recording equipment, but it didn't necessarily make him expert enough to conceal his tracks on social media. The man had nothing to gain from threatening his golden goose, but it wouldn't do any harm to confirm he could be excluded from the list of suspects.

"Are we done here, guys? I want to go for a swim."

Linzi might have been in her early twenties, but at that precise moment, she sounded a decade younger, justifying Rocco's assumption that liaising with Sasha would be a much more effective way of achieving his professional objectives. He doubted Linzi would be able to answer any of his questions without deferring to her assistant, anyway.

"We're done, Ms. Suto. We'll leave you to get on. Please excuse us. Enjoy your swim."

Sasha didn't miss the cue, and together they left the recording studio. They hadn't gone very far when Sasha laid her hand on his arm and brought them both to a halt. "I'm sorry."

"What for?"

Sasha glanced back toward the studio. "The car crash back there. I can set up a more helpful meeting tomorrow—Linzi has time in her schedule."

The expression of regret was the last thing he expected. "Hey, it's okay, don't worry. If anything, it… gave me a useful insight into my client."

Sasha raised an eyebrow. "As first impressions go, it can't have been a great one."

Rocco gave a short bark of humorless laughter. "Trust me, I've worked with worse. If it helps, I don't see that I'll need much contact with her unless or until she leaves the estate, and on those occasions, I'll make sure she has a thorough briefing before we leave. You mentioned she's attending some sort of event?"

"Yes, the Diamond ACE Music Awards, in a couple weeks."

They resumed their stroll back to the main house, but Rocco's mind was on what might happen between now and the event. Depending on the progress made with tracking down the perpetrator, he might not even still be here by then. "Does she have anything scheduled before then? Any PR commitments, personal appearances or the like?"

"Nothing. She may be impulsive, but that rarely extends to making spontaneous trips into the outside world."

"Not even for shopping?"

"Not even for shopping," Sasha confirmed. "I put a call in to her favorite stores, and they come here."

"Isn't that unusual?"

"Not really. If she shows up someplace unexpectedly, with social media there's always the risk that word will get out and the place will be overrun with fans. The first couple times it happened, people got hurt—minor injuries, thankfully, but even that was too much. After that, we decided it would be safer for all concerned if shopping trips—impromptu or otherwise—stayed off the menu, for a while, at least."

That made sense. Rocco had seen something similar with previous clients, but the reasoning behind it had been very different—they didn't want to mix with people whom they considered beneath them, so they either had the store closed for a private visit or made the store come to them. He seldom had strong feelings one way or another about the people he protected, but in their case, he'd been prepared to make an exception.

"Fine, but if that changes, please keep me informed. I want to be there if she makes an unplanned departure from the property."

"Yes, sir!"

And to his surprise, Sasha snapped off a salute. Rocco smiled and shook his head. "Okay, okay. What can I say?"

"Nothing."

He heard the smile in her voice before he saw it. The

genuine amusement in it was a jolt to his system, as if something deep inside him cracked open. Before he could reply, Sasha continued.

"Look, you need some time to unpack and settle in, so how about we call it a day? If you like, we can meet over breakfast in the morning to discuss strategy."

"Sounds good to me."

And how many *assistants* talked about discussing strategy with security consultants as easily as if they were arranging a stroll in the park?

At long last, Rocco closed the door behind him and allowed himself a moment or two to take a breath. He had a lot to assimilate at the end of a day that wasn't quite over yet. Nick Blackmore was expecting a report on his first impressions and immediate plans.

After Sasha had escorted him back to his suite, he hadn't let the grass grow under his feet. Unpacking hadn't taken long, and then he'd carried out his own reconnaissance of the area around the house. Everything had been pretty much as he'd expected.

Having stashed his jacket in the closet, he made himself comfortable at the writing desk where he'd left his laptop. Referring to the notes he'd recorded during his exploration, he quickly typed up his initial observations, and, together with his plans for the next few days, sent them via secure email to Nick.

He wasn't surprised when Nick's face popped up on Skype a few minutes later.

"Thanks for the report, Rocco. I've given it a quick once-over, but you seem to have made a good start. Is there anything you need?"

Rocco was about to reply in the negative but thought better of it. No harm in asking about what was on his mind—after all, Nick himself had told Rocco they were going to do some more digging. "Sasha Morgan, the PA. Do we have any more information on her yet? Like who she really is? Or was, before she started working for Linzi."

Nick's expression became more serious. "Not yet, we're still working on it. While we do have a little clout here, it doesn't compare to what HQ back home has with the UK government—added to which, the situation here is more complex because of state and federal jurisdiction. As soon as we uncover anything material, I'll be in touch. What's your gut telling you about her?"

"In the context of her past? This is going to sound crazy, but..." On the verge of saying it aloud, it sounded crazier than ever, even in his head. "I think she's ex-Agency."

Nick quirked an eyebrow. "What makes you say that?"

"Little things—where she's lived, the words she uses. Things that could add up to three interesting initials."

"But equally could not. If she is, though, it could also explain the lack of information about her, although not how and why she's come to be working for Linzi Suto."

Good question, and Rocco didn't have an answer—yet. "Whether I'm right or not, there's one thing I am sure about—she's not behind the threats."

"Why? Because she was the one who raised the alarm?"

"That, and... I've only caught of glimpse of her interaction with Linzi, but I didn't see anything that suggested the kind of hostility that has to be in play here. If anything, I think she could be a useful ally."

He thought other things about Sasha, too, but they weren't for public consumption.

Charity came into view behind her husband, draped her arms over his shoulders, and bent so that she also appeared on the screen. "How're you doing, Rocco? Everything good?"

"Everything's fine, thanks, Charity. Just getting started."

"So are we," she replied. "And I just had an idea."

"Uh-oh, now we're in trouble," Nick muttered.

"Oh hush, you. I'm working on tracing the source of the threats with a guy called Tex, who is a genius with computers."

"Tex?"

"A friend of a friend," Nick explained. "If what you're looking for is on a computer anywhere in the world, he can find it. And I have a feeling I know what my better half's idea is. You tell him—I wouldn't want to steal your thunder."

Charity dropped a swift kiss on her husband's cheek. "I should think not. Rocco, I'm going to ask Tex to see what he can find out about Sasha. Whatever she's hiding, he'll uncover it."

Charity had called him a genius, but to Rocco, Tex sounded more like a wizard. People might be difficult to deal with at times, but he'd take them over technology any day of the week—unless it was directly connected to his occupation. "Thanks, Charity. In the meantime, I'll focus on the staff and see what I can find out."

Nick agreed. "That sounds like a plan. Now, is there anything else you need?"

Rocco debated the question for a moment, then shook his head. "I don't think so."

"If anything comes to mind, let us know—especially if it's reinforcements."

Rocco couldn't see any reason why he would need backup and said so. "Besides, who would you send?"

The smile made Nick's eyes crease up with genuine humor. "Lucas Brand arrives tomorrow—I could always throw him in at the deep end. Having said that, I have some friends who might be able to help out if the shit really hits the fan. Have we covered everything?"

"I believe so."

"Then I have one more question before I let you go."

"Yes?"

"From a personal point of view, how's your first day on the job been?"

Rocco shrugged. "Busy. Interesting. Relatively warm, even though everyone around here keeps telling me how cold it is."

Nick nodded. "You'll get used to the weather. Sounds like a pretty good start. If anything happens, night or day, and you need assistance, call me. Other than that, have a good evening."

Rocco signed off. Now he could relax—as much as his training and experience ever did let him relax, whether on a mission or not. At least this one, for now, didn't involve being shot at by some crazed lunatic with enough munitions to equip a battalion. And here, he could keep his firearm handy if he needed it. That was a big plus in the pro column for taking on this job.

A shower, something to eat, and then bed. It was a pity Sasha wouldn't be sharing it with him, but a guy had to walk before he could run, and at the moment—to extend the metaphor—he hadn't even begun to crawl.

Hazel eyes and frosted honey-blonde hair shimmered and took form in his mind. She'd truly captivated him—the process had started with the photo in her file, and today had only added fuel to the flames. He couldn't even begin to count the number of times he'd looked at her and had to rein in the impulse to take her in his arms and kiss her. Her mouth would be the death of him.

Rocco wandered out to the terrace and leaned against the wall that gave the area, with its serious-looking barbecue station, a measure of privacy. What he needed most right now was that shower, and the stall in the decadent bathroom was calling to him. Another plus for this gig. The enclosure would easily take two occupants—great for sexy times—but for now, he'd settle for a spray that would pound the tightness out of his shoulders.

The luxury of a few minutes under the powerful jets was all he needed. When he was done, Rocco dried off and wrapped a fresh towel around his hips, before heading back to the bedroom. In spite of his determination to clear it, his mind was already racing ahead to the next day, and the answers he wanted from the head of security at their meeting. The last thing he expected was a knock on the door.

Old habits died hard. Instantly on alert, he extracted the Glock from its holster and went to answer it. A swift look through the viewer revealed his unexpected visitor was a member of the household domestic staff—an armed response was probably a little over the top. Rocco laid his weapon carefully on the nearby table, ensuring it was still within reach if needed, before opening the door.

The young man greeted him with a dazzling smile. "Good evening, Mr. Equizi. My apologies for disturbing you, but Chef thought you might not have time to prepare dinner tonight."

Which explained the cart off to one side. Rocco's stomach rumbled in convenient agreement with Chef's assumption. "Thank you. That's… I appreciate it. Please thank Chef for me."

"My pleasure… sir." As he turned to leave, his speculative gaze raked Rocco from head to foot and back again, and the last thing Rocco was aware of was the entirely different kind of smile that appeared on his departing visitor's face.

Rocco raised an eyebrow. At least one person was going to go to bed happy tonight.

An enticing aroma reached him from the covered dishes on the cart, and when he lifted the lid on the first one, he discovered a thick, perfectly grilled steak. And he would bet dollars to donuts that, beyond grilling it, Linzi's Cordon Bleu import wasn't the one responsible for its presence.

There was only one way to find out if he was right. He picked up his cell phone, brought up the number he'd made sure to acquire during the day, and touched the icon to make the call.

After a day that could best be described as "interesting", the sound of the bath tub filling was especially soothing, as was the floral scent of the bath oil she'd added to the steaming water. Sasha rotated her shoulders, trying to release the aftereffects of her second encounter with Linzi that day. There were occasions when, if it hadn't been for her sense of loyalty to her former supervisor, she'd have walked out on this job, and that had come perilously close to being one of them.

At least here, in the haven of her suite, she could relax and regroup. Tomorrow, Linzi would have forgotten all about her difference of opinion with Sasha… and Sasha would not let Rocco Equizi's presence stir up a hornets' nest of memories and impulsive desires again. He reminded her too much of what she'd lost, and many of the dangerous reasons why she'd walked away from her previous life.

You gotta get back on the horse sooner or later, sugar.

She could hear him say the words in that lazy drawl of his —Jack Ward, her former partner. All blond charisma and a perpetual smile that had charmed her into his bed with ease. They'd been great as a team and great in the sack together, and even though they'd both known what they had wasn't the real-deal love-for-a-lifetime, they'd been more than merely friends with benefits.

And if it hadn't been for him getting in the way of that bullet, she'd be the one in the ground, and her family would have been left to grieve, not his.

On that disastrous mission, the only saving grace had been their proximity to the exfil point, and the fact that extraction had been imminent. If it hadn't been for the special forces team, her fate would probably have matched Jack's. He'd lived long enough to know they'd made it to safety, but his wounds had been too severe for even a combat medic to prevent him from slipping away.

So why on earth did thinking about Rocco lead almost seamlessly to thoughts of the last man to grace her bed? Yeah, like it would take a genius to answer *that* one. Her brain was as dumb as her hormones. Both men, though physically very different, were devastatingly attractive, but while her attraction to Jack had been based on friendship and proximity, Rocco appealed in other, more basic ways that had nothing to do with either.

Physical need, for one. She'd stuffed that away in a dark corner, where it couldn't encourage her to make bad choices. Consequently, her recent sex life would have made a nun proud. Now Rocco had come along, and suddenly she was in danger, the kind that had nothing to do with drug cartels and everything to do with what her rampant imagination was doing with him.

This had to stop. She was physically exhausted, but her mind was running a marathon. If she didn't relax and unwind, she'd never get any sleep. Hopefully a long, hot soak in the tub would help.

For one person, the rooms she called home were ridiculously extravagant, and that included the bathroom. The white suite was set off by the geometric style of the ivory, taupe, and gold color scheme, which included gold-toned fittings, and as the steaming water filled the huge tub, Sasha finally stripped out of the clothes that were starting to feel as if they were glued to her body. She swirled her hand in the water and inhaled deeply, the scent alone enough for her to start relaxing.

Until, from the sitting room, she heard the shrill call of her cell announcing the arrival of a text message.

Please, not again. Not tonight.

She'd thought Linzi was at last showing signs of maturing over the last few weeks. Her off-duty calls and texts had tailed off considerably, and those she had made had been for valid reasons. Was this her way of getting back at Sasha for their earlier altercation? As a precaution, Sasha switched off the faucet. She didn't need to come back to a flooded bathroom as well.

The text, however, was not from Linzi, but from Rocco. Sasha's brow furrowed. What on earth could he want at this time of night? Unless…

I take it I have you to thank for organising dinner?

Her mood eased, teasing her lips into a slow smile at the Brit spelling. So he had worked it out. She quickly texted her reply.

No need to thank me. Figured you might not be in the mood to cook tonight, so I talked to Chef. Hope you like your steak rare. There are only two acceptable ways to serve a steak in his eyes—rare or still mooing.

. . .

Thanks. Appreciate it. Rare is fine. And thanks for stocking the kitchen too.

No problem.

Sasha waited. Crazy though it was, she as convinced the exchange wasn't done yet. Then, just when she was ready to blame tiredness and a deprived libido, her phone chirped again.

Perhaps you'd let me return your hospitality by cooking dinner for you one evening?

She blinked, and read the message again. He wanted to cook for her? The mere thought was enough to put her sex-starved imagination into overdrive, which was a ridiculous reaction, because sex with Rocco was not on the menu.

You don't have to do that.

I know, but I'd like to. Besides, it'd be a great way of interrogating you ;-)

"Rocco, I did not have you down as a smiley kind of guy," she murmured as she formulated her response.

. . .

Okay. We can discuss tomorrow. After your meeting with Frank?

Great. Shouldn't take more than an hour, unless the conversation turns up something. How's your schedule?

Sounds as if you'll be done by the time I break for coffee. My office?

I'll be there. Sleep well, Ms. Morgan. And thanks again.

Now the exchange was over. Sasha set her cell to one side and returned to the bathroom. While the tub continued to fill, she lit some scented candles on the ledge that surrounded it, and also on the vanity. With the lights dimmed, the atmosphere would be both relaxing and intimate. Music would make it perfect.

As she slid beneath the fragrant water, Sasha let out a long, heartfelt sigh. She needed this so much. If there was one thing she could thank the job that had taken her to France for, it was introducing her to the sheer luxury of investing in quality bathing products. Paris had been another difficult assignment, but for this, it had been worth it.

Then again, working for her former employer was never meant to be easy. One day, she would finally be able to let the memories go. Today was not going to be that day.

Sasha closed her eyes. Unable to lie completely still, her restlessness disturbed the water enough for it to add a delicious caress to her skin. Her imagination taunted her remorselessly by turning the silken sensation into a lover's hands, then dialed it up another level by bestowing the kiss of a golden tan on her anonymous admirer's skin.

Except her admirer wasn't truly anonymous. His accent was English, yet his dark good looks spoke of a Mediterranean heritage. As her own hands explored her body, so did his in her mind. Her touch became his as he cupped her breast. His thumb gave the dusky nipple a lazy flick. His head lowered, and the softness of his lips replaced his fingers. His tongue flirted with the taut bud, while his hand roamed further, to explore the dip of her waist and the flare of her hips. He stroked her mound and wove his magical spell around her. Her thighs parted, and when his finger touched her already hypersensitive clit, she couldn't hold in the soft, anguished moan of arousal.

It had been so long. No one since Jack. More than eighteen months. Almost two years without a lover to warm her bed and help her believe she still had a heart. She should never have sat so close to him while they were waiting for Linzi in the recording studio. Without visual input to distract her, she even fancied she could still smell the subtle scent of his aftershave.

She stroked her clit again. Her hips lifted and the water washed and swirled over her, as turbulent as her inner unrest. Her work was her life, but she had needs it couldn't satisfy. Her mind transported her to a different place—to a soft, warm bed in a bedroom lit by a blazing log fire.

Sounds of movement in the adjacent bathroom... the door opening... a man silhouetted in the doorway.

He came toward the bed, lifted the sheets and slid beneath them. Lying on his side, he simply looked at her, and the longer he looked, the more aroused she became.

Sasha's fingers parted her labia once more and tormented the slick pearl concealed beneath. This time she didn't stop stroking—she carried on, and her mind returned to her fantasy.

He leaned toward her and touched his lips to hers, deepening the kiss as he laced their fingers and trapped her hand against the pillow. Momentum carried him further. His body covered hers and her thighs parted to accommodate his hips. He was hot and hard, and though he wasn't inside her, his hips moved as if he were.

She wanted him inside her. Her fingers tightened on his and she pushed, rolling him onto his back so that she was astride him and that thick shaft bobbed between them.

She rose to her knees, lifted one clear of the bed so she could guide him inside her. Slowly, so slowly, she lowered herself until he filled her, the full length of him, the girth of him stretching her. She threw her head back in ecstasy at the sublime sensation, then opened her eyes, looked down at him, and breathed his name.

"Rocco..."

CHAPTER 4

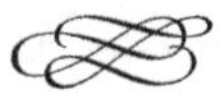

"The steak was cooked to perfection—thank you."

Sasha lifted her gaze from the email she'd printed off, to see Rocco leaning against the door frame, arms folded and looking like a tall drink of something cool and incredibly sexy. Once again, she was impressed by how comfortable he looked around the Glock 19 in the shoulder holster, as if he'd been born with it—so much for the awkward Brit of her assumptions, who wouldn't know a gun if it bit him on the ass. "I'll be sure to tell Chef. Good morning. Did you sleep well?"

"Very well, thank you." He pushed away from the door frame. "Almost too well."

Sasha raised an eyebrow. "Too well? How can *anyone* sleep too well?"

Rocco shrugged. "Let's just say, it's a very large and very comfortable bed, and in the past I've slept in some much less... hospitable locations."

Intriguing. "You're ex-military, right?"

"Yes—but you already knew that. I'm sure Gerry would have mentioned it."

She shrugged and smiled. "True. Do you mind if I ask—"

"Army."

And the way he said it told her he wasn't going to elaborate. She could take a hint. She wasn't stupid, either. The special forces guys whose paths had crossed hers in the past never talked about who they really were and what they really did. "I take it you haven't had breakfast yet?"

"No, unless black coffee constitutes breakfast in Texas."

She wasn't surprised—he looked like a black coffee kind of guy. And then, completely unbidden, another thought occurred to her—was he a morning sex kind of guy, too?

"Sasha? Are you all right?"

"What? I'm fine—absolutely fine, thank you." Apart from the furnace blazing in her cheeks. She was way too old to have that kind of reaction to a man, yet here she was, blushing like a virgin. "Yes, breakfast—and no, black coffee does not constitute breakfast around here. Come with me."

The house was quiet—hardly surprising, since it was barely light. While her employer would probably be dead to the world until almost lunchtime, Sasha liked an early start when it was practical.

So, apparently, did Rocco. Visions of intimate first meals of the day filled Sasha's head as she led the way to the kitchen. Chef didn't come in for this shift, but his assistant did, and she made the most amazing breakfast dishes imaginable.

"Tell me, is this your normal daily routine?" Rocco asked over his plateful of pancakes with all the trimmings.

"Pretty much." Sasha forked up her first mouthful of fluffy omelet and almost moaned as the delicious flavors bathed her taste buds. "Geri, this is amazing."

The young woman in chef's whites laughed as she continued to prepare vegetables. "You say that every time."

"And I mean it every time. Thank you."

"You're welcome."

Sasha turned back to Rocco. "Unless I've accompanied Linzi to a show or some other event the previous evening and we've arrived back late, I'm normally in the office by zero six thirty at the latest, in case anything urgent's come in from Europe overnight."

"What could be that urgent?"

"The entertainment industry works fast twenty-four seven, and it also works on rumors. It could be anything—a request for an interview, a guest appearance on a talk show, that kind of thing. Normally activities like that are booked well in advance, but there are times when we have to respond to something that's happened overnight."

"Does that mean a long day for you?"

Sasha shrugged. "It can do, but I'm paid very well for the… inconvenience. I've worked irregular hours before, so I'm not hung up on finishing at five."

"I know that feeling."

Rocco cut another piece of pancake, smothered it with maple syrup, and carried the fork to his mouth. That mouth had given Sasha some sinful dreams overnight. He had the most perfect lips. Even watching the movement of his Adam's apple as he swallowed was having a disorientating effect on her.

He sighed. "Delicious as this is, I am going to have to up my workouts. I don't think a portion of blueberries, no matter how generous, is going to compensate for pancakes like that."

Sasha tried to suppress her sympathetic laughter. "That's partly why I switched to omelets. I hate the gym, so this way, I don't have to spend too long in there. We have one on the second floor," she explained, before Rocco could ask. "You can use it if you want to, although you might want to give

Monday, Wednesday and Friday afternoons a miss—that's when Linzi's personal trainer comes over. Her sessions can be a battle between the two of them, you know?"

"She doesn't like exercise?"

"Just the gym. She prefers to swim, but when you're a performer, there's a lot of pressure to look good all the time. That means time in the gym as well as the pool."

"You said you don't like the gym, either—is there something else you prefer to do for exercise?"

Sasha almost gulped down her orange juice—it was the closest thing to hand to try to cool the hot flash burning her up inside at the imagined innuendo in Rocco's question. "I use the dance studios a few times during the week, for things like yoga, and I run most days. Either first thing in the morning, or when it cools down—relatively—later in the day. With the size of the estate, there's plenty of places to run."

"I see. Do you prefer to run on your own, or do you have company?"

She leaned her elbows on the counter and studied Rocco over the rim of her glass. She couldn't escape the feeling that his questions were leading somewhere, and her hormones were only too eager to follow. The damn man was an enigma, even with her training. She could appreciate the irony, though—*his* training was probably responsible. Maybe it would become easier, the more time she spent around him…

Yes, she was certifiably insane.

"I usually run alone. In the morning, it's too early for most people around here who aren't already at work. That's my favorite time, but at this time of year, unless I have other priorities, I run after work."

Rocco took a moment to refill his coffee cup. "Would you like some company later on? You'd be doing me a favor."

When he put it like that, how on earth was she supposed to refuse? "How is running with me doing a favor for you?"

"It's a way of learning more about the property, and with you there, if I have any questions, I have someone I can ask."

She couldn't argue with that. She also tried to tell herself it was a good thing, because it proved there'd been no double meaning behind his earlier questions. "Seventeen hundred, at the main door. We can fit a half-hour in easily before we start losing daylight."

His gaze snagged hers and held it. "It's a date, then."

And that blew her sense of relief out of the water. A date. Did he have to phrase it like that? An image flashed into her mind—Rocco sitting opposite her in a restaurant. A candle on the table, a glass of wine in her hand, and him studying her as if he'd like to eat her alive. Crazy—she was barely even acquainted with the man.

Doesn't stop you wanting him, though.

Yes, definitely crazy—now she was hearing voices, too. It didn't matter that the voices were right—the mischievous one that belonged to the devil took control of her mouth and responded for her. "First date I'll have been on in a long... long... time."

Rocco's expression became one of disbelief. "Not possible. Any man would give his left—eye teeth to take you out."

His unwavering gaze pinned her in place, while her brain struggled to find something to say that wouldn't give away her unbridled urge to rip his clothes off. "Hey. Professional workaholic here. Not enough hours in the day."

She expected him to take his cue from her and laugh it off. However, his expression remained unchanged, and now she was even more hot and bothered, and almost squirming in her seat.

His dark gaze mesmerized her. "There are always enough hours in the day for something you really... really... want."

Energy crackled between them. In her mind's eye, he pushed aside the plate of pancakes, stood, and leaned across the counter. His face came closer, until she could no longer focus properly, and his mouth claimed hers with a deep, bewitching kiss.

In reality, he remained completely still as he continued. "Of course… sometimes, what you really, really want doesn't need hours."

His brown eyes—the richest, most sinful chocolate she'd ever seen—darkened even more, and suddenly, Sasha was consumed by a craving to find out if that chocolate was as wicked as she suspected.

To kill some time before his meeting with the head of security, Rocco was examining the plans of Casa Millefiori laid out on the table before him—at least, that was what he hoped it looked like. His mind was occupied elsewhere, replaying the conversation he'd had with Sasha over breakfast, and berating himself for overestimating his self-control so badly. What the hell had come over him?

He was also hoping that, whoever the mysterious Tex was —the computer expert's computer expert, by all accounts— he could come up with not only an explanation for the missing history in Sasha's file, but what was in that history. If he could do that, Rocco would gladly take the man out for a drink. Especially if what he discovered meant there was nothing to stand in the way of Rocco pursuing his personal interest in her.

He was, to put it bluntly, obsessed, and all it had taken was a few hours of being around her. He'd spent most of the previous evening putting the contents of the file on her under the microscope, trying to tease out information that simply wasn't there. Defeated and frustrated, he'd lain in bed and stared at the photographs of her, going from one to the next until he'd finally fallen asleep, only to wake up this morning and find them strewn across the unoccupied side of the massive bed.

And then he'd had to sit opposite her over breakfast, watching those luscious lips, in the full knowledge he could do nothing about claiming them yet. Right now, he could only be thankful she was away from her office on some errand or other, leaving him free to regain his self-control.

"Rocco?"

A gentle touch to his upper arm accompanied the voice washing around him with the freshness of a crystal-clear stream at dawn. An image flashed through his mind of her coming up behind him, wrapping her arms around his waist, and as he turned to look at her, her lips took his in a deep kiss.

So much for self-control. In spite of that, he had to leave the fantasy behind. When he turned to face her for real, there was no kiss awaiting him. Even so, his body still responded—to her closeness, her scent, her touch, her voice. "Hi. Everything okay?"

"Fine, thank you. It was no big deal." She held up a slip of paper. "You might find this useful—it's a superuser login for our HR and payroll system. I'd just ask you to be mindful of the confidential nature of the data. You'll be asked to change your password the first time you use it, so please make sure you keep it secure."

"I will, thanks." Rocco took the paper from her. When her fingertips made brief contact with his, a jolt of electricity zinged between them. Judging by her reaction, she felt it too, and was almost as successful as he was at hiding it. "Who else has access to the system?"

"I do. Frank Schofield, as head of security, though he never uses it, as far as I'm aware. The IT consultants who installed it, for remote support. That's it."

Rocco nodded. "Who's the system administrator? Who do you call to reset a forgotten password?"

"It should be Frank, but he's about as IT-literate as a stump, so I'm the on-site system administrator. If I forget my password, I have to call the consultants. Haven't needed to call them yet."

Rocco would have been more surprised if she had. There was something about Sasha that said attention to detail wasn't a problem for her. "I don't doubt it for one moment. I have to go and see Frank now, but I'll see you later."

"Would you still like to meet for a cup of coffee when you get back?"

He should decline. "If you can take a break then, but don't wait for me if I'm running late."

She smiled as if he'd promised her something special. "I think I can wait a few without going into caffeine withdrawal."

Rocco took her smile and her words with him on the short stroll to the security block, along the access road that led to the outside world. There was no one around as he entered the functional, box-shaped building that housed Schofield's office, the closed circuit TV control room, and facilities for the guards who patrolled the estate and manned the main gate. He made his way past the closed door of the control room and straight down the corridor to the one that bore the name of the man he'd come to see. He knocked, and when prompted, entered.

The man behind the big desk rose as Rocco approached. The image he'd been given of the security chief was obviously a few years old, but he was still recognizable. Taller than average, built like a brick wall, and wearing a smile that, on close examination, wasn't as friendly as it seemed, Frank Schofield was well into his fifties and looked it. He also had the unmistakable air of having spent a number of years in law enforcement.

Rocco offered his hand. "Good morning, Mr. Schofield. Thanks for seeing me at such short notice."

"My pleasure. Why don't you take a seat? Can I get you some coffee?"

Schofield spoke with the characteristic drawl of a Texas native. Rocco moved to the chair across the desk from him and sat. "I'm fine, thank you, but please don't let me stop you."

"Don't mind if I do. I'll be right with you, Rocco. You don't mind if I call you Rocco, seeing as how we're in the same line of business?"

"Not at all… Frank."

He watched Schofield as he filled his cup from the filter coffee machine on top of a low cabinet at the side of the office. Schofield took his coffee black, and it looked as if it had the consistency of tar. Having acquired his taste for coffee via his Sicilian genes, Rocco had clearly dodged a caffeinated bullet there.

"Now, what can I do for you, Rocco? We're all one big happy family here."

Again the man's face creased into that overly friendly smile. If what Rocco suspected about Sasha was true, he'd be interested to find out her opinion of the head of security. "This is by way of a courtesy call. I'm not sure how much you've been told about why I'm here—"

"Ms. Suto's manager just said there'd be a security consultant coming in to make sure we're doing what we're paid to do. I run a tight ship here, Rocco—"

Rocco noted the falsely jovial, defensive undertone. "Of

that I have no doubt. I'm merely here to review the systems and protocols in place, and offer suggestions for improvements, should any be necessary. Fresh eyes, that's all. I'd appreciate your cooperation so I can present a full and accurate report at the end of my visit."

Schofield eased off a little. "Of course, son—you let me know what you need and I'll get right on it."

"Thank you. To begin with, I'd like to take a look at your staff roster for the next month, with particular emphasis on who will be accompanying Ms. Suto to any events or on any activities that will take her outside the compound. In the interests of full disclosure, I have access to the personnel system and I will be looking into the backgrounds of all the security personnel, as well as the domestic staff."

"You don't need to waste your time looking into my men. They're all good boys and—"

So much for "getting right on it". Rocco filed the genial blustering under the same heading as the saccharine overuse of his forename and the false bonhomie—all for show. "And I need to carry out my assignment in a thorough manner, in accordance with my orders. Part of my brief is to assess your people for suitability for the duties required of them. If that's going to be a problem—"

"No, no, it won't be a problem, Rocco. I'm sure we can all get along."

Schofield seemed to lose a little of his faux buddy-buddy manner—someone less observant might never have noticed. "I'm sure we can." Rocco removed his billfold from his pants pocket and withdrew a business card. He offered it to Schofield. "I'd also like to see a schedule of all known visitors for the next month, if you have that information to hand. If you need to contact me, all my details are there. I would appreciate the roster information by email as soon as possible, if that's not inconvenient for you."

"Of course. I'll get it to you by the end of the day." Schofield's smile didn't quite reach his eyes.

"Thank you. I appreciate your assistance." Rocco stood. "I know you'll be busy, so I'll leave you to get back to work. Thank you for your time. I'll see myself out."

Rocco closed the office door behind him, and before he'd taken three steps, reached the conclusion that he didn't like Frank Schofield, and more to the point, didn't trust him. In Rocco's opinion, he should probably have stayed retired from the police department, rather than seeking out a position in private security. It wouldn't take much for Rocco to recommend he be replaced.

"Hey. Hold it right there."

Rocco stopped dead. An order delivered in exactly that tone was usually backed up by a weapon. When it came from behind him, it was especially bad news. He raised his hands and kept them well away from his head and his shoulder holster. "My name is Rocco Equizi, and I'm here—"

"Oh shit. I am so sorry, sir."

Rocco let out a long, low breath. He lowered his hands as slowly as he'd raised them, and turned to see who had challenged him.

The tall, blond man finished holstering his sidearm as he stepped out of the cover provided by the doorway to the locker room. In his mid to late twenties, he was almost wearing the uniform of one of the estate security guards. His shirt wasn't quite buttoned up, and he was missing the ball cap—as if he'd just arrived and had been interrupted in his preparations to go on shift.

"No problem. You didn't know who I was. What's your name?"

"Scott Monroe, sir."

"Nice to meet you, Scott." Rocco held out his hand in

greeting. "And it's Rocco, not 'sir'. Have you worked here long?"

"Only about six months—I'm still the new guy. I usually pull the night shift, but someone called in sick, so I volunteered to cover some extra shifts."

An impressive work ethic. Rocco nodded. "You'll probably see me around for a few weeks. I'll try not to get in your way."

"I doubt you'll do that, sir."

Rocco chose not to remind the other man about using his name. The respectful form of address was clearly second nature to the other man, so Rocco left it at that, and after chatting for a few more minutes, he resumed his walk back to Sasha's office. He'd arrive just in time for coffee, and when he did, there was something very specific Rocco wanted to discuss with her. It related to Scott Monroe, and depending on what Rocco found—or didn't find—in his records, he had a somewhat different duty in mind for the security team's latest recruit.

Sasha screwed her eyes up and pinched the bridge of her nose. Getting older sucked sometimes, but it beat the alternative.

She was more than ready to take a break from her computer. She wondered if Rocco was on his way back from seeing Frank Schofield, and it wasn't only because she was craving an injection of caffeine. She was keen to hear his assessment of the head of security, and how closely—if at all—it matched hers.

Frank was already working for Linzi by the time Sasha came along. The way Gerry told it, he'd been recruited in a hurry because someone had sent Linzi some packages containing "gifts" that clearly hadn't come from her legions of adoring fans. Sasha's instincts were probably doing Frank a disservice, but she'd never been able to shake the feeling that there was something not quite legit about him—that he was pretending to be something he wasn't. She had no proof, and there was no evidence—the man had never, to the best of her knowledge, done anything that could be construed as threatening, but the suspicion wouldn't go away.

"Now there's a serious expression. Got something on your mind?"

A delicious quiver of awakening shimmered down Sasha's spine at the mere sound of that English accent. If Rocco recited the alphabet, she'd be in a puddle before he reached H for Hot-As-Sin—a perfect description for the man standing in the doorway to her office. "No. Yes. I don't know... Maybe."

A frown creased Rocco's brow. "Sounds to me like you need a good, strong coffee. Why don't we grab one and take a breath of fresh air?"

"Fresh air? Are you kidding me? It's winter," she complained, almost to the point of whining.

"It's Texas, and it's sunny. Did you or did you not tell me just yesterday you're more used to seeing snow in winter? Back home, we don't always have *summers* as good as this. Come on—I need to talk to you about something."

That snagged Sasha's attention. Had he detected something sketchy about their head of security? She rose and came out from behind her desk. "Sure. Let's get that coffee and we'll find a quiet corner."

Having sneaked a couple of mugs of the constant supply of superior coffee from the kitchen, Sasha led the way around to the secluded area of the garden that was perfect for a discreet discussion that shouldn't be overheard. Ever the gentleman, Rocco waited until she was seated in one of the Adirondack chairs before taking the one beside her. She refused to feel bad about being wrapped up in a warm coat while Rocco was dressed as if it were spring.

Sasha took a sip of liquid bliss and gave a soft sigh of contentment. "So, what's on your mind?"

"A couple of things. What can you tell me about Frank Schofield?"

This was promising—he was asking about the ex-cop after only one conversation with him. Maybe it wasn't her imagination after all, if Rocco's instincts were in line with hers. "I'll give you the details when we get back to the office, but, as you probably know, he's a retired police officer from up north. Good at his job in his day, if his records are to be believed. Gerry hired him on Linzi's behalf about a year before I started working for her, in circumstances not unlike the current situation. Why do you ask?"

Rocco set his coffee down on the low table between them. "I don't know. Maybe it's a lack of cultural awareness on my part—for which I apologize—but... I can't put my finger on it yet, but there's something not right about him. You say this has happened before?"

Sasha wrapped her hands around her mug for extra warmth. "It's why Frank was hired. The threats and packages stopped soon after he started."

Rocco frowned. "What sort of packages? What was in them?"

Sasha shuddered. "Nothing good, according to what I was told. Dead animals, mostly—you get the idea."

"If he was so successful last time, is there a reason why you haven't told him this time?"

How could she explain the inexplicable? "If I said it was instinct, that I have no proof, that I can't even point to any specific incidents that give me reason to suspect him, would you believe me?"

"Yes."

"But why? You don't even know me."

Rocco chuckled. "I have instincts too, and they tell me I can trust yours. Anyway, we were talking about Frank. He doesn't live on site, does he?"

"No, none of the security team do. Frank has a house about twenty, thirty miles away, I believe." Unless he'd relocated since she'd first felt the need to look into him.

"And when he's not on duty, who's his deputy?"

"Brian Schofield—his son." Sasha had never been happy about the nepotistic arrangement. "Why do you ask?"

"What do you know about him?"

Sasha thought about that one and came up short. "Not a lot. By that, I mean he doesn't stand out for any particular reason. I think he started a few months after his father. Does his job, doesn't ruffle any feathers—or hasn't so far."

"When we get back to the office, I'd like to take a look at his records."

"You've got your login—help yourself. Just, please... don't delete everybody by accident."

Rocco chuckled. "I'll try not to." Then he sobered. "There is something else, though."

"Go on."

"I ran into one of the guards in the block while I was there—Scott Monroe. You know anything about him?"

"Again, for the details, I'll need to check the personnel records. If I recall, he's a recent recruit—Army vet, with an exemplary service record. Why's he attracted your attention?"

Rocco raised an eyebrow. "He got the drop on me as I was leaving the security block. You might not think it's important, but it shows he's alert, with good situational awareness. Good to know he has military experience; it might come in useful. I have a proposition, but before I put it to him, I'd like your agreement. Out of professional courtesy I should also speak to Schofield, but I'd rather leave him out of this particular loop if I can."

"If you think that's best, I'm not going to argue. So what's this proposition?"

"When Linzi attends the awards, I want someone else there who I know I can rely on implicitly. She'll be out in the open, and it'll be an ideal opportunity for someone who means her harm."

"You really think that's likely? On what basis?" The subtle shift in Rocco's expression told her there was more to this than met the eye.

"I've seen some of the online threats, and while I'm no expert, I believe there's an escalation. If whoever's behind it intends to make those threats real, the awards will be their first opportunity to do it. That, and instinct. The first time I ignored instinct was also the last."

She didn't want to ask, but she couldn't stop herself. "What happened?"

Rocco picked up his coffee and took a fortifying drink. "Good people died."

Like a perfectly aimed punch, the short, bleak answer hit home with breathtaking accuracy. Sasha could identify with the deeply buried emotion behind it only too well. She'd seen good people die, too—including Jack. "Then if your proposition is designed to prevent that from happening again, you have my full support. What do you intend to do?"

"If Monroe agrees, I'd like to train him up—build on the experience he has, give him some close protection skills. Hopefully, he won't have to use them, but I think he'd be a good man in a crisis, and someone you could rely on one hundred percent."

Especially when Rocco was no longer there. The back of

Sasha's neck prickled with tension. "You think we're going to need that level of extra protection?"

"I don't know, but like I said, it'd be a good idea. Better to have someone and not need them than need them and not have them."

The words were a chilling reminder of the reason why Rocco had come to Casa Millefiori. "Do you really think we'll be able to find out who's behind the threats?"

Rocco sat forward, his forearms resting on his thighs while he rotated the mug between his hands. "Cybersecurity —the technology behind it—isn't my forte, but we have people on it. If they can tie the threats back to an identifiable individual, then we can take action."

"Sounds simple, doesn't it?"

"On the face of it, yes, but if it's someone who really knows what they're doing, we could chase our tails forever and not track them down."

Much as she'd suspected. "What happens then?"

"A heightened state of vigilance becomes a way of life, but no one can live like that for the long term. It's fortunate that criminals make more mistakes than you'd think—if they didn't, if they all planned and executed the perfect crime, prisons would be empty and crime rates would be sky-high."

An unexpected surge of frustration clawed at Sasha. She had skills that would make her far more useful in this situation than the persona she'd adopted as Linzi's assistant. She could work with Rocco as an equal, but that would mean informing him about the past she was determined to leave behind her. Still, it was a sacrifice she was willing to make. "Rocco—"

He stood. "Try not to worry. I know my job, and I have a good team backing me up. By the time I leave here, Linzi will be safe, there'll be no more threats, and security on this site will be upgraded to a far more effective level. Are you ready to go back to the office now? The sooner I start, the sooner I finish and get out of your way."

Sasha had to bite her tongue. She had the oddest, strongest impulse to tell Rocco—a virtual stranger—that he could stay in her way for as long as he liked. What made it especially odd was that it didn't feel odd at all.

CHAPTER 5

"Can you find out more about Frank Schofield, the head of security? I think the file we have on him might have some extensive gaps."

Rocco hadn't intended to report back to his boss that evening, but something about his meeting with Schofield hadn't sat right with him all day. The more he'd thought about it, the worse it had become, until finally he made a Skype call to Nick before he went to meet Sasha for dinner.

At the other end of the video call, Nick's eyes narrowed. "Why are you asking about him? I thought he was barely IT-literate."

"That's right, but there's something about him that's bothering me. I can't say what it is, but my instincts are telling me there's more to him than meets the eye, and it's not good."

Nick's expression became pensive. "If he's bothering you, that's good enough for me. I'll get Charity and Tex onto it."

"Thank you—and thank them for me."

"Will do. Have you eaten yet?"

"Just about to."

"Good. On your own… or with company?"

There was an air of speculation to the question that didn't escape Rocco. "With company. I'm not fraternizing with the client, if that's what's worrying you."

Such fraternization was neither allowed nor disallowed according to the terms of Spectrum's standard employee contract. There was only an understanding that if fraternization took place, it would be discreet and would not jeopardize the client's safety. After all, that was how Ros Northwood, his boss back in the UK, had come to meet the man who was now her husband. And her submissive, if what he'd heard about the couple was true. Each to their own...

"Wouldn't worry me if you were, so long as it didn't get in the way of the mission, and I have it on good authority you wouldn't let it. However, I doubt Miss Suto's your type," Nick said with a wry smile. "Her PA on the other hand..."

Having come to know his boss and his better half fairly well during the week of his induction, Rocco covered the sensation of being caught out like a child with his hand in the cookie jar with his own little humorous dig. "Have you been married long enough to get away with saying things like that about other women?"

Charity's voice came from off the screen. "He hasn't, but I'll give him a hall pass just this once. I'll ask Tex about this Schofield guy, see if he'll give us a twofer on him and Sasha."

"Has there been any word from Tex about her yet?"

"No, which is why he thinks—and I agree—there must be something to hide, but he's hoping to uncover something soon." Charity appeared behind her husband. "If it means anything, even if she does have something to hide, I still think she's good people. I don't think she's the bad guy in this."

"For what it's worth, I agree," Nick added.

Rocco wanted to think the same. He told himself it was because he wanted the person closest to his principal to be someone she could trust and rely on, but the truth probably had a lot more to do with his very personal interest in Sasha, and involved indulging some of his baser instincts. "I hope you're right."

Nick shrugged. "Time will tell—hopefully fairly soon. Anything else you need?"

"That's about it for now."

"Okay. Enjoy your dinner." Nick raised a knowing eyebrow. "It's a school night—don't stay up too late."

Rocco closed his eyes and shook his head. "I left home a long time ago… Dad."

As he signed off, Rocco kept his features carefully schooled, so as not to betray even the slightest hint about the link between his last word to his boss and the single most toxic relationship he'd ever experienced.

His cell pinged with a text alert. It was from Sasha.

We're in the kitchen for dinner—sorry. Linzi's boyfriend's staying over, so they're using the small dining room.

Rocco couldn't say he was sorry. Given a choice between very informal dining in the kitchen and the formal dining room—a space that was only marginally smaller than the flight deck of an aircraft carrier—he was glad Sasha had opted for the kitchen rather than the larger of the two dining rooms.

All thoughts of his conversation with Nick disappeared as Rocco made his way through the house. It was, without doubt, a beautiful residence, but a home it was not. Would he feel any differently if he lived there permanently? He doubted it, but the question was irrelevant. When he was done here, he'd move on. *Wash. Rinse. Repeat.* Until he no longer wanted to do the job—or something happened that meant he couldn't do it.

There was no sign of his dinner companion yet, so Rocco gave Chef a wide berth and took the long way around the kitchen to the counter where he'd enjoyed breakfast with Sasha that morning. He almost made it, too, until Geri waylaid him.

"Rocco, hi. Hope you've had a good day."

"I have, Geri, thanks. You work evenings as well?"

"I have the breakfast shift, and help Chef with dinner."

"So you get lunch off for good behavior?"

The petite blonde grinned. "Something like that. Now, where are you going?"

Rocco glanced toward the counter where he and Sasha had had breakfast. "Over there seemed to be a reasonable assumption."

Geri folded her arms and treated him to a disapproving shake of the head. "Absolutely not. Come this way."

Rocco followed her around a corner and straight into a secluded alcove where a table for two had been prepared, complete with a dazzling white linen tablecloth, coruscating crystal glassware, and what Rocco's mother would have called "the posh cutlery". He turned to Geri.

"I think there's been some kind of mistake. Unless you're expecting—"

"Only you and Sasha. Oh, she sends her apologies—she'll be here in about ten minutes. Linzi wanted her for something. Now, can I get you a drink?"

"Water will be fine, thanks." Nick's comment about it being a school night might well have been a joke, but when he was working, Rocco preferred to keep a clear head whenever possible.

"One pitcher of ice water coming right up. You sit down,

make yourself comfortable, and relax. I'll take care of everything."

In the absence of any better ideas, Rocco did as he was told. This was crazy. All the table needed was candlelight, and anyone would think it was a date.

With nothing else to do, Rocco took the opportunity to look through what amounted to a glass wall to the gardens beyond. With the sun now well and truly set, the solar garden lights had come on, giving the place an almost fairy-tale appearance.

All in all, the day had gone well. No real surprises, which was always good, and then there'd been that twenty-minute run with Sasha. The perfect way to end the working day, or so he'd thought—until she'd invited him to join her for dinner and perfection had taken on a whole new meaning.

He sensed a presence to his right at the same moment he became aware of the scent of flowers. She was there, just beyond his peripheral vision, but for some reason, she'd come to a halt.

Rocco resisted the temptation to look around. Instead, he reached for his glass, took a sip of water, and waited.

Being unexpectedly waylaid by Linzi had been frustrating at the time, but at this moment, Sasha could only give thanks for the consequences. If she hadn't been running late, she wouldn't be standing here, out of Rocco's line of sight, drinking in a vision that had her ovaries throwing the party to end all parties. She really needed to get a grip.

He'd beaten her to the kitchen, as she'd suspected he might. The man had been nothing but punctual all day. Then again, he was ex-military, probably ex-special forces, and disciplined to the nth degree. His middle name was probably *self-control.*

She'd imagined him turning up in jeans and a short-sleeved t-shirt, given he was off the clock, and had worried that the dress she'd chosen would be too much. Now she was glad she'd made the effort.

Her dinner partner was wearing black dress shoes, black tailored pants, and a crisp, white, open-necked dress shirt with the sleeves rolled up to mid-forearm, revealing the light smattering of hair that mirrored the glimpses she'd caught of his chest on their run earlier. His dark hair—slightly messy in a way that had her itching to run her fingers through it—curled a little over his collar.

With a glass of water in one hand, he sat at ease, one ankle resting on the other knee. In another reality, the one fabricated by lust and imagination, she'd go over to him, lay a hand on his shoulder, and when he lifted his head to look at her, she'd stoop and kiss him in greeting.

But that was a fantasy. Real life was very different—unfortunately. Sasha smoothed her dress down over her hips, straightened her shoulders, and stepped forward.

"Hi," she greeted him as he rose to meet her. "I'm sorry I kept you waiting."

He gave her a smile that made butterflies loop-the-loop in her stomach. "It's no problem. Geri let me know you'd be delayed. I've been enjoying the view."

Sasha glanced toward the windows. She'd grown so accustomed to her surroundings, both inside the house and out, that she'd almost become blind to them. Seeing them through Rocco's eyes breathed new life into her perception. "The gardens are pretty, aren't they? You should see them in summer."

She continued to the vacant chair, and somehow Rocco was there, drawing it back for her. He made sure she was comfortable, then returned to his seat. Before he sat down, though, he offered to pour her a glass of water.

"That would be lovely, thank you."

Now that she had a better view of Rocco, Sasha was truly impressed. She'd last seen him in sweatpants and a tee with a V-neck—now he was the epitome of casual elegance, and every bit as devastating as he'd been in his suit during the day. The man sure did know how to dress.

On her way down for dinner, Sasha had promised herself she was going to keep the conversation strictly to business, but Rocco Equizi was pure living, breathing temptation. Just looking at him gave her a delicious tingle in places that had been in hibernation for too long. She wanted to know about *him,* not the work that had steered his path her way. And she didn't care how unwise it might be.

"Did you manage to resolve Linzi's issue for her?"

"I did. She has a service that comes to Millefiori to style her hair, makeup and nails, and she was… concerned about the scheduling of her next appointment."

"Concerned" being a euphemism for a full-on meltdown. Fortunately, Sasha was well-versed in placating her employer. When Linzi got a bee in her bonnet about something, she was harder work than usual anyway, but this time had been even worse and had taken longer. At times like this, Sasha seriously wondered how much longer she was going to stay in the job, threat or no threat. Loyalty to her former supervisor was one thing, but for the sake of her sanity, it couldn't be an infinite resource.

Rocco's expression intrigued her. If she had to identify the sentiment behind it, she would have said it was sympathy, as if he understood. His next words, in response to her unspoken question, confirmed it.

"A whole day visiting every department store in the West End. His husband had given my principal carte blanche to buy whatever he wanted while he was in session at some conference, and he wanted everything—except it took about three circuits of each store to make sure he got it. I've had easier deployments to the Middle East."

Sasha dissolved into laughter. "Oh, that sounds painful. How did you survive?"

A panty-melting half-smile curved his mouth. "I'm not sure, but when they returned to the UK on their next visit and requested my services, my boss wove a fairly elaborate tale around my... unavailability for the duration of their trip. The two guys who drew the short straw and got the gig were not happy."

"I'm sure they weren't." Sasha could imagine only too well how bad it could get.

"I'm guessing you don't rate shopping as a pastime."

"More like a necessary evil." There hadn't been much time for treating it as a recreational activity in her previous life, and her attitude toward it hadn't changed in the intervening years.

Rocco raised his water glass in salute. "Music to a man's ears."

A discreet cough sounded to the side of them. Geri was peering around the wall that shielded them from the frantic activity going on in the kitchen. The young chef was wearing a smile that suggested she was reading way too much into the situation between Sasha and Rocco.

"Good evening. I hope you both had a good day today. Now, what can I get you to eat?"

Rocco shrugged. "Whatever's easiest. We know you have your hands full with catering for Linzi and her guest."

A thrill of pleasure zinged down Sasha's spine. Part of her wanted to protest at the way he'd spoken for both of them, but on the other hand, she agreed with him, so why cause a commotion? Besides, she could do exactly the same. "Surprise us. Whatever it is, I know it'll be delicious."

"Is there anything we can do to help?" Rocco asked.

Geri raised her eyebrows. "Thanks for the offer, but it'll only stress Chef if he has untrained newbies under his feet. Sure I can't get you a bottle of wine or something?"

"Sasha?"

The way he said her name almost had her squirming in her seat. "I'm fine with water, if you are?"

"Absolutely."

"Great," Geri said. "I'll be back in a few moments."

Having delivered the replacement pitcher, the young woman took the almost empty one away, leaving Sasha and Rocco alone once more. Sasha turned a wry smile on her companion. "She's right about Chef—he can be a little temperamental when things don't go his way."

"Something tells me there's a story there?"

Sasha shrugged. "It was a showbiz party. A lot of guests, and some of them got a little carried away. Illicit substances may or may not have been involved, but there was definitely an abundance of alcohol. Some of the guests found their way to the kitchen, and... Let's just say, Chef nearly had a meltdown to rival Chernobyl, and Geri earned every last cent of the bonus I authorized for her that week."

Rocco laughed, and something turned a somersault in Sasha's chest. The lighthearted reaction revealed a whole different side to him. A man like him could have any woman he wanted. Especially when he looked at her the way he was looking at Sasha, now that the laughter had died away.

"I enjoyed our run tonight."

A certain kind of warmth suffused her body, something she hadn't felt in a long time. "So did I. It was good to have some company."

Especially such delectable company. Rocco had inspired

her to up her game, so her regular run had suddenly become a lot more interesting.

"So tell me—when you switch off your computer for the day, and you've been for a run and dinner's out of the way, what do you find to do? How do you fill your spare time?"

Spare time was a luxury she didn't waste. "Sleep, usually. Or I sometimes read. Why are you looking at me like that?" Sasha tried not to respond in kind to the smile he was trying to stifle.

"I… can't really imagine you lazing round, reading."

"Why not? Reading is a perfectly honorable way to pass the time."

He didn't look convinced. "So what do you read?"

"Books, of course," she hedged.

"You know that's not what I meant. What kind of books? Fiction? Non-fiction? Biographies?"

Sasha shook her head. "What is this? The third degree? Some sort of weird psychological evaluation?"

"Not at all." Rocco raised his glass to his lips. "I'm interested. What about days off? What do you do when you have a whole day away from your desk?"

She gave a short laugh. "I'll let you know when it happens. Linzi usually needs me for something at least once a day."

Rocco's brow creased in disapproval. "That's harsh."

"Says the man who works in close protection, a field not known for keeping regular office hours."

"Touché." He raised his glass in salute. "That's probably why being able to go for that run tonight was a welcome change."

"Does that mean you'd like to do it again?" They hadn't really discussed it, but Sasha had more than a passing interest in the answer.

Rocco's gaze pinned her to her seat. "I'd love to."

Before Sasha could respond, Geri reappeared with two steaming plates. "Here you go. Enjoy."

"That smells delicious."

Sasha liked the way Rocco directed his comment to Geri. She also liked the sheepish grin that appeared on Geri's face. "Are you responsible for this, Geri?"

"Chef told me to get on with it, so I got on with it." A male voice suddenly roared Geri's name. She rolled her eyes. "I think I'm wanted elsewhere. I'd better go. Enjoy your evening."

The spicy chicken dish was a favorite of Sasha's, and she was pleased to hear it met with Rocco's approval, too. Not that he said anything intelligible—the giveaway was the hum of satisfaction that accompanied his first taste.

Confirmation came at the end of the meal, including the light dessert Geri presented them with when she arrived to bus the dishes.

"She's good. I thought breakfast was amazing, but that was something special." He pushed his dessert plate to one side.

Sasha agreed with a groan. "Tell me about it. In some ways, she's wasted here. She should have a restaurant of her own."

Rocco agreed. "She'd make a fortune."

Under the influence of an exquisite meal, they sat in a comfortable silence. The sounds of activity coming from the kitchen gradually diminished, eventually broken only by the sound of footsteps heading in their direction.

"Hi, guys. Everything okay with your food tonight?"

Sasha turned to see Geri peering around the wall that separated their table from the kitchen. She was wearing a mischievous grin and a teasing expression that Sasha knew was meant primarily for her. "Delicious as always, Geri, thank you. Shouldn't you be off duty by now?"

"Just on my way, ma'am. Leave the dishes to one side—I'll stack them in the washer in the morning. Enjoy your evening!"

And with that, she disappeared from view.

Somewhat perplexed, Sasha was still looking into the space the other woman had occupied when a question from Rocco sent fire to her cheeks.

"Did she just wink at you?"

Sasha winced. "You saw it too? I was kind of hoping I imagined it."

"If you did, then both of us did. What was—"

"Nothing." Sasha fixed a bright smile in place to cover up the abruptness of her response. "Absolutely nothing, she has a crazy sense of humor. Now—where were we?"

"I was about to ask you if you were ready to call it a night."

She was… and she wasn't. Sasha had enjoyed his company even more than she'd anticipated, leaving her reluctant to end the evening. And while she wondered how he'd react if she asked him back for coffee in her apartment, another part of her wasn't keen on the idea of hearing him turn her down. "I guess so."

She automatically made to pick up the plates, but Rocco beat her to it. She did, however, manage to call dibs on the glassware. Rocco followed her to the dishwasher, and once he set the dishes in the racks, he offered Sasha his arm. "Allow me."

His accent and his smile would be any woman's undoing. She slipped her hand into the crook of his elbow, and at once was struck by twin impressions of heat and strength.

In no particular hurry to rush back to her suite, Sasha let Rocco set the pace. Apparently, he was in no rush either. They strolled together through the silent house, along the hall to the main atrium, and from there, to their accommodation. As they stopped outside her door, he moved his elbow to release her and turned to face her.

"I enjoyed this evening. Thank you very much for the pleasure of your company."

His sincerity warmed her through. "The pleasure was all mine."

Her gaze connected with his, and suddenly the undercurrent of attraction that had been bubbling away all evening burst to the surface. Sasha couldn't help herself. She drew closer to him, her focus narrowing to concentrate on his mouth, and just as she was mentally preparing for her lips to collide with his, the shutters came down and he backed off.

"Enjoy the rest of your evening, Sasha. I'll see you in the morning. Sleep well."

And with a crushing sense of loss mingled with growing frustration, she watched him walk away.

He'd come so close to kissing her. The woman he wanted, warm and willing, and right there in front of him, and like a craven coward, he'd retreated. What the hell was wrong with him?

Stupid question. He was only using it to avoid the truth.

Rocco leaned against the wall and gazed out into the darkness beyond the terrace outside his suite and reflected on an evening spent with the woman who, to put it bluntly, had knocked him on his ass. The woman who had driven him to abandon his principles and make a beeline to the refrigerator for the beer that now chilled his fingers. He put the bottle to his lips and took a healthy swallow of the ice-cold beverage.

So close. Another couple of seconds, maybe even less, and he'd have known the sweet taste of her lips, were it not for the swift assault of a guilty conscience striking through him like a spear.

It had been so easy when all he'd known of her was that photograph. Back then, she'd been a woman he wanted to bed, no different from any of his previous lovers, no different from the women who'd come after her.

Meeting her, being with her, had changed all that, and with a speed that left him as breathless as she did. With her, he wanted more than some fun at the end of the day. She wasn't an easy lay he could walk away from when his job was done.

Rocco didn't remember much of his early childhood in Sicily, but he did remember something Dario had told him during one of his summer visits in later years.

"When I first saw your mother, she was alone and scared. She was also the most beautiful girl I'd ever seen in my life, and I vowed to God that one day, I would marry her. I loved her from the moment I met her, and I will continue to love her until the day I die."

As a teen, he'd never understood that, but now? One thought looped through his mind, and no matter how hard he tried, he couldn't rid himself of it.

Like father, like son.

Did he have more in common with Dario than he'd always thought?

The concept was unsettling. Rocco didn't want to admit he had anything at all in common with the man who'd sired him, yet he couldn't deny his deep, spontaneous attraction to Sasha.

Or how, over the course of the evening, it had taken the first few steps toward evolving into something all-consuming and infinitely more complex than a primal urge to have sex with her.

CHAPTER 6

After a restless night, Rocco rose early and visited the deserted gym for a short but rigorous workout. He then left a message of apology for Geri for not making it to the kitchen to sample her amazing cooking again, and resigned himself to a substantially inferior breakfast of strong black coffee instead.

Which was how he came to be buried in his examination of personnel records when Sasha arrived in her office the morning after he blew his chance to become intimately acquainted with the taste of her lips.

"Good morning, Mr. Equizi. I hope you slept well."

Rocco stiffened—and not in a good way. To describe Sasha's manner as cool would be an understatement of epic proportions. Not that he could blame her. The way he'd walked away from her had been… abrupt. And insulting.

"I did, thank you," he lied. "You?"

Her reply completely ignored his question. "I'm going to be with Linzi all day, going over her schedule for the next twelve months, so you'll have the office to yourself for the rest of the day. If you need anything, text me."

Without another word, she scooped up her tablet and notebook, and departed. Rocco couldn't shake the feeling he'd been summarily dismissed, especially with the storm-force deafening silence that filled the room following the explosive slam of the door.

Rocco crossed off the last name he'd checked on the list of employees and brought the next one up on the laptop screen.

It was going to be a long day…

And at the end of a long day came an even longer evening. Rocco was used to dining alone, but tonight had been a trial. He'd prepared dinner for one, the way he had thousands of times before, but by the time it was ready, his appetite had all but vanished.

Though he'd remained focused on his work all day, Rocco had still missed Sasha's presence in her office. True to her word, she hadn't returned. He'd skipped lunch, so he should have been hungry, but the pasta dish had nonetheless ended up in the waste disposal.

He still hadn't heard from Nick or Charity, and not knowing Sasha's history—and that she was in the clear—was making him itch from the inside out. He paced the room like a caged jungle cat, to the point where he had to get outside or he'd end up punching something. He tucked the Glock into the waistband of his pants as a precaution, grabbed his jacket, and made good his escape from the suffocating apartment.

Although the stillness and quietness made a pleasant change from the hustle and bustle of the house during the daytime, it didn't mean Rocco was any less observant. Vigilance was a way of life, had been for years, and that didn't change just because he was playing nursemaid to an overindulged brat in a glitzy mansion. His next assignment could come with a much higher level of risk, so he couldn't afford to lower his guard for a cushy job like this one.

With no particular route in mind, Rocco wound up on the path that would take him to the studio annex. He hadn't been down here since his introduction to Linzi. Of course, there was still a hell of a lot of the compound he hadn't seen at all, but tonight, for a reason he couldn't identify, he felt drawn to this place.

Trees and shrubs rustled in the light breeze, accompanied by the gentle lapping sound of the water in the pool. Thoughts of skinny-dipping with Sasha on hot nights sprang to life and kicked his libido into high gear—until he saw the light spilling from the studio block. His hand automatically retrieved the weapon nestling against his spine and, dropping low, he ran to the building. With his free hand, he punched in the access code, silently cursing the chirps as he did so.

Not only was light spilling from—if memory served—the dance studio, there was music, too. Without lowering his guard or his weapon, Rocco hugged the wall, crept to the open doorway, and peered into the room.

From his vantage point, the studio looked typical of its kind—a light-colored, presumably sprung wooden floor, with a floor-to-ceiling mirror along one wall. What was atypical was the chrome pole fixed to the floor and ceiling a few feet in front of the gigantic mirror.

Reflected movement caught his eye. He edged forward inch by inch, until he could get a line on who was to the left of the room.

Of all the people it could have been, it had to be *her*. He pressed his lips together. Sasha hadn't seen him yet, and if he stepped back now, she wouldn't. Except… he couldn't step back. Curiosity kept him rooted to the spot. He made his weapon safe and returned it to the waist of his pants.

She was using the touch screen on some sort of control panel, but that was a minor detail—his focus was on the woman herself, and in response to the vision before him, interest spiked in every cell in his body.

Sasha was barefoot, clad only in boy shorts and a crop top that left little to the imagination. He'd had no idea her crisp, professional appearance concealed a body a woman fifteen years her junior would have been proud of. Both his hormones and his cock sprang to attention.

A new piece of music started up, one Rocco recognized. It was an instrumental version of *Love Me Like You Do,* and as he stood there in silence, he could only watch in awe.

Swaying in perfect time with the music, Sasha grasped the pole with one hand, spun and pirouetted around it, and then somehow, using both hands and maybe some weird kind of esoteric magic, she was a foot off the ground. The series of elegant spins and fan-like kicks that followed left him mesmerized by her strength and agility.

He'd never seen anything more graceful in his life. Some of her moves seemed impossible—one leg wrapped around the pole, with the rest of her body arranged in a way that left both hands free as she rotated. Then she grasped the pole again, and all of a sudden she was upside down and making gravity-defying moves even a ballet dancer might envy.

And while the athleticism was impressive, the sheer sensuality of her dance was off the charts. She moved as if the pole were her lover, caressing it, twining her body around it in a way that left him hard as granite, wanting even more to be the lover she'd wrap herself around in search of the most basic of human pleasures.

When it came to anything arty, Rocco would readily admit he was pretty much a philistine—he wouldn't know a good painting from a hole in the ground. On the other hand, he knew what he liked, and he liked what he saw—even if it was an oncoming tsunami of living, breathing temptation. And the longer he watched her, the more intense his internal conflict became. With each passing second his desire for her grew ever more feral, and the consequences of surrendering to it ever more insignificant.

In spite of that inner turmoil, he recognized the song was coming to an end, and when it did, she'd stop dancing. He should disappear—right now—and leave their relationship at its frosty, business-only status quo, but his feet still refused to move. At least, not in the direction they should. Instead, he pushed the door further open and knocked.

Towel in hand, Sasha spun around to face him. For a split second she reminded him of a delicate bird caught in a net, unable to escape, but then a veil of glacial composure slipped into place. "Mr. Equizi. What are you doing here?"

"I couldn't sleep, so I thought I'd make a start on familiarizing myself with the place."

"By coming to an area you've already visited?"

She pointed out the blatant flaw in his response with cutting objectivity. Rocco refused to be deterred.

"I was going to take the path around the rear of the building, but I saw the lights and thought it would be a good idea to make sure nothing was amiss."

"Really?" She lifted the towel and pressed it to her glistening cheeks. "So did you find anything 'amiss'?"

Rocco folded his arms—it was the only way to make sure they didn't go anywhere near her. "Only you."

"So how long have you been there?" She folded her towel and dropped it on the table beside her.

"Since the beginning of that last track."

Her lips pinched together. "I see. Do you always spy on defenseless women, Mr. Equizi?"

No matter how he answered that, with the way things were between them, there was a very good chance she'd spit-roast his balls over a barbecue—she was far from defenseless. "How can I possibly answer that, Miss Morgan? If I say yes, then it's an instant admission I'm a stalker, yet if I say no, it might imply I sometimes spy on… defenseless women."

He was goading her, and he had to be crazy to do it. The only sensible course of action was to walk away, so that was what he'd do. Any. Minute. Now.

A raised eyebrow told him he hadn't won her over. "But, Mr. Equizi, I didn't specify a yes or no answer. Give me an answer that'll… convince me."

She prowled toward him, all sinuous female grace and predatory feline intent. Some men—men with more intelligence than he possessed—might take the prudent action of beating a hasty retreat, but not Rocco. He shifted his weight to both feet and waited, prepared for whatever she fired in his direction.

She stopped inches away from him, all lush woman at the peak of her attraction. He didn't care that she was older than him—four years was nothing, and age was only a number anyway. The only thing that mattered was this insane, intense attraction that wouldn't go away.

"So, how do I do that?"

Now he was pushing her. Those words should never have left his mouth. Any second now, she was going to tell him in no uncertain terms to fuck off and stay out of her way.

Except… she didn't.

"I was hoping for something like this." Her hands framed his face and she stepped closer, one knee opening up the space between his legs, so his cock and balls became intimately acquainted with her thigh. "Rocco."

The husky way she spoke his name, sweet honey and smooth whisky, was hypnotic and enthralling, and when her arms went around his neck, his craving to take her soared into orbit. She claimed his mouth, and when the tip of her tongue swept across the seam of his lips, his hunger for her surrendered easily to her demand.

A wild game of tease sprang to life. He responded in kind, kissing her the way he'd wanted to since he'd first seen her. Her lips closed on his lower lip, gentle suction teasing him into her mouth, and his dick responded as if it were the lucky recipient of her attention. He sensed her smile—it didn't take a genius to work out what she was smiling about. She'd have felt his body's reaction through a suit of armor.

"Basta!"

Reality gatecrashed the party, reminding him of what still stood in the way of what he wanted. He couldn't let this continue until he was certain Sasha wasn't implicated, and getting involved with her wouldn't compromise his ability to see the job through. He had to get the hell out of there fast, before his willpower crumbled.

"I'm sorry to have interrupted you, Miss Morgan. Enjoy the rest of your evening."

And with that, he left, before he did anything even crazier.

After allowing her pride to get the better of her the moment she'd laid eyes on Rocco that morning, Sasha had not expected the day to end like this.

Until that moment, she hadn't realized exactly how deep the impact of his entrance into her orderly existence was. He'd left her a churning mass of frustration and conflict, torn between running after him to climb him like a tree and running after him to punch some sense into him and make him acknowledge their mutual attraction. He wanted her as much as she wanted him, and now that she had an idea what he was packing in those tailored pants of his, she wanted him *tonight*.

But not like this. She'd thrown herself body and soul into her dance session, leaving her hot and sweaty. Her hair was a mess, and her outfit, while scanty, was hardly a seductive little number. There was no way she was getting any more up close and personal until she'd cleaned up and changed into something far more suitable. She pulled on her yoga pants, pushed her feet into her sneakers, and crouched to tie the laces.

Fully intending to dive under the shower when she reached her apartment, Sasha jogged back to the main house, keeping a watch out for Rocco as she did so. There was no sign of him, but she was banking on him sequestering himself in his quarters after he left her. If he'd gone anywhere else, it would derail the wild plan taking shape in her mind.

However, at the door to her apartment, she hesitated. What if he was there right now, but disappeared while she was getting cleaned up? She ducked inside and considered her options.

There was no time to lose. A shower would take too long, so she washed her face and brushed out her hair instead, before darting back to the bedroom, stripping as she went. Clothes flew in all directions. Determined to waste as little time as possible, she didn't replace her sports bra and panties, pulling on a clean top and another pair of yoga pants instead. After stuffing her feet into a pair of ballet flats, she paused briefly to check her appearance in the mirror, and seconds later, she was knocking on Rocco's door.

Her heart thudded in her chest. If anyone had been within six feet of her, they'd have heard it pounding against her ribs. She hadn't been this nervous in years, but she wasn't going to let that stop her now.

The door opened and there he stood, his brow furrowed in a questioning frown. She waited for him to ask her what she was doing there, but then she noticed something. His jaw was rigid, as if he were fighting to maintain control.

Or was he fighting the memory of what he'd felt with her body pressed up close to his?

"May I come in?"

For a fraction of a second, indecision flared in his burning gaze, but then, without a word, he stepped back and opened the door wide enough to allow her to enter. She heard it close behind her and turned to face him.

Rocco's expression communicated only one thing—that he was a man whose will power was being tested to its limits. Maybe even beyond. All because of her. Didn't he understand she wasn't here to disrespect his boundaries, but to tell him they weren't necessary?

Rocco broke the silence. "Why are you here? What do you want?"

His voice was as taut as the atmosphere surrounding them like an invisible firestorm. She closed the gap between them and placed a butterfly-light kiss at one side of his mouth. "This."

She repeated the action with a second kiss at the other side. "And this."

Then she placed the third directly on his lips. "And you."

He didn't know the effect he had on her. He couldn't. Just as he couldn't know she'd been waiting all her life—for this moment, for him, the man who could make her heart race the way no other ever had.

And having come this far, she had to continue. If she was wrong… well, she could only die of embarrassment once when she had to face him the next day. She laid her palms on his chest, waiting for him to flinch or move away.

He did neither.

He was still wearing the white dress shirt and tailored black pants. The combination suited him—masculine, uncompromising, confidant. Dominant without needing to prove it. He let her unfasten the top two buttons of his shirt before he manacled her wrists with his hands and lowered them to her sides.

Even as she waited for him to reject her, every feminine instinct Sasha possessed responded to the light dusting of dark hair on the V of flesh exposed by her efforts. The urge to plaster herself to him came back with a vengeance. When he didn't push her away, just held her there, she leaned forward, trying to tempt him with another kiss.

His gaze glittered with intensity, as if he were searching her face for the answer to a question that was tearing him apart. Then, as abruptly as if he'd been stung, he released her hands and framed her face with his palms, to tilt her head so she was looking directly into his eyes. The need in them swept through her like a tornado, accelerating her pulse to breakneck speed. Heart racing, Sasha stood on her toes, placed a hand either side of Rocco's head, and urged him to lower his head for a kiss.

His mouth was lethal—what he could do with it, deadly. He kissed her like no other man had ever kissed her before, and it was intoxicating. She parted her lips to invite him in, and his response was immediate. His tongue flirted with hers, teasing and tasting, luring her to a place she was only too eager to go.

He walked her back until she hit the wall. Before she could recover her breath, he had her wrists pinned against the wall above her head. His lips crashed into hers again, and wave after wave of desire rolled remorselessly through her body, leaving her gasping for breath when his mouth moved to the side of her neck. "Rocco…"

"Shh."

Using one hand to keep her wrists tethered to the wall, he used his free hand to lift her top and palm her breast, growling his satisfaction when his flesh met hers. Tempestuous and demanding, the contact gave her a thrilling glimpse of the rough soldier beneath the urbane exterior. He pinched her nipple hard and her pussy throbbed in response, preparing for the cock she needed with increasing desperation. In her mind, she begged him to thrust his fingers between her legs, to do whatever it took to banish the agony of unfulfilled desire.

He didn't heed her silent plea. Instead, his hand stroked down her side and found the top of her yoga pants. He pushed the material down over her hip and groaned when he discovered the absence of panties. Strong fingers squeezed her bottom, then his hand moved to her lower belly, never losing contact with her skin. Instinct tilted her hips up, trying to coax him into doing what she craved, what her body cried out for.

"What do you want, Sasha?" he whispered against her cheek. "Tell me."

She squirmed against his free hand. "I want you to touch me."

"I am touching you."

She whimpered in frustration. "Not where I want you to."

"Then where do you want me to touch you?"

The primitive male prowling beneath the question tapped into her inner, equally primal female. "Between my legs."

"Here?"

He wasn't playing around. Sasha pressed her shoulders against the wall for more leverage as her hips writhed beneath his touch. The moan that escaped her lips could have been one of pain or pleasure—she had no way of knowing. While his thumb punished her clit, his fingers worked inside her, slipping in and out in a punishing rhythm that would drive her insane if he didn't let her finish.

He didn't. Without giving her time to think, much less protest, he spun her around so she was facing the wall. He released her long enough to strip her of her top and fling it aside, and yank her yoga pants down to her ankles. Then he resumed his hold on her and trapped her wrists against the wall above her head. In spite of his clothing, the steel bar of his cock digging into her told its own story of carnal desire.

"Sono pazzo di te."

Even though her Italian was almost nonexistent, she still got the message he was conveying through the low words he ground out against her shoulder. She wasn't about to break the mood by asking for a translation. Instead, she concentrated on the pressure of his chest against her naked back, the leashed power in his muscles. He was using just enough strength to hold her where he wanted her.

Which was *exactly* where she wanted to be.

Just when he'd thought the danger was over.

He should tell her to go, to get out and not come back.

And yet...

She'd come to him.

She wanted him.

His conscience could go to hell, and take his common sense with it.

He loosened his grip on her wrists. She lowered her arms and turned to face him, without even a hint of self-consciousness. There was nothing coy about Sasha Morgan. There was, however, something very, very beautiful. A woman who was as secure in her body as she was should be appreciated as a rare and precious treasure. Rocco appreciated every perfect, stunning inch.

Sasha lifted her chin and flashed a bold, confident smile. "What's wrong? We're both adults, and we both know what we want. No harm, no foul. What's stopping us?"

If only she knew.

To hell with it. At that moment, he didn't give a flying fuck if he torpedoed his career and ended up as a rent-a-cop in a shopping mall in the ass end of nowhere. Wanting Sasha had been the devil on his shoulder from the day he'd arrived in Texas, and now she was right where he wanted her.

Willingly.

His to take.

And he, it appeared, was where she wanted him. "Get rid of the pants," he growled.

Her gaze challenged his order for a few seconds, then he was peripherally aware of her toeing off her shoes and pushing them to one side, before doing some fancy footwork to carry out his instruction and shove the offending garment bunched around her ankles in the same direction.

Totally naked now, she was heaven in human form, all lush curves and golden skin. He wanted to strip down and take her there, up against the wall, to drive himself so deeply into her she'd never want any other lover but him. She'd wrap those incredible, long, dancer's legs around his hips, and once she'd screamed his name as one explosive orgasm after another ripped through her body, he'd empty himself inside her, and she'd be his forever.

"Whatever you're thinking right now," she whispered, "hold that thought. There's something I need before we get down and dirty."

He almost growled in frustration. "What's that?"

She ducked around him and put a couple of feet between them. "I could really use a shower."

He watched the hypnotic sway of her hips as she headed toward his bathroom. When she reached the doorway, she stopped and turned.

"Well? Are you going stand there all night, or join me?"

CHAPTER 7

In the past, Rocco had enjoyed the thrill of the chase when he'd set his sights on a woman he wanted in his bed. Conversely, there'd also been more than one occasion, while he'd still been serving with the Regiment, when he'd been the target for a woman who wanted to win bragging rights among her friends for spending the night with a trooper.

None of those women would come close to the classy lady in front of him and for that, he thanked God.

He took her hand, intending to lead her into the shower enclosure. "Let's get you cleaned up."

She didn't move. "I need to finish unwrapping my present first."

"What present?"

"You."

Rocco raised an eyebrow. "Finish? Seems to me you've barely even started. Come here."

He lifted her onto the bathroom counter, grinning at her shocked shriek when her bare ass came into contact with the marble surface. From his point of view, it was a small price to pay to have her at pretty much the perfect height.

He couldn't help himself—he had to kiss her, because kissing her was becoming as essential for his survival as breathing. Fingertips under her chin were enough to guide her into the perfect position for their lips to meet. He tasted her as delicately as if she were his father's finest vintage. Her skin was soft beneath his fingertips, her body sleek and taut like a jungle cat. She quivered as he explored the dips and swells of her lusciously feminine body, and when he finally rested his hands on her thighs, she parted them willingly, allowing him to step closer. He lowered his head to suckle at her breast and almost lost it when her palm cradled the back of his head.

"You're still wearing too many clothes."

Her mournful complaint coaxed his lips into a smile, and in the process, he released her nipple.

"Whose fault is that?" Rocco straightened up. "I'm still waiting for you to finish with my shirt."

Her hands returned to the place they'd occupied, burning his skin through the material that separated his flesh from hers, but this time, as if she'd finally tuned into his most intimate thoughts, she wrapped her delectable legs around his hips, too.

Rocco felt the smooth pull of fabric across his skin as Sasha eased the next button through the hole and drew his shirt to one side. She leaned forward, and before he knew it, her lips were branding his skin. To take his mind off the incendiary effect on his nervous system, Rocco stroked her hair and pushed it back, so he could kiss the side of her neck. Her quiet hum of pleasure stoked his inner blaze even higher.

"You smell so good," he murmured, his nose buried in her hair, while his hands busied themselves with caressing her.

"I've been working out for over an hour, remember? I smell anything but good."

Her protest made him chuckle. "You should try getting to the end of a long-range foot patrol with a bunch of soldiers whose personal hygiene was questionable to start with. I think we'll have to agree to disagree."

"What we'll have to do is get you undressed." Her mouth curved into a devious, feline smile, the kind that had been the death of unsuspecting men for centuries.

For a split second, he expected her to rip his shirt open and send buttons ricocheting around the bathroom. Instead, she took the civilized approach of using a more orthodox method to dispense with the remaining buttons, before turning her attention to the cufflinks at his wrists. With great care, she removed them, set them to one side, and turned her sultry gaze back to him.

"Now we can even things up."

Her hands stroked slowly down his chest. The sensation sent waves of arousal through his body. When she reached his pants, she tugged the garment free, but rather than finish the job and remove it, she slipped her hands beneath the cool cotton, and the next thing he was aware of was her palms skimming around his waist to his back.

Rocco growled in frustration.

Her fingers danced up his back, exploring every pad of muscle, the dip to his spine, until, without warning, without breaking contact with his body, she brought her hands back to his chest, and pushed the garment over his shoulders. She even managed to snatch it before it fell to the floor, and in a continuation of the movement, tossed it to one side.

Then she leaned back and stared at him, eyes wide and unreadable.

Bereft at the abrupt loss of contact, Rocco wasn't used to that kind of reaction from the women he dated. While he was no bodybuilder—that kind of muscle could easily be more of an impediment than an asset in a combat zone—he worked out regularly and his job kept him mission-fit. Most women seemed to be drawn to that, rather than recoiling from it.

Then she spoke.

"Sweet. Baby. Jesus."

Not exactly the reaction he'd expected. "Is that good or bad?"

Sasha's immediate response wasn't reassuring. "Neither." Her gaze met his. "It's… I used to think…" She pursed her lips and frowned. "I normally have more control over my words than this. Let me put it this way… No woman in her right mind would complain about perfection."

She leaned into him once more. This time, she put one arm around his waist, while the other hand cradled the side of his head and coaxed him into bending so she could kiss him. This time, her lips lingered. This time, at the butterfly-light touch of her tongue, he parted his lips to let her in.

Suddenly aroused beyond belief, Rocco was only distantly aware of the discomfort of his cock pushing against the zipper on his pants. Sasha's honeyed mouth was an elemental force, whipping up a firestorm of desire and need. When they broke contact, body trembling, she collapsed against him.

"Holy cats," she whispered. "I never knew kissing could be so good. I don't think I'll ever get enough of kissing you."

So, it was mutual. Good to know. "Likewise," he murmured.

"May I ask you something?"

Now he was intrigued. "Ask me anything you like."

Her gaze was soft and gentle when it met his. "Has anyone ever told you you should be an artist's model?"

He'd have laughed, but for the fact she asked the question without any trace of humor. She deserved a more respectful response. "No. Who'd want to paint this, anyway?"

"This" was a body that had seen active service on too many black ops missions to count. He was one of the lucky ones—he'd never suffered any serious, life-changing injuries, but his body bore visible traces of armed conflict.

"Any artist with any sense. You're beautiful."

~

How could any woman look at him and not see beauty?

Perfection as a concept could be defined a million different ways. For a lot of people, Rocco wouldn't be it, but for Sasha, she could think of nothing more flawless than the man standing before her, from his unruly black hair all the way down to his gleaming black shoes.

If she couldn't get enough of kissing him, then the same applied to touching him. The light covering of chest hair thrilled her. So different from the men she'd dated who'd mistakenly thought manscaping made them more attractive. Rocco was natural, all the way down to the darker arrow on his lower abdomen, pointing the way to the treasure awaiting her beneath the pants that still preserved his modesty.

Although, as a former soldier, it was likely all traces of modesty had deserted him a long time ago, if her past dealings with the military were any indication.

"If you want to talk about beautiful, have you looked in the mirror lately?"

Her cheeks warmed with an unexpected blush and she looked down, fixing her focus on his washboard abs. Rocco wasn't the first man to have told her that, but he was the first to have said it with complete sincerity when she was literally a hot mess. What would it be like if her fantasy turned into reality, and from now on, he were the only man to say it, too?

Sasha wriggled a little closer to the edge of the counter—

and a little closer to Rocco, so she could frame his face with her hands. While a smooth chest wasn't to her taste, she usually preferred a clean-shaven lover when it came to facial hair. The slight rasp of dark stubble over her palms was electrifyingly erotic. She loved touching him.

Her right thumb caressed the fullness of his lower lip. "Is it bad that I want you to kiss me again?"

"No—but I want to do more to you than that."

He swayed toward her, reinforcing the message when his thick, rock-hard cock pressed snugly against her, in spite of the clothing that separated them. One arm encircled her waist, while his free hand lifted her thigh and drew her into even more intimate contact with his groin. The pressure, the sensation, was amazing. A playful touch or two of his lips to her mouth and cheeks, and then he went into full attack mode, devouring her with his kisses.

Pure lust consumed her from the inside out. A fierce, intense craving to feel Rocco in every cell of her being engulfed her. Overwhelmed, she broke away, barely long enough to catch her breath before Rocco yanked her back, mashing her breasts against his chest. The abrasion from the crisp hair turned her tormented nipples into even tighter buds, a reaction that instantly dialed her level of arousal up to eleven. She couldn't get enough of him—as he kissed and nibbled the side of her neck, one hand roamed freely over his back while the other, curved around the back of his head, clutched at the cool silk strands of his hair. Almost delirious and barely able to think straight, she gave a soft moan and bit lightly on his earlobe.

Oh God, I want you inside me.

"I will be."

The ragged promise shocked her back into some semblance of awareness. Had she truly said those words aloud or had he read her mind? Either way, she didn't really care. Then she remembered why they were in the bathroom —it wasn't to make out on the counter. "Shower."

"Not yet."

Strong hands bracketed her waist and guided her back from the edge of the counter. Sasha whimpered, and then shrieked when her shoulder blades made contact with the cool tiles on the wall behind her, but her attention was swiftly diverted to Rocco's hands grasping her ankles.

"What are you doing?"

"Feet on the counter, legs apart. Can you do that?"

If she'd ever needed to know why she attended yoga classes, this would have been the answer. A hot flush seared her body as she let him position her feet exactly where he wanted them, leaving her totally exposed.

Without preamble, he thrust the middle finger of his right hand inside her, and without a hint of a fumble, found the spot that curled her toes. She gasped and whimpered, trying to hold on even though she wanted to scream.

"You're soaking wet."

Her core clamped down hard on his finger in response to his blunt observation, but she couldn't prevent him from withdrawing. The loss was almost a physical pain. Then her jaw dropped as he licked his glistening finger.

His dark, hooded eyes held her enthralled. Even if her life had been in danger, she wouldn't have been able to tear her eyes away. Her breath stalled in her chest at his next words.

"Now I know what I'm having for dinner."

Sasha reeled. On the precipice of melting into a useless puddle, she fought to regain an even keel on an ocean of bubbling, boiling, clamoring lust. Her self-control was fading fast, and she still had to get him out of his remaining garments.

"Please take your clothes off," she implored. "I want to see you. All of you."

Rocco took a step away from her but before he could unfasten his pants, she jumped down from the counter and did it for him. Slowly, so she could savor every moment of her exploration of the rigid bulge behind the zipper.

He gave a grunt of discomfort, mirrored by the unyielding set of his jaw and the way his hands clenched into fists at his sides. He'd gone commando too, allowing her to protect the heated steel of his erection with one hand, while the other slowly guided the zipper tab down. It was only when she tugged the tailored fabric over his hips that she could fully appreciate what was going to fill her.

His cock bobbed free of the restriction of clothing and strained upwards, almost touching his flat belly. The head was swollen and already glistening with the evidence of a need as urgent as her own. He was long, thick and hard, and at the sight of him, Sasha had to grit her teeth against the impulse to rub her aching clit until she came. Going into a semi-crouch, she continued pulling his pants down, only for him to stop her.

"No. Shoes."

He sounded as if he could barely get the words out. Sasha glanced down. Oh, that would have killed the moment, trying to get his pants off over his footwear. Once the offending items were disposed of, she carried on toward her goal of getting Rocco naked. When he stepped out of the puddle of black fabric, she had to admit he was the most exquisite man she'd ever laid eyes on.

Only now did she fully recognize the true beauty of what she'd missed. Not only that, she was in the perfect, eye-level position to appreciate Rocco's most… prominent attributes. While he didn't shave the way they had, he clearly still took care of himself—his balls and the base of his cock were framed by neatly trimmed pubic hair. Unable to resist, she leaned forward and licked his shaft from root to tip. She finished the maneuver with a swirl of her tongue around the crown, with the finale of a satisfying pop as she released him.

If only her previous role had taken her to Italy, then she'd have known exactly what his words meant. Not that it made much difference—the vehemence of the short, sharp utterance above her head communicated the impact of her action perfectly. She rose in one fluid movement, and before Rocco could take both of them on another sensual detour, she took him by the hand and led him to the spacious shower enclosure.

Typical of every male she'd ever met, Rocco had the temperature set just a little too cool for Sasha's liking. After adjusting it to a far more sensible and acceptable level, she turned the controls to the tropical rainfall setting and ducked under the cascade. With a tug on his hand, Rocco followed her, unwittingly standing in precisely the right position for her to drape her arms around his neck and share another lingering kiss.

"So you won't forget what comes next," she whispered.

"No chance," Rocco replied, as he ran his fingers down her spine and his hand curved over her hip. "I know exactly… *who* comes next."

As Rocco wrapped the huge, warm towel around the woman who'd just tested his resolve to its limits, he was still trying to work out what had happened during the shower they'd just shared.

He'd done the same thing many times before—there was nothing quite as intimate as getting to know a lover's body by bathing together. In the shower or in the bathtub, it didn't much matter, but this time, something different had happened.

What had proved it had been his reaction when she'd slipped and almost fallen. He'd caught her, as he would have done for any other woman in that situation, but the near-accident had triggered a surge of protectiveness, the like of which he'd never experienced before. She'd grabbed his arms, and when their eyes met, a powerful blast of emotion had hit him square in the solar plexus.

As he'd already known, there was more to this than lust and primal need, but heaven help him, he didn't care. What he did care about was standing in his arms right now, and unless he missed his guess, she was as reluctant to step away from him as he was to let her.

"You're still wet."

Her quiet voice broke the trance he'd fallen into. Rocco blinked and took a deep breath. "No problem."

He grabbed a second towel from the rail, but before he could do anything with it, Sasha took it from him.

"Let me."

He was about to protest, but at the first touch he was lost. All he could do was watch her, vaguely aware that with each passing second, he was tumbling deeper into the rabbit hole. Common sense tried to warn him he was opening himself up for a heap of trouble on so many levels, but his brain was short-circuiting from the sparks flying between him and Sasha.

Reality gave way to the desire in her gaze as she went about the task of drying him off. When she reached his cock and balls, he had to grit his teeth and mentally strip down his Glock and put it back together again, so he wouldn't go off like a rocket in her hands. His self-control was completely shredded.

Finally, he couldn't take the torment any longer. "Sasha, that's enough."

He tried to keep his voice gentle, but the words were

rough and gravelly. As she turned away to drop the towel in the laundry hamper, he hooked a finger in her towel, pulled it loose, and tossed it in, too.

Sasha spun around to face him. "What—"

"That's better. I can't wait any longer."

"My hair…"

Although he'd toweled it dry, her hair was still damp. "I think I saw a dryer somewhere—"

"I'll tie it up. I don't even know why I mentioned it…"

Nerves, probably. Hopefully anticipation, too. "Hey." He laid his palm against her cheek. "Come to bed with me?"

The question had the desired effect. She visibly relaxed—he could almost feel the waves of tension flooding away from her. "Yes, please. It's been a while, though."

Cristo. How was he supposed to hold onto the veneer of civilization when he heard a confession like that? He swept her up in his arms, and grinned when she shrieked in surprise. He loved the way her arms ended up around his neck.

"Wait."

Almost at the doorway, Rocco stopped. "What's wrong?"

"Nothing, but there's something we need. Can you put me down, please?"

He had no intention of doing that—not until they reached the bed, anyway. "Tell me what it is."

The bathroom had more storage than he'd need in three lifetimes, and it was at one of the many drawers he hadn't opened yet that Sasha glanced. He carried her to it, and held her tightly while she retrieved a small box from it. "We're going to need these."

Rocco raised an eyebrow. *Condoms.* "Why are they there, and how did you know?"

"I put them there," she confessed. "Part of the housekeeping we provide when there are guests staying overnight. I believe in being prepared, but not everyone does."

Rocco believed the same, but compared to this, his supply was meager. "Now that we *are* prepared—"

She laid a finger over his lips. "It's time to stop talking."

He carried her back to the bedroom, and with great care, set her down in the center of the huge bed. She was perfect—and exactly where she belonged. He went around the room and dimmed the lights, then returned to where his lover awaited him.

Sasha had rolled onto her side and was watching him. There was no way she could miss his body's response to her attention. Lasting long enough to ensure he gave her all the pleasure she deserved could prove a challenge, but it was one he was eager and ready to... rise to.

Rocco lay down beside her. For long moments, he simply drank his fill of the visual, of Sasha in his bed, naked, available and wanting him as much as he wanted her. She'd tied her hair back while he'd been attending to the lights, and now primitive instincts urged him to grasp the ponytail and anchor her in place while he plundered her mouth and claimed her properly for himself. However, the gentleman his mother had taught him to be encouraged him to take his time, to make it so good for her, she'd never forget him.

He didn't want her to forget him.

Rocco raised his hand. He had to touch her, reassure himself she wasn't a dream, yet as he would have laid his palm against her cheek, the differences between the two of them came sharply into focus—her skin was so soft, so flawless, so perfect, while his hands were the brutal hands of a killer.

"Whatever you're thinking of, it has no place here." Sasha pressed his hand to her cheek. "I know you want me, and if it really needs to be said, I want you, too. It's just you and me,

Rocco. There's no room in this bed for anything but us… What we can give to each other… What we can be to each other."

Her soft words of encouragement were all he needed. He stroked her cheek, marveling again that she was with him, then leaned in to claim her mouth.

She responded with a hunger that equaled his own. Her warmth and softness sent a thrill of pure ecstasy through him.

He needed her to be closer, though. He moved his hand to the small of her back and pulled her to him, knowing he wouldn't be satisfied until their bodies became one.

Being around Rocco had driven her to the brink of insanity. Sasha had only needed to hear his voice and that deliciously sexy accent, and her bones started to melt. Her ability to think straight was disintegrating, which was why she'd vacillated between wanting him so badly even her teeth ached with it, and behaving with cool impartiality.

She closed her eyes and inhaled deeply. The scent of him was dizzying, all clean male and the masculine fragrance of his body wash. She hadn't been able to keep her hands off him in the shower. He'd wanted to shave but the light scrape of his scruff against her palms had made her spine tingle with anticipation. The delay while he removed it would have been untenable.

He was truly a banquet for the eyes. Simply looking at him tore her in two—one half wanted to spend a lifetime getting to know every inch of him, while the other half was all revved up and ready to get down and dirty. She might not have a lifetime, but when Fate dropped a gift like Rocco into a woman's lap, she owed it to Fate to treat that gift with the respect it deserved. To live in the moment, enjoy it, and make it last as long as possible.

Sasha wrapped her free arm around his torso and draped her leg over his thigh. As she nuzzled his neck, peppering his skin with light kisses and nibbles, her hand explored the muscular contours of his back. He was lean and strong, and though he went running and visited the gym regularly, these muscles came from hard work in the field.

Lying like this, his cock was a thick bar of hot steel against her belly—dear heaven, when she'd first seen him naked, all she could think of was how it would feel when he filled her. Even the thought of him inside her was enough to plunge her into a frenzy of smoldering, carnal hunger.

She wanted contact with him over every inch of her body, to brand every inch of him as hers, so a part of him would always remember her and want her, no matter who he was with in the future. She wanted to put him on his back and ride him until they both reached the peak, until he came inside her and she could feel the jackhammer pulse of his release in every cell in her body.

Intending to maneuver him into the position she wanted, she pushed at his shoulder, but Rocco was too quick. He finished the movement she started and ended up looming over her, big and male and oh so desirable. She wailed her surrender when his hand parted her thighs and his fingers pushed inside her.

He muttered some dark, Italian profanity. "You're so wet."

"What do you expect?" She tugged at his lower lip with her teeth. "I've thought about having you since the day you arrived, when I saw you come around the front of the Escalade."

He rubbed her clit and she almost howled. Her thighs clamped together, imprisoning his hand, and he retaliated by zeroing in on her G-spot. This time she did howl—an explosive orgasm soared way beyond her control and into vertical takeoff, taking her straight to paradise.

"How…?"

Sasha could barely get the word out. She wasn't even sure what she was trying to ask, but none of that mattered as Rocco kissed her forehead.

"The night's only just started," he whispered against her temple. "So have I."

Sasha growled. At the same time, she pushed against him. He resisted for a moment, but then he was exactly where she wanted him—on his back.

She straddled his thighs and gazed down at her fallen angel—sinful and divine, he promised her heaven, but only through the purgatory of his terms. Even in this submissive position, he radiated dominance.

She knew her advantage wouldn't last long. His abdominal muscles contracted and he sat upright, one arm tight around her, while he used the other hand to guide her nipple to his mouth. The pull as he suckled made her head swim, until all she could do was cling to him because her knees were about to fail her.

The sensations pulsing through her were intense… unbearable. Soft whimpers didn't help. All she could do was hold on tight as he maneuvered her back beneath him.

"Cara."

He whispered the word as he caressed her cheek, and with a brief kiss to her mouth, he moved away from her. She tried to pull him back, but he evaded her grasp and settled into a new position between her parted thighs. If he was even only half as skilled there as he'd already proved he was elsewhere…

What the man could do with his mouth and tongue was positively wicked. He urged her closer and closer to the edge, then drew back before she could topple over it into ecstasy.

Each crackling jolt scrambled her ability to think even more. With no chance to recover, she couldn't give voice to the wayward thoughts rioting inside her head, and when he finally teased her beyond the point of no return, all she could do was cry out his name.

"Rocco!"

He returned to her side, and when he kissed her again, she tasted herself on his lips. As normality seeped into her consciousness and her racing pulse calmed once more, Sasha became aware of an uncontrollable tremor, saw it when she tried to touch him with trembling fingers. "What did you do?"

He smiled as with an incredibly tender touch, he brushed her hair away from her face. "You mean no lover has ever—"

"They have," she gasped, "but it's never been like that."

"I thought it would be a good way to get things started."

If she'd had the energy, she might have punched him, but as her frazzled mind cleared, a sweeter revenge struck her. Turnabout was fair play, after all.

"My turn now." Sasha licked her lips.

Rocco groaned.

She tilted her head to one side. "What was that for?"

"Seeing you do that," he replied. "Do it again, and I won't be responsible for the consequences."

Her gaze followed his down the length of his body, and... yeah, with an erection like that, there would be consequences. Delicious, delightful consequences. Maybe she'd better plan on tasting *all* of him another time. "Then I guess I'd better be ready, huh?"

Her inner devil drove her to lean over him for the box of condoms. Her intention had been to torment him with the graze of her pebble-hard nipples over his chest, but her strategy backfired when his chest hair made contact with her supersensitive flesh.

Rocco took the box from her, ripped it open and took out a foil packet. “Keep it handy,” he growled. “We may need it fast.”

“Oh, I know exactly when we’ll need it, soldier.” She took it from him and set it to one side, close enough to grab in a hurry, but far enough away not to get in the way. Right now, she had something else to take care of.

He gave a low moan at the first contact of her tongue swirling around the small, tight nipple. The dusky brown flesh tasted of clean male, a delicious accompaniment to the scent of him. Her hand stroked his flank, mapping out the ridges of muscle all the way to his hip, where she took a detour to the apex of his thighs.

His straining cock was a bar of fire against her palm. Her fingers closed around him and he groaned again. This time, Sasha shifted slightly, just enough to bring his mouth into range while keeping him captive in her hand. As she peppered his skin with kisses, she moved her hand up and down his shaft, gauging the effect by the sounds Rocco made, and the way he closed his eyes and writhed restlessly beside her. He reached his limit when she cupped her hand around his balls and lifted them with tender care.

“Stop.” He ground the word out, and at the same time, clamped his hand around her wrist, bringing an end to the torment she was inflicting on him. “Carry on like that, and I’ll never last.”

“But I haven’t finished.”

His gaze locked onto hers. “Neither have I.”

Rocco moved like lightning, and before she knew it, her back was against the cool sheets once more. This time, though, he pressed closer, and the hand that caressed her waist moved lower, over her hip to lift her leg and drape it over his thigh, bringing their lower bodies into sensual contact.

Hungry for more, Sasha pressed even closer. The heated sensation of his cock and balls against her mound made her want to wrap her legs around him and pull him into her body. That need was reflected in the gaze of a man starving for the intimacy to come.

She wouldn't let Rocco take the wrapped condom from her—she wanted to cover him herself, craved it, because he was hers, and no one was taking that away from her, not even him. She took it slow, tantalizing him with every little adjustment and reveling in the muttered curses that spilled from his lips.

Swearing sure sounded colorful in Italian.

"Sasha… enough."

The frustrated growl came as, with a speed that almost blindsided her, he scooped her up and deposited her beside him. The sheer, naked hunger in his eyes robbed her of her ability to breathe. "Rocco?"

"I think it's time."

And now the moment had come, all Sasha could think about was how long it had been. "It's been a while, remember?"

Not to mention the fact she was probably the oldest woman he'd ever made love to. She shuddered at the thought.

"I remember." A muscle in his cheek twitched as he swallowed. "I'd never hurt you, *cara*."

She cupped his jaw. The rasp of stubble across her palm made this—made *him*—thrillingly real. "I know."

He eased inside her slowly, holding back until she visibly relaxed. He felt so good, in ways her toys could never emulate. It had been so long since she'd enjoyed the attention of a hot, aroused male that she rejoiced in the passion and power of him, the weight of him on her, pressing her into the pillows. At the first rock of his hips, she gave a soft moan that was part arousal, part anguish at the spear of pleasure that reminded her what it was like to be alive.

"Sasha? You okay?"

The question was accompanied by a slow thrust that took him deep inside her. "Uh-huh. Just keep on doing what you're doing."

She hoped he would. She couldn't get enough of him, of exploring and enjoying the play of muscles as he surged and withdrew. She murmured her inarticulate approval as he unleashed more of the power he'd been holding in check, and as he did so, her need for him exploded out of control. No longer able to think logically or even string a couple of words together to make a half-assed sentence, Sasha let her inner primal female take control, until all that remained was the pleasure and release she and Rocco could give one another.

The developing connection between them remained even when he took his weight on his arms and arched over her. His kisses slowed, synced up with the rock of his hips, and the combined assault annihilated every higher thought process she possessed.

All she wanted was this.

All she needed was him.

Her hips rolled with his as her fingers dug in so hard, her nails would leave crescent-shaped grooves where she tried to pull him more deeply inside her. He wasn't close enough, he could never be close enough until he was inside her, until she was inside him, until they merged into one indistinguishable creature of lust and need.

"Harder. Please. *Please*."

His hips slammed into her, the sharp sound of flesh colliding with flesh intensifying the primal atmosphere that filled the room. Civilization banished to the outside world, all that remained was need to fulfill the most basic human need of all, to celebrate life with the very act that could create it.

Arousal spiraled and spiked. Any second now, she was going to fly straight into the sun, where she'd explode like a thousand stars, and she needed Rocco to soar with her. She needed eye contact with him, and as her gaze connected with his, her core contracted around him and he cried out her name.

His shaft pulsed inside her, marking time for her own seemingly endless orgasm, wave after wave of pleasure pounding at her as every muscle in Rocco's beautiful body strained under the impact of his own climax. An anguished cry broke from him, and in response, Sasha wrapped her arms around him, took his weight as he collapsed against her. The aftershocks of his orgasm racked his body as she held him, until he finally raised his head from her shoulder.

When she looked into his eyes this time, she realized he was contemplating her as if she were a puzzle, something he couldn't quite work out, but at the same time, was important to him. His chest heaved with the effort of dragging each breath into his body, mirroring the physical effects of their lovemaking on her. Then he rolled away—his cock abandoned her body, but before the space between them could destroy the moment, Rocco gathered her in his arms and held her close. As they slowly returned to reality, Sasha became aware of a new emotion—a sensation of coming home, as if she were finally where she'd always been meant to be.

Which probably explained the sense of loss when Rocco left her with a kiss, telling her he'd be right back. Compensation came in the form of the magnificent view as he made his way to the bathroom—the man had an ass she could bounce dimes off. That was the only reason she wasn't wishing she'd gone with him to freshen up while he disposed of the condom.

He reappeared a few moments later, and as he drew closer to the bed, she saw what he was carrying.

"I thought this only happened in romance novels," she murmured, watching as he used the warm, damp wash cloth between her legs and then used the soft towel to dry her. She was further puzzled by the amused expression that suddenly appeared on his face. "What are you laughing at?"

"Not laughing." He moved the towel to her mound and applied a gentle pressure. "Now I know what you read. What genre of romance?"

Sasha groaned and let her head fall back on the pillow. "Not telling. If I tell you, I'll have to kill you."

"Any sexy bodyguards in those stories? I might need to pick up a few hints."

There was something comfortingly intimate about this crazy conversation. "Oh trust me, you don't need any hints. Your technique is flawless."

He wrapped the cloth in the towel and left the bundle on one side. The unsettled feeling in Sasha's chest quieted as he lifted the sheet and returned to his place beside her. Though he'd only been gone from the bed a few minutes, in that short time, she'd missed him.

With Rocco's arms wrapped tightly around her, his body spooning hers, Sasha was safer than she'd been in what seemed like forever. Tonight the dreams would be different, and as if to prove it, as her eyelids closed and the sleep of exhaustion stilled her mind, Jack came back one last time.

You're back on the horse now, hon. You don't need me no more. Be brave. You got this...

Maybe so, but a couple hours later, instead of guilt about Jack rousing her from sleep, it was a growing anxiety about what she hadn't told Rocco about her past. Hiding it during a brief fling was one thing, but now Sasha wanted more than an extended one-night stand. How she could achieve that, she had no idea, but she was drawn to this man on much more than a physical level.

Making what she wanted happen came with a price, and that price was the truth about what she'd once been. She couldn't assume that Rocco's past would make it easier for him to accept hers. She was no closer to a solution the next morning, when she woke to kisses and caresses from the man with whom she was perilously close to falling in love.

CHAPTER 8

Rocco's belly clenched at the blast of arousal that powered straight to his cock at the sensual sigh of pure pleasure that came from his dinner guest when she tasted her first mouthful of the steak he'd prepared for her.

"This is incredible. So tender. If Chef tried this, I think he'd be worried about his position here." Sasha took a sip of water. "Where did you learn to cook like this? It's perfect."

Rocco chuckled. "I don't think Chef needs to be too concerned. And to answer your question, my mother taught me."

As soon as he was old enough and tall enough, Claire Equizi had taken her son into the kitchen and shown him how to make a slice of toast. From there, his culinary skills had progressed in leaps and bounds, and had even survived the minor setback of his years in the military.

"She did a great job. You even looked as if you enjoy doing it."

That was another thing his mother had given him—her love of taking care of and providing for others. Although it had partly translated into his military service and the career that had brought him to Texas, he still missed the more… personal aspects. "I do. It's very therapeutic—especially after a bad day at the office."

It was a subjective judgement, but going through personnel records with a fine-toothed comb was not his natural go-to for fun times, especially when it produced nothing worth further investigation. Then again, sitting at a computer for *any* reason was not his preferred way of working, period. He preferred to be out and about—even if that did mean following his principal on a shopping expedition.

"A bad day at the office? And yet you don't seem unhappy about it. Am I missing something?"

The corner of Rocco's mouth curved up in a half-smile. "I'm not unhappy now. There's more to life than work."

Sasha looked at him with renewed focus. "Oh?"

"Finish your dinner before it gets cold. I'll get rid of the dishes and then we'll talk."

"Should I worry?"

"I don't think so. I hope you won't."

A gentle lift of her eyebrows signaled a mix of curiosity and acceptance. She wasn't stupid—she'd know it was connected with the previous evening, the kiss that hadn't happened, and what had come after it.

When they finished eating, Rocco cleared the table while his guest went to make herself comfortable on the long couch. He took heart from the fact she wasn't trying to shrink into one of the corners, so she'd be as far away from him as possible.

Having learned a little about her preferences already, he retrieved two ice-cold beers—he wasn't about to let her drink alone—from the chiller, opened them, and went to join Sasha. She smiled when he offered her one of the bottles before making himself comfortable beside her.

"Thanks. And thanks for dinner, too."

"You don't have to keep thanking me. It was my pleasure. We'll have to do it again."

"Soon?"

He liked the hint of hope in her voice. "Whenever you're ready."

He watched Sasha as she took a delicate drink directly from the bottle. She caught him looking at her and deposited the bottle on the low table in front of them. Rocco took a drink from his and did the same. For the conversation they were about to have, he wanted his hands free, in case of an emergency, like needing to take Sasha in his arms, hold her, and…

Before doing that—maybe—they needed to clear the air, and from the way she was watching him, Sasha expected him to go first. It was only fair, considering he was the one who'd said they had to talk.

There was no point in prevaricating. The sooner this was done the better. "It's about last night."

Her expression didn't alter—apart from a shadow that appeared in her steady gaze. "Ah. Is this where you tell me you don't usually sleep with clients and last night was a mistake?"

He had to remove that shadow, and the sooner, the better. "Technically, you're not my client. As for last night… I don't see it as a mistake. It didn't feel like a mistake when I woke up this morning and you were in my bed. Did it feel like a mistake to you?"

He'd blow it off if she said yes. He was a grown man, he'd had relationships before, from one-night stands to one where thoughts of engagement rings had even occurred to him. He'd seen rejection from both sides of the deed, and if this conversation was going to add to the tally, so be it.

Sasha quirked an eyebrow. "I wasn't expecting that. Given

I agreed to dinner tonight and made it clear I want to do it again, what do you think my answer is?"

He was fairly sure he knew the answer. "I think it's a no. Am I right?"

Her lips twitched. "Since it seems to matter so much to you, yes, you are correct." Sasha shifted so she mirrored his sideways position on the couch and leaned her elbow on the low back. "And before you ask, not only would I like to have dinner with you again, I'd like to do what we did last night again, too."

She leaned toward him and her lips touched the corner of his mouth. The contact was lighter than a butterfly's wing, but the cautious tenderness of it made him ache for more. He turned his head a fraction of an inch, enough to pay her back with an equally gentle kiss full on her lips.

"Mm, nice," she murmured. "You're not going to get into trouble with your boss for engaging in nonprofessional activity, are you?"

If only she knew about the conversation he'd had with Nick. He might not number his boss among his closest friends, but Rocco had a hunch the other man would probably offer encouragement if he had any idea what had happened between him and Sasha. "Unlikely. Are you planning to tell him?"

"No chance of that." Sasha laid her hand against his cheek, leaned forward, and when she kissed him this time, she didn't hold back.

Momentarily outflanked, Rocco recovered quickly, wrapped his arms around his woman, and lifted her onto his lap, all without breaking contact with her luscious mouth. To help him out, she draped an arm around his neck and wriggled into a more comfortable position.

"You know this is crazy, don't you?" she whispered when they had to come up for air.

“Probably as crazy as it gets,” Rocco agreed.

“There’s one thing you should know, though.”

He wanted to know more than one thing. He wanted her to share, so he’d know everything here was to know about this fascinating, totally incredible woman.

“In case you didn’t have a file on me coming into this… I’m older than you.”

That was it? “And your point is? It’s numbers—they’re nothing, and they sure as hell don’t bother me. Don’t let them stop you. You see something you want? Go for it.”

Because a person spent a long time dead. He’d learned that through losing too many good friends in too many conflicts in too many putrid hellholes around the world.

“You didn’t. Go for it, I mean, when you almost kissed me. What stopped you?”

“Sanity. Insanity. Take your pick. I’ve been attracted to you since the first time I saw you.”

A confused frown creased her brow. “But that was only a couple of days ago.”

Rocco shook his head. “No. It was a week before that. Nick did give me a briefing pack for the job. There were photos of you in it. You… bowled me over on sight. Then I met you, and the reality blew me away.”

“Apart from the part about the file and the photos, I could say the same about you,” Sasha admitted. “You weren’t at all what I expected.”

Rocco laughed. “Do I want to know what you did expect?”

“I don’t know—do you?” Challenge lit her gaze as she studied him. “That’s not quite true—I was partly right.”

“Now I’m worried. Which part?”

“These.” She laid her hand on his biceps.

His self-control protested. “Ah. I get it. All brawn, no brains. Very flattering—thank you for that.”

For a moment she took him at his word, until she registered the wry grin he almost succeeded in stifling. Then her expression changed. "Men. Although this... this is a Brit thing, right? The dry humor?"

He held a hand up. "Busted. I guess I inherited it from my mother. She could do sarcasm to Olympic standards."

Her expression softened. "Is your mother still...?"

Rocco shook his head. "She died a while ago. She was an amazing woman."

"I'm not surprised. I think her son's pretty amazing, too. And your father?"

An all-too-familiar iron band clamped Rocco's chest. The question was an inevitable extension of the conversation, so he'd seen it coming, but the prospect of talking about Dario —especially to Sasha—was still anathema to him. "Dario and I don't talk."

He hated shutting her down like that, yet at the same time was infinitely grateful when she didn't press the issue.

"Then tell me about Rocco Equizi."

When that question came from a woman he was dating, it usually set his inner alarm bells ringing. In his experience, it meant there was a better than even chance she was looking for more from the relationship than he was prepared to give. For Sasha, however, those bells remained silent. "What do you want to know?"

"Everything, of course."

Still no alarm bells. Rocco groaned. "Suffer from insomnia much? It's pretty boring stuff."

Sasha's eyes narrowed. "I don't think it is. I don't think anything about you is the least bit boring. Come on—tell me *something*," she pleaded.

He racked his brain for something lighthearted and frivolous. "All right, then. My star sign's Cancer."

"And I'm a Capricorn."

"Hmm. That's tropical."

Sasha groaned and gestured toward the end of the couch. "If I could reach that cushion, I'd hit you with it. Is your sense of humor always so lame?" she asked with feigned disappointment.

He shrugged. "I usually have better material to work with."

She rolled her eyes. "Then tell me something else."

Rocco shook his head. For so long he'd been little more than the sum total of his work, and his work had, for the most part, not been a subject suitable for conversation, polite or otherwise. "Why don't you tell me about you instead?"

The look she gave him conveyed caution. "What do you want to know?"

His answer to that was simple—everything that had made her the woman she was today, and that started with where she'd come from. "Tell me about your family. I know you're an Army brat and you weren't born in Texas. That leaves forty-nine other possibilities. Since it would be a terrible waste of an evening if I were to sit here reciting the names of all the other states, why don't you put us out of my misery and tell me?"

She relaxed visibly. "Colorado. Dad was stationed at Fort Carson at the time. We left there when I was about seven. I grew up in a lot of places."

"Tell me more," he prompted.

"Okay—you asked for it, remember."

Rocco helped her settle more comfortably in his lap. As she regaled him with various tales of her childhood—including time spent on American bases in Europe—he found himself more and more bewitched. Everything about her drew him even more deeply under her spell—her smile, her voice, even the way her hand rested on his forearm, as if she couldn't get enough of the skin-to-skin contact. He had no complaints about that.

He could have listened to her all night, but sooner or later, they'd have to go to bed, and he wanted to know if she wanted to spend the night with him again. He was about to ask her when she gave a deep sigh and laid her head on his shoulder.

"I wish I didn't have to get up so early tomorrow, but Linzi has a Zoom interview with a European entertainment news channel, and I need to help her get set up. I'd better go."

She started to get up, but he wasn't about to let her go so easily. "You don't have to. You could still stay here until the morning. The bed's big enough, and I get up early anyway."

She leveled a narrow-eyed glare at him. "Not making this any easier, Equizi. I'll tell you now, if we share that bed, there's no way my ass is staying on my side, and if I don't stay on my side, there's no way I'm going to get enough sleep to push the right buttons tomorrow. Besides, when I say early, I mean *early*." She laid her palm against his cheek. "I'd hate to disturb you on my way out. How about if I make dinner tomorrow night to make it up to you?"

It sounded like an excellent idea on the face of it, but a memory clamored to make itself heard. "Wait. Didn't you tell me you don't cook?"

Indignation swirled around her. "I don't. Much. Doesn't mean I can't."

He was tempted to agree, but his mother had raised him to be a gentleman. "Why don't we have dinner on Saturday, when you won't have to get up so early?"

Sasha curled her fingers into his shirt and tugged, bringing his face closer to hers. "You calling me old, mister? You don't think I've got it in me to last the day?"

"Oh, I think you've got it in you to last the day, *cara*, but will you last the night?" With a grin, he waggled his eyebrows in what he hoped was a suggestive manner.

The way she kissed him was pure sin wrapped in hot seduction. There was nothing more alluring than a woman who believed in the power of her own sensuality and sexuality.

When their lips finally parted, something odd happened in his chest when he read the reluctance in her gaze. She didn't want to leave any more than he wanted to let her, and the lack of resolve in her next words proved it.

"I think I'd better go now. If I stay any longer, you may not get rid of me."

"Then stay. I told you—I don't mind if you wake me up early."

She pressed her forehead to his. "Don't do this to me, please. I really have to go."

He'd have given anything for her to stay, but he didn't want to make it any more difficult for her than it already was, so he conceded. "All right, but take this thought with you—you're always welcome here."

"In your apartment?"

"And in my bed."

A flash of understanding passed between them, and in one lithe, sinuous movement, she dismounted his lap and stood. Rocco watched her supple, feline stretch, before following her and offering her his hand. "Come on—I'll see you to your door."

Sasha gave him a pained look. "I'm only a few feet away down the hall. I think I can find my way home safely."

"I know you can, but I never leave my date to find her own way home." And didn't that make him his own worst enemy?

She raised her eyebrows. "Is that what I am now, your date?"

"If you want to be."

Her radiant smile hit him like a runaway train. She draped her arms over his shoulders and touched a light kiss to his lips. He'd never get enough of her kisses. "I want to be."

"Then I'm taking you home."

The house was quiet as they strolled down the hall to Sasha's suite. With luck, this was the last night he'd have to leave her at her door. When she opened that door but didn't go in, he hoped it was because she felt the same way. When she turned to him, all soft, delicious female, pupils dilated with the same want and need pulsing through his veins, he knew it was.

She licked her lips. "I guess this changes things now."

Rocco couldn't disagree. "I guess it does."

CHAPTER 9

Rocco rubbed the back of his neck and rolled his shoulders. He'd been sitting in one position, staring at the computer screen, for too long. He was no profiler, but then again, he didn't have to be—it was eminently clear from the vitriolic nature of the social media posts that the person behind them had some serious issues, and looking through their history, Linzi was their only target. It would take someone with a different skill set from his to glean anything further.

A hand landed on his shoulder and squeezed it, heralding the arrival of a mug of coffee on the desk. "Here, this might help."

He looked up and to the left, timing the movement perfectly for Sasha to brush her lips across his. He stretched. "Mm, I know what would help more."

"Insatiable man."

Around her, he was—and that was after only one night together. He'd been intensely aware of her absence from his bed the previous night, but the fact that he'd missed her over breakfast this morning would have been enough to convince him—had he needed convincing—there was more to it than sex and scratching a fundamental human itch. His reaction when she'd finally made it to her office after Linzi's European interview had proved it.

Impossible though it should have been, given they'd known each other mere days, his connection to Sasha was becoming more vital with each passing moment. At the same time, whatever secrets might be lurking in her past were becoming less and less relevant.

Rocco returned his attention to the task at hand, and was so deeply engrossed in it that, when his cell phone vibrated, he picked it up without a thought. When he saw the caller ID, his stomach clenched. He was due to Skype Nick that evening, so what was so urgent it couldn't wait until then? He glanced over at Sasha, and as if she could feel his gaze on her, she looked up from her computer screen. For a split second, he thought he caught an almost haunted look in her eyes, but then she gave him the kind of smile that only lovers shared.

Whatever Nick wanted, it had better not be to tell him Sasha was behind the threats.

Rocco answered the call. "Nick. What's up?"

"Can you talk? This won't take long."

The words he'd been dreading. "Sure. Give me a minute."

Rocco rose, aware that Sasha's eyes were on him. He adopted what he hoped was a reassuring expression and gestured toward the phone. Sasha nodded and returned to her work.

A few long strides took him far enough away from the office. "Sorry about that. Go ahead."

"I thought you might like to know Tex came through with his inquiries about Sasha."

And here it came. She had no history because she'd been in jail. Or she was in the witness protection program. Or there was some wild reason he couldn't even begin to fathom for her only springing into existence when she started working for Linzi. He had to know the truth, little though he wanted to. "Go on."

"Turns out you were right—Sasha Morgan *is* ex-CIA. She left the Agency not long after her partner was killed overseas."

"Her partner?" Rocco knew Nick meant her work partner, but even so, the green-eyed demon of jealousy flashed at the word.

"Jack Ward. He was shot multiple times, but survived just long enough for exfil. She returned to the States, was on compassionate leave for a while, then she went to work for Linzi. By a strange coincidence, her former supervisor is Linzi's godfather." Nick's tone implied he believed coincidence had nothing to do with it.

"You think she's here to protect Linzi?"

"I don't think it's so much that as just to watch over her, and maybe watch out for the very circumstance that led Brookes to engage us. Without Sasha to catch the nuances of the messages, I suspect they'd have been dismissed as the ravings of your average internet weirdo, and I doubt very much we or any other security consultants would be involved."

"Is there any particular way you'd like me to handle letting Sasha know we know? Seems to me someone went to a lot of trouble to cover up her past."

"I don't know that her past is particularly relevant. I'll leave it up to you to decide how to handle it… if it needs to be handled."

"Understood. Thank Tex for me, will you?" Mentioning the name of Nick's "friend of a friend" reminded Rocco of what else the other man was working on. "Have he and Charity made any progress with tracking down our real target?"

"That's proving to be more problematic than either of them anticipated. Whoever it is is bloody good at hiding their tracks. Far more skilled than the average keyboard warrior. They started explaining the technology to me, but within about thirty seconds, they'd gone way over my head. Give me numbers any day," Nick grumbled.

Rocco chuckled. Before heading up Spectrum Security Inc., Nick had been the bean counter-in-chief for Spectrum Security, the parent company back home. He was still double-hatting the two roles, but as soon as they found a replacement CFO, his time would be dedicated one hundred percent to the stateside operation.

"That reminds me—I stumbled across something in the financial records I'd like you to take a look at, if you have time. I'm no expert, but what I found feels wrong."

"No problem. If you can send me the details today, I'll take a look over the weekend."

"Thanks, I will, but I need to clear it with Sasha first. I know it's not really part of our remit and I can't see any connection with the threats, but my gut's telling me not to let it go."

"That's good enough for me. Better to look into it and discount it, than find out later we should have investigated. Talking of Sasha, how are things between you two?"

"We have a good working relationship. Everything's going very smoothly."

Silence at the other end of the call made Rocco wonder if Nick was expecting a different kind of answer. If he was, then he'd be disappointed. There was no way Rocco was admitting to any other kind of relationship—not yet, at any rate.

"Good to know. Anything else?" Nick asked.

"Just one thing—have you managed to dig up anything on Frank Schofield yet?"

"Nothing out of the ordinary, only what you'd expect of someone with his kind of history. Run-of-the-mill record as a cop, with nothing to indicate or explain any involvement in this campaign against Linzi. I'll send it to you. Did you expect there to be anything suspicious?"

Rocco wasn't sure. "Maybe, maybe not."

"You aren't convinced."

"No, but if that's all there is, that's all there is. Thanks anyway."

"No problem. Unless there's anything else, I'll just wish you good luck with Sasha—let me know how you get on."

Nick's tone hinted at a degree of amusement, but unless he was way off track, Rocco also thought he detected a certain level of sympathy. The implications of that gave him food for thought. Nick had originally come to the US to provide financial oversight of the company's plans to expand into the country, and had ended up staying when he met the woman who became both his wife and his world. Now Rocco could understand why. It could also end up being an option open to him, too.

Having wandered as far as the atrium during the course of the conversation with his boss, Rocco stepped outside for a breath of fresh air. He didn't like secrets, but sometimes they were necessary. His service in the SAS had pretty much mandated them, so he could understand why Sasha hadn't divulged anything about her past.

And that just about decided it for him. He wouldn't stand by forever while this was bothering her, as it so clearly had all morning. He'd give her another day to come clean, but that was all—there was no way he'd risk letting her past or his come between them.

~

Sasha automatically looked up at the sound of the door opening. The expression on Rocco's face stalled her smile before it was even half-formed. "Not bad news, I hope?"

"Huh? No, everything's fine."

Rocco's preoccupied tone would have been enough to tell her everything was not fine, but add to that a smile that wasn't reflected in his eyes, and Sasha was pretty damn certain the conversation he'd just had hadn't been all sunshine and roses. "You look like you could use another cup of coffee. I could use a break." She checked the time. "In fact, how about we take an early lunch?"

"That's a great idea. Besides, there's something I want to talk to you about."

Hopefully, it would be whatever was on his mind. "Okay. We'll grab something to eat, and… do you want to talk here or find a corner someplace else?"

"Somewhere quiet where we won't be interrupted or overheard would be ideal."

Now she was more concerned. They were already careful about what they discussed and where they discussed it, but for Rocco to make a point of it, he must have had something major on his mind. "In that case, how about we have this conversation in my apartment? Or yours, if you'd be more comfortable there?"

"Yours would be perfect."

A couple of minutes later, Sasha was checking the contents of her fridge, while Rocco was making coffee. He made the best cup of coffee she'd ever tasted, which was another reason why she wouldn't mind keeping him around.

Phenomenal sex, great cooking, and fantastic coffee. Man, he was ticking all her boxes…

Sasha banished the frivolous thought from her mind. "So, how would you like to try my homemade chili? I usually have rice with it—is that okay?"

"Rice will be fine. It'll be amazing. And delicious. Anything I can do to help?"

"Thanks, but I've got it. Should be ready in about twenty minutes—will that be long enough to talk about what's on your mind?"

"I imagine so."

A hundred possibilities exploded in her mind. She could cope with any of them, except maybe one—the one where he told her he was being reassigned with immediate effect. She'd need time to process that. "You go sit down, and I'll be right with you."

A couple minutes later, she took a seat beside him on the long couch, where her coffee was waiting for her on the low table in front. After an initial reviving sip, she turned to Rocco—to her lover. Thinking of him that way made her lady parts turn jubilant somersaults, which was perhaps not ideal for the middle of the working day—or during a serious conversation. "So what happened this morning?"

"I need your permission to send some information over to Nick. It's connected to the financial records."

Okay, so, not what she'd expected. "You have it, but I'm not sure how this could be connected to the threats."

"It probably isn't—at least, I can't see how it would be. I stumbled across it by accident. If I'm right, I think you have a tag team of embezzlers on your hands."

She hadn't expected that, either. "You're saying we have two thieves on the payroll? No, I don't believe it. It can't be true. I'd know if it was true."

Questions sprayed across her mind like machine-gun fire. Rocco had to be wrong. If something like that was going on, she'd know. She spent anywhere from a few minutes to a couple of hours in the financial systems every day—she'd know if a crime was being committed.

Wouldn't she?

Perhaps if Rocco told her who he suspected, she could tell him it was out of the question. The only person she had real doubts about was Frank Schofield, and not only did he not have access to the financial systems, he barely knew his way around a smartphone, never mind a sophisticated computer system.

So who was it?

Rocco shaking his head brought her out of her mental turmoil, to the realization she must have asked the question aloud.

"I can't tell you anything until I have more than a suspicion to go on. Look, I could be wrong. I'm not an expert, but Nick's an accountant—he'll know if I'm reading this right, and if I am, he'll know what we need by way of evidence. At least, enough to take it to the police."

"I'm stunned. I had no idea. How could I have no idea?" She was fuming as well as in shock.

"Because you can't control everything. If you tried, you'd be working twenty-four hours a day, and you'd burn out in no time. No one can do that day after day. We all have our limits."

"If there's something going on, I should have—"

"No, you told me yourself—there aren't enough hours in the day. I still need to talk to these people, but I'm going to wait until I hear from Nick."

Rocco was right, although Sasha was reluctant to admit it.

"Hey." Rocco's fingers on her jaw coaxed her into looking at him. "Don't beat yourself up about it. You put people you believe are honest in positions of trust, and you expect them to behave in an honorable way. It's also human nature to see yourself reflected in others—"

"I know that!" she snapped, and immediately regretted it. Wounded professional pride was making an ass out of her. "I'm sorry, I shouldn't take it out on you."

Rocco's arm went around her and drew her against him. There was a wonderful sense of warmth and comfort about him, and she couldn't help but relax.

"Don't worry—the shoulders can take it."

Sasha doubted there was anything those broad, muscular shoulders couldn't take. They certainly held up well when she was gripping them in the throes of the most intense orgasms she'd ever experienced. She sighed at the memory and snuggled—since when did Sasha Morgan *snuggle*?—into Rocco's side. He made an irresistibly comfortable, but more to the point sexy, pillow. "Do we really have to go back to work this afternoon?"

She moved with his shrug. "It's Friday. We can always POETS."

Sasha groaned. "What? Is that another Brit thing?"

"POETS. Piss—Push Off Early, Tomorrow's Saturday."

Sasha suspected in the circles he used to run in, his initial definition of the P was the accurate one. "Is every Brit as crazy as you?"

"Only the half-Sicilian ones. I have an idea."

"About what? What we do this afternoon instead of work?" She was so tempted. She'd put in some long days in the run-up to Rocco arriving at the estate, and the thought of quitting early for the weekend was so, so seductive. Not to mention she'd missed having him beside her the previous night.

"Don't reject this out of hand. How about if we have lunch, take an hour—ninety minutes max—to tidy up today's loose ends, then spend some time together, and maybe, later on, go for a swim?"

"A swim? That's it? That's the best you can do to entice me into finishing early? I can swim any day of the week," she scoffed, knowing Rocco would take it with the humor she intended.

"Uh-huh. See, I didn't say how much later we'd go for that swim. I was thinking much… much… later."

Now he was making it start to sound interesting. "'When everyone's asleep' later? Does this include skinny-dipping, by any chance?"

"If you like. We could use the smaller pool," he suggested.

Good choice. Linzi had used that particular pool less than half a dozen times since she'd moved in. Sasha didn't relish the thought of being caught swimming in the nude by her petite, skinny boss. "How many lengths are you planning to swim?"

"The length I have in mind has nothing to do with swimming, and you can have it inside you as many times as you like."

His low voice, full of intimacy and promise, and the images it conjured up curled her toes and made her squirm with a sudden desire to straddle his lap and grind herself against him until they both saw stars. "You're leading me astray, Mr. Equizi."

"Glad to hear it, Ms. Morgan. My plan is working."

She lifted her face, and with perfect synchronicity, her lips were ideally placed for Rocco to kiss them. She cupped the back of his head, increased the pressure of her demand, and was rewarded with a deepening of the kiss that intensified her craving to climb all over him to the limit of her self-control.

His hand landed on her hip. "Damn skirt," he growled into her mouth.

Her instincts had protested when she'd chosen the pencil skirt in her closet that morning. The fit was so tight, it looked as if she'd visited a paint shop and had it sprayed on. Her instincts had been proved right, and as Rocco's fingers squeezed her ass, she offered up a silent apology for ignoring them.

"Patience. You can take it off later," she promised.

When lunch was ready, they sat opposite one another at the counter. Sasha was especially pleased when Rocco signaled his approval of her cooking, but what startled her was the thrill she experienced simply having lunch with him in her apartment. For a wild, reckless moment, she allowed herself to imagine what it would be like if they could do this for the longer term... maybe even permanently... as if Rocco was going to stay and they were in it for the long haul.

It was complete and utter fantasy, of course. She waited for common sense to tell her not to be so silly, but that inner voice remained silent.

"Sasha? Are you all right?" The genuine concern in Rocco's words was mirrored in his frown.

She gave herself a mental shake. "Yes, of course."

"Are you sure? It's just that—"

"Believe me, it was nothing. Cramps in my leg. It's gone now."

The excuse sounded so lame. For a second or two, she wondered if Rocco would press her further, but after a second or two, he continued to eat his lunch.

When they returned to her office after lunch, Sasha was for once glad that where she'd set up desk space for Rocco, he had to sit with his back to her. It made it incredibly easy for her to carry on with her work and steal surreptitious glances at the same time. He almost caught her, though, when he turned to her during a phone call with Nick Blackmore.

"Sasha? Nick would like a word with you, if it's convenient?"

"Yeah, sure."

Rocco came to her to hand over his cell phone. Their fingers touched briefly, and the look on his face told her it wasn't by accident. Sasha's pulse jumped, then she greeted Rocco's boss.

"Good afternoon, Mr. Blackmore. What can I do for you?"

She listened intently as the Brit explained what he needed and why. During the conversation, she glanced over at Rocco. He was watching her with a neutral expression, but it was clear he was waiting for something.

"I have to admit, Nick, this isn't what I expected when Gerry told me he was bringing your company on board, but if you really think there's a problem, I'll get something set up for you as soon as we finish talking. Thanks for taking a look at this. I never imagined anyone would steal from Linzi like that. I'll pass you back to Rocco and get onto it now."

Rocco took the phone from her, and while he carried on his conversation, Sasha logged into the administrative module of the web-based financial system and created a superuser login for Nick. She wrote the details on a note and took it to Rocco, who was still talking to his boss.

Back at her desk, Sasha stared blankly at the computer screen, unable to concentrate on what she was supposed to be doing. If Rocco and Nick were right, two of the most trusted employees on the payroll were committing embezzlement on a grand scale, and possibly had been for some time. She still didn't know for certain who they were, but the list of candidates with access to the financial system was small—small enough for her to zero in on two names.

Her first thought was that she was wrong—completely and utterly wrong. It couldn't be them. However, the more she brooded about it, the stronger her anger grew, and without thinking, she started taking it out on her keyboard.

"Come with me."

Rocco was standing by her desk, holding out his hand. Her first response was automatic, then she found her voice.

"What?" She stared at her hand, now firmly enclosed in his. "Why?"

"If you hit those keys any harder, you'll break your keyboard. I'm taking you to bed—whatever you're feeling right now, you can take it out on me."

Sasha's jaw dropped as her lady parts rippled and all but purred. For a second, the stark declaration took the wind out of her sails and all the fire out of her temper, but then something much more primitive kicked in. Having her wicked way with that gorgeous body? She could get on board with that. "Your place or mine?"

"Whichever you prefer."

It was a no-brainer, and she almost snarled the word. "Mine."

Rocco would have put his arm around her shoulders but counted himself lucky she was letting him hold her hand.

She truly hadn't expected the news he'd given her, and the resulting anger rolled from her in waves. Her trust and judgment had been gravely wounded, generating feelings that were best released, rather than being kept bottled up. And when they were released, he was going to be there for her.

As soon as they reached her quarters, Sasha led the way inside. Rocco barely had time to cross the threshold before she spun around and flung herself at him, managing to slam the door shut behind him as momentum almost forced him off-balance. Her lips smashed into his, while her fingers tangled in his hair to anchor him in place for a kiss that scorched and sizzled through his whole body.

When Sasha came up for air, she took a step back from him, panting for breath. "I know what you said, but tell me who it is. I need to know if I'm right."

She was frustrated, and he didn't blame her. He hated being the source of that frustration, but until they had sufficient evidence to back up what he'd found, he didn't want to put her working relationships at risk with unfounded accusations. "You know I can't," he said gently, reaching toward her to pull her back against him. "What if I'm wrong?"

"What if you're not? What if I'm right and it's who I think it is? I can help."

"Listen. I don't know who you think it is, but we can't name names until we have solid proof. Nick knows his way around financial records, and if there's anything else that looks suspicious, he'll find it. He knows what to look for. For all I know, what I found could be a genuine error." He didn't think so, but there was an element of doubt.

"And whoever it is could be committing more crimes right now. The longer we wait, the more damage they can do."

"Agreed, but look at it this way—if they are, they're providing us with more evidence to build a case against them."

He studied Sasha for a moment. Reluctant acceptance haunted her eyes, but she was still surrounded by a boiling cloud of nervous energy. Rocco held out his hand, unwavering in the face of her fiery, assessing stare.

Sasha laid her fingers across his. Slowly, he stroked them with his thumb. As he did so, he watched out for changes in her level of agitation. Not that he had her fooled for one moment—she knew exactly what he was trying to do. For a second or two she held his gaze, then her grip on his hand tightened. "Bed. Now."

Rocco didn't argue.

The suite was so quiet, he could almost hear his own heart beating. Even though this wasn't exactly what he'd had in mind when he'd encouraged Sasha to finish work early, he didn't regret what had happened, and he couldn't complain about the result—not when that result was Sasha nestled against him, deep in an untroubled sleep after a session that had made wild monkey sex look like a vicarage tea party.

Not that Rocco had attended too many of those in his time.

Although Sasha was finally resting after the earlier upset, Rocco couldn't say the same for himself. His inner turmoil was severely at odds with the tranquility surrounding them. Soft, low-key lighting was supposed to be soothing, but he had too much going on in his mind for it to work.

He knew he was right not to disclose the names of the two alleged embezzlers to Sasha, no matter how much she'd tried to coax him into divulging the information. If it turned out he was wrong and he'd divulged their identities, those working relationships could be permanently wrecked. He wasn't here to make Sasha's life harder.

"What time is it?"

The sleepy question returned his focus where it belonged. He glanced at his watch. "Almost eight. Are you hungry?"

Her sigh skimmed over his chest, breathing new life into his desire for her. "I don't know."

Rocco waited. He couldn't say why, but he had a feeling she had something on her mind.

"I'm sorry."

An apology was the last thing he expected. "What the hell for?"

"Being a bitch."

Not what he expected, but he had no intention of playing stupid games when she sounded so unhappy. "You weren't a bitch. Right now, you feel let down… angry. It's understandable."

"I shouldn't have taken it out on you." She shifted position, as if she were trying to extricate herself from the arm he'd had around her for the last hour. "You need to let me take a look at your back."

"You didn't draw blood, if that's what you're worried about."

He'd checked when he went to the bathroom to dispose of the used condoms. The rake of her fingernails down his back had left red weals, but she hadn't broken the skin. The prognosis was favorable that he'd survive. After all, his body had endured far worse.

"Turn over—let me see."

The quickest way to get this over with was to comply. This time he did lift his arm to release her, then rolled onto his side with his back to her. He braced himself for her touch.

At first it was almost clinical, but then the contact changed, became softer, slower, and when her lips joined her fingers, his body's response was predictable. "Sasha."

The low growl of warning didn't deter her.

"I overreacted today," she said quietly. "That's not like me."

"I told you—you were let down—"

"No." Movement behind him had him imagining her shaking her head. "Even if that's true, I've been—"

Sasha broke off suddenly. Rocco would have bet his left nut she'd been about to say something about having been trained to deal with the unexpected. Joint ops with US special forces had given him some idea of the training CIA agents underwent. "Sasha?"

"It doesn't matter. But I am sorry for ruining our plans for this evening."

He couldn't keep his back to her a moment longer—the strain in her voice was too obvious for him to ignore. Seeing it in the sadness of her expression was even worse. He drew her back into his arms, where she belonged. "It wasn't that much of a hardship. Skinny-dipping with a beautiful woman versus hours of crazy sex with her? I'll take the latter any day."

A playful punch landed on his biceps. "You are such a man."

He grinned, more out of relief at hearing some of the tension ease out of her voice. "Glad you noticed." He paused. "There's something I need to ask you."

"Go on."

"Would you like me to stay with you tonight, or would you prefer me to go?"

Because this was her territory, tomorrow was Saturday, and people's routines were less predictable. Anyone could catch him leaving here in the morning—and trash her reputation—but tonight, there'd be hardly anyone around.

"Stay—please. I… need you."

The naked honesty in her expression pierced him through. He wondered how she'd react if he told her he needed her, too.

"Then I'll stay."

Because just for tonight, it really was as simple as that.

CHAPTER 10

Sasha opened her eyes. He was still there. Then again, he'd promised.

He was still asleep, too. Lying on his side with his back to the terrace doors and the subtle lights illuminating the gardens beyond, his face was in shadow, but she didn't need to see his features to know he hadn't roused when she stirred. His breathing was shallow and even, telling her he was likely resting peacefully.

She could feast on Rocco Equizi for hours, lie there doing nothing more than looking at him, taking in every perfect detail of the man. The glow from the lights highlighted the muscular curve of his shoulder and the dip where the deltoid ended, but her memory revealed what the shadows concealed. The sculpted perfection of a body honed by hard work. Her body warmed with the reminder of the perfect fit of his hips between her thighs as he drove into her, hard and deep, until the universe exploded in a million orgasmic stars.

She was poised on the cusp of falling in love with him—if it wasn't already too late. In spite of her best efforts to deny them, the fantasies she'd woven around him were gaining strength and becoming more difficult to dismiss. Like it or not, she'd become emotionally involved, and there was every chance her heart would break because of it.

Her eyes stung for a moment. She lifted her hand to wipe the tears away before they could betray her, only for it to be enclosed in a strong, gentle grip.

"Hey, what's this for?"

Caught out, Sasha rolled her eyes. "I thought you were asleep."

"Haven't been asleep for the last ten minutes—I was watching you."

Thank God for the darkness hiding the heat rushing to her cheeks. Wait—she was *blushing*? It was half a lifetime since she'd last been capable of doing that. "You know how that sounds, right?"

He chuckled. "As if I'm stalking you?"

"Something like that, although I'm not sure it counts as stalking when we're in the same bed." Sasha trembled at the sensation of his hand stroking her side.

"Mind if I turn a light on?"

Sasha gave a pained moan. "Do you realize what time it is?"

"Literally or figuratively?"

What in the name of heaven was he talking about now? "I was thinking literally."

He consulted the Omega Seamaster that rarely left his wrist. "In that case, it's almost zero three hundred, and I wondered if you meant figuratively."

Sasha groaned. "Please don't ask me riddles when half my brain's still asleep. If there's something you want to know, just spit it out." She slapped a hand over her mouth and yawned.

He reached behind him for the control on the nightstand. Soft, warm light bathed the room, subdued enough not to disrupt their mood and strong enough for her to fall victim to Rocco's charismatic good looks all over again. "All right, I will. You've had something on your mind—I've been waiting for you to start the conversation, but enough is enough."

She used to be real good at keeping a poker face, but all of a sudden, she realized it didn't much matter. For one thing, Rocco would have worked alongside British Intelligence agents during his military service, and for another, she owed it to him to tell him the truth. After all, that was what anyone would do when it came to the person they loved. She'd thought she was close to falling in love with him, but she was wrong—it had already happened.

"You're right." Sasha wriggled away from him, just enough so that she could see his face without contorting her neck through a ninety-degree angle. "There is something. First of all, I couldn't work out if I should tell you or not, but now, I can't work out how. At least, I haven't been able to."

"I find words are usually fairly effective," he said with a touch of wry humor. "Interpretive dance is so yesterday."

Now she had to laugh. "You're crazy."

"About you, I am. So, tell me what's bothering you."

Sasha's heart skipped. The emotion behind it was something to store away for discussion later—if he still felt the same way after he learned what she had to tell him. She took a deep, cleansing breath.

"So…What's bothering me is… I don't think you know who I really am. Or was. If I came in here to do what you're doing, I'd want a full background check on everyone closest to Linzi, including me. Maybe even especially me. All I'd find out is how long I've been doing this job and a big, fat, black hole leading up to it."

"Go on."

Rocco's tone revealed nothing—at least he wasn't mad at

her. *Yet.* "Did that file tell you I worked for the government for over fifteen years? I was with—"

"The CIA?"

Sasha's eyes widened. "You know?"

"I know, but not from the file." He shrugged. "You mentioned Virginia. Taking that into account, along with other observations—the way you move, the way you behave, even the words you use—I suspected you might have been connected with Langley, so I asked Nick to find out what he could. If it's any consolation, it took a couple of experts a while to track down the information."

"Does it bother you?" Sasha's stomach churned in anticipation of the response she didn't want to hear.

"No. Why would it? We both know how the world we inhabited works."

"What world did you inhabit? Special forces of some kind?"

Rocco nodded. "SAS. I think it's safe to say we both understand the need for caution and secrecy."

He was right. Had their positions been reversed, she'd have done exactly the same. She was still curious, though. "As badass as I thought. So, you had me checked out—was that before or after the first time you kissed me?"

"Both. I asked my boss what he could find out about you, but I kissed you before he could tell me what his contact discovered. Not that it mattered—they only confirmed what I already knew. My instincts told me you weren't involved in this, and they're rarely wrong."

"Know-it-all," she groused with good humor.

This time, Rocco's body shook with laughter. "I can't begin to tell you how many times in the past I've wished that were true. Good instincts can only take you so far." He became serious again. "You were a spook for a long time.

Nick told me why you walked away from it—what happened to your partner—but that was about it."

The memory of grief rippled from the past to the present. She and Jack had never been in love with one another but they had loved one another as true friends, as well as close colleagues and partners. Losing him had been bad enough, but the circumstances in which he'd lost his life would remain with her always. No matter how this thing with Rocco ended up, he deserved the truth.

"His name was Jack Ward. We'd been partners for over five years, went on dozens of assignments all over the world. The last one... It was in South America. The details don't matter, but it went sour. We were compromised and called for emergency evac. We almost made it, too. The cartel came out of nowhere. I didn't see them, but Jack did. He took the bullets that were meant for me. We made it to cover, and he survived long enough for the Delta Force team to get us out. He died on the transport plane. At least we were able to bring him home."

To a funeral where only she among the attendees had known the true extent of his heroism.

Rocco pulled her closer, kissed her forehead, and tucked her into his body.

"I'm sorry. Were you and he...?"

Rocco was a man and only human—of course he'd want to know. "Yes. He was my friend as well as my partner, and... we were probably closer than we ideally should have been."

The arms around her tightened. "We all need someone to be there for us. We need that person even more when we're in a hostile environment."

She should have known Rocco would understand, more than anyone—more than the average joe, anyway. The pain around her heart eased a little more. "All of us? What about you? Who do you have?"

His chest rose and fell beneath her cheek. "I think you can guess the answer to that, Sasha. We wouldn't be here, like this, if I had someone."

"Or if I had someone."

It was important that he know that. Neither she nor Jack had been with anyone else while they were finding comfort with each other, something they'd agreed as friends, and there'd been no one in her life since.

"Do you miss it?"

For a split second, Sasha wasn't sure what the "it" was. "Ah. You mean the adrenaline rush of saving the world one more time?"

"Something like that."

Sasha considered her response. "It's an easy question to ask, but not so easy to answer. One of the reasons I took this job was to ease my way out of the Agency. I had to get out after losing Jack, but the thought of stopping cold was… daunting. This was a halfway house."

"So you'll have a way back in at some point?"

"No. No way, not now. I may not know what I'll end up doing when I leave here yet, but I do know that when I do leave—when, not if—it won't be to go back there."

"Good choice."

"I think so. You're probably wondering how I came to be here. After all, it's not an obvious move. My former supervisor is Linzi's godfather. I already told you she made enough of a name for herself to attract the wrong kind of attention before I came along. Even though that stopped, her godfather was still worried, so when I told him I was about to quit but had no idea what I was going to do, he came up with the idea that I become Linzi's assistant. It was a win for everyone. I got myself a job, my supervisor got someone he could trust on the inside, and Linzi got someone to watch over her."

"Makes sense."

Rocco fell silent, but Sasha had the impression there was more he wanted to say. She wasn't wrong.

"Are you happy, working for her?"

From the cautious way he asked the question, she wondered if there was more to it than the casual inquiry it appeared to be. She opened her mouth to give the glib response she'd offer anyone else, but then thought better of it. "Happy enough for now—for the long term, who knows? For all any of us know, it could all end tomorrow, not that I'm wishing that for Linzi. She may be difficult, but she's also talented, and she has a drive to succeed. You've seen what she's like in the studio."

"Focused, I think is the polite word," Rocco said dryly. "She knows what she wants."

"And she isn't going to let anything get in her way." Sasha had seen plenty of Linzi's single-minded determination, and the drive to achieve what she wanted that had sometimes mown down the unsuspecting. "What about you? Do you see yourself still in close protection five, ten years from now?"

Sasha didn't want to admit to herself how invested she was in his reply, or why she was—that way lay madness. Instead, she tried to convince herself that the answer didn't matter and she was merely making small talk.

At this time of the morning when you're in bed with the man? Please.

Rocco rolled onto his back. "*Cristo,* I hope not. There has to be more to life than this."

For half a second, her heart thudded into her stomach, fearing he somehow meant casual liaisons with women he met while on assignment, but then common sense reasserted itself. "You mean, putting yourself between a celebrity and some crazy with a gun?"

He gave a short, humorless laugh. "When you put it like

that, this job doesn't have much going for it. Only a lunatic would do this for a living."

"I believe we make life choices for a reason. Every choice you've made in your life, every choice I've made in mine... without those choices, we wouldn't be here, together, in this moment."

Sasha wasn't sure where the words had come from, but the more she thought about it, the more she believed it to be true.

"You're saying we were meant to meet?" The way he asked the question made it sound as if he was taking it seriously.

Desire shivered through Sasha's body at the low, sexy tone that transformed the atmosphere between them. "I guess I am."

Rocco moved again, and he was almost on top of her. "We might not know what's in the future for either of us, *cara*," he growled, "but I do know what I want for now—you."

He was already hard against her belly. Pure lust consumed her as she wrapped her free leg around his thigh and pressed closer to him.

"The feeling," she whispered, "is very, very mutual."

The mattress barely moved as Rocco left it, but it was enough to rouse Sasha from slumber.

"What time is it?" she murmured, reluctant to move from the position where she'd drifted off to sleep with Rocco spooning her. Which he was no longer doing, and she wished to hell he'd get his delectable body back where it belonged.

He came back to the bed, pulling his shirt on as he did so. "Zero four hundred. I have to go. Go back to sleep."

Rocco stooped. His lips brushed her shoulder, and a deliciously sensual tremor rippled through her. Sasha sighed. Sometimes a woman had to play dirty to get what she wanted. She rolled onto her back so she could get a good view of him. Somehow, in doing so, she accidentally on purpose managed to dislodge the sheet and present him with an eyeful of her most prized assets.

If she'd blinked at the wrong moment, she'd have missed the flicker of distraction that had him fumbling with his shirt button. Her inner siren gave a smug, knowing smile, and followed it with an invisible fist-pump when he sat on the edge of the bed and leaned over her, bracing himself with a hand on either side of her.

"You did that deliberately," he accused, fixing her with a steely glare. "Tell me, do all women go on some secret course to learn how to seduce a man, or does it just come naturally?"

Supporting herself on one elbow, Sasha rose to meet him. She caressed the back of his head with her free hand, fingers tangling in his hair, and kissed him. "The answer to your question is… it's a secret, and I will never betray the sisterhood."

"Tease." He groaned and rested his forehead against hers, muttering something Italian under his breath. If they carried on like this, she was going to have to get a better handle on the language.

His open-mouthed kisses pulled at her flesh, sending sizzles of electricity through her nervous system. He traced a sensual path from her cheek and down her neck, finally arriving at her breast, where he licked and bit the pebbled nipple before suckling on it hard enough to make her squirm with a level of need that made her core pulsate.

"Stay," she whispered.

"Can't," he murmured. "Training session with Scott, then it's the day job."

A pang of guilt hit her. They'd spent most of the night

wrapped in the throes of the hottest sex she'd ever known and gotten barely any sleep. Maybe she shouldn't have been quite so demanding.

"Wait—it's Saturday." As the words sank in, her brain finally kicked into gear. "It's Saturday," she repeated. There was something fundamentally incompatible between what Rocco was doing and the day of the week. Of course, officially, she didn't work weekends, but in reality, it never worked out that way.

Rocco gave her a wry grin. "Ten out of ten for observation."

"So why are you working? Don't you get time off?"

"It's the job."

Then the answer to her question was no. It was so unfair—what would she find to do without him? "What are you going to do?"

"After training with Scott? See if there's anything I've missed." He lowered his head to lavish attention on her other breast.

Sasha's eyes almost rolled out of her head. The man's mouth was a lethal weapon when it came to lovemaking. "You think that's possible?" She just about managed to string the sentence together.

"It's always possible. Sometimes you just don't see things first time around, or even the second. Sometimes you take another look, and in the context of new information you've uncovered in the meantime, everything adds up differently. More variables, different outcomes." He pinched her nipple and soothed it immediately with his tongue.

"I see. And how long..." Sasha's teeth clamped down on her lower lip. The attention he was lavishing on her was dissolving her ability to think. "How long are you planning to do that? All day?"

A delicate bite to her sensitized flesh made her moan with

frustration. He was doing this to her just as he was about to go? If he left her like this...

"Not all day. I have a couple of ideas I want to check out, and then I'm all yours."

And now she was melting. "Say that again, and I'll handcuff you to the bed."

Rocco winked. "Promises, promises. Be good, and I'll bring you back something nice."

That woke her up. "What?"

He straightened up, hands held out at his sides in a gesture that clearly indicated he was the "something nice" he had in mind.

"Ah, okay, you've convinced me. After you've finished with Scott, are you coming back for breakfast? It's Geri's day off, so you'll have to take your chances with me."

For an instant, he looked aghast, and then grinned. "You know how to make a man an offer he can't refuse."

"Good. Now go. Don't work too hard." She crooked her finger, and when he bent toward her, she pressed a swift kiss to his mouth. "I'll see you later."

"And tonight?" He nuzzled her cheek.

The husky directness of the question thrilled her. "Unless something happens, I think I'll go to bed early—say, by nine?"

God, that smile of his made her toes curl. Being with Rocco was like nothing she'd ever experienced before.

"Sounds good. Now get some sleep and I'll see you later."

She watched him finish dressing. Seconds later, he melted into the darkness. Two doors clicked closed, and it was as if he'd never been there.

Sasha settled beneath the cool, cotton sheet and grabbed the pillow Rocco had used. She hugged it close, and when she inhaled, the scent of him wove its magic around her senses. With a couple of hours before her day was due to start, she could allow herself a little extra dream time.

Or at least, she could have, had she not been assaulted by an insistent voice asking silent questions about what was happening between her and Rocco, and the accusation that it was all happening way too fast.

Not only that—where did she expect it to go?

It was a question for which she had no answer, but worrying about it was pointless. She closed her eyes, and eventually she drifted off to a parallel world where her relationship with Rocco wasn't limited by the length of his assignment.

CHAPTER 11

Trying to make as little noise as possible, Rocco pulled the door closed behind him. A few long strides covered the distance from Sasha's apartment to his. In spite of his fears, there was no one around at this ungodly hour, so he remained unseen.

He'd hated leaving her. He could still smell her wildflower scent on him, and though the last thing he wanted was to wash it off, he didn't want to give Scott any reason to suspect what was going on between him and Sasha.

After all, she'd still have to work here when he was long gone to his next assignment.

The thought of leaving her didn't settle well in his belly. As he ran the shower, Rocco considered his options, and none of them were a good fit. If he stayed in Texas, there was no guarantee he'd be working close enough to Casa Millefiori to see Sasha on a regular basis—he could end up anywhere from Alaska to Florida. Or even Hawaii. Even if his next assignment were in Texas, he could still be hundreds of miles from her. The damn state was three times bigger than the entire country he called home.

Home. That was an option, too, but if he chose it, he'd be thousands of miles away from her and thousands of miles closer to his father.

Rocco stripped off his clothes and stepped into the shower enclosure. He braced his arms against the wall and let the spray pound down on his neck and shoulders. So far, since he'd arrived in the US, his father hadn't called, but it was only a matter of time. The old man was as stubborn as they came—he refused to accept that Rocco had no intention of returning to Sicily to be shackled to the family business until the day he died. He lived his own life, and that included the ability to make decisions for himself.

One of those decisions was that running a vineyard and winery wasn't for him. When he'd moved into close protection, he'd known it wouldn't be forever, but giving it up was always some vague, indefinable point in the future. Now he wondered if his conversation with Sasha would be instrumental in bringing it a lot closer.

What his immediate future held, however, was the first training session with Scott Monroe. For this one, Rocco wanted to focus on assessing the other man's existing skills against what might be required when Linzi attended the Diamond ACE Music Awards in Austin in a little over a week from now. Rocco wanted at least one man there on whom he could rely without question.

Half a cup of strong, black coffee later, Rocco was making his way to the gym located in the guest house. The facility was rarely used, but that didn't mean it had been mothballed. When he arrived, Scott was ready and waiting.

"Good morning, sir."

"It's Rocco, remember?" He smiled. "Thanks for coming in today and giving up part of your day off. I hope it hasn't caused any problems at home."

"It's no problem, s—no problem at all. Thank you for the opportunity."

"You might not be quite so grateful by the time we're done." Rocco rolled his shoulders. "We'll warm up with some stretches, and then start off with a look at your unarmed combat skills. That okay?"

One brutally demanding session later, when they were both on their knees and panting with exertion, Rocco had a pretty good idea of Scott's ability to defend himself when he didn't have a weapon to hand. It was easily on a par with his impressive scores on the shooting range, which were recorded on his personnel file. It would be interesting to see how current those scores were.

"I think that'll do for today. I've seen enough."

Scott straightened up and looked Rocco straight in the eye. "With respect, sir, I can do better. If you'll give me a chance—"

"You did great, and you will do even better when I show you additional techniques you can't find in a basic training manual."

Scott sat back on his heels, his expression one of perceptive curiosity. "I know you're ex-military, but were you in the British special forces?"

Without using his hands for leverage, Rocco stood in a single fluid movement. He approached Scott, offered him a hand, and helped him to his feet. "Yes."

To Rocco's surprise, a broad smile appeared on Scott's face. "That makes me feel a hell of a lot better, sir—Rocco. Whatever you want to teach me, I can do it."

Rocco lifted his chin in acknowledgement. "I know you can. Over the next week, if you can, I want you to report here, starting tomorrow. We can get your shifts changed to accommodate that. I'll take you through those techniques I mentioned. I'm also going to set up a firing range—I don't imagine I can show you much there, but I'd like an idea of how you handle a weapon."

"You don't need to set anything up. We already have an indoor range on site. Some of the guys like to practice before they go on shift or go home."

That was interesting. Rocco couldn't recall seeing a range on the plans, but then again, there'd been quite a few anonymous structures that could have functioned as one. "Thanks for that. When you were serving, were you ever assigned any close protection duties?"

"No, never—I was just an average grunt."

"Nothing wrong with that. I'll set you up with some basic close protection skills—enough for you to be 2IC when we escort Linzi to an event in Austin a week from tomorrow. I want someone there I know I can rely on."

Scott was already standing ramrod straight, but at that comment, he was almost standing at attention. "You can rely on me... and I won't say a word about this to the other guys."

He was discreet as well—promising. Discretion was always a good quality for a bodyguard. "Good. That's enough for today—can you be here same time tomorrow?"

"Sure can. I'm looking forward to working with you."

"Same here, Scott. I'll see you tomorrow."

Rocco let Scott leave ahead of him, then checked the gym to make sure they hadn't left any obvious signs of it being used. This arrangement had to be kept as low-profile as possible. If Frank Schofield was as sketchy as both he and Sasha believed, then it cast doubt on the men he'd hired. Scott, being the latest recruit, was probably least likely to have been drawn into any shady activities, and the vibe Rocco was picking up from him seemed to bear that out.

A steady jog would take Rocco back to the main house in minutes. After another quick shower, he'd set to work on his to-do list, then take another look at the estate plans. He grinned to himself. He needed Sasha's help to locate the shooting range, so he had an excellent excuse to tell her to get her sweet ass out of bed.

Maybe he'd switch those around. He'd been away from her for too long, and besides, looking in on her before he started work wouldn't be that big a distraction, just a fix to see him keep him going until they could get together later.

Grinning like an idiot, he picked up his pace.

Sasha's stomach growled, once again making known its displeasure with the lack of food. If Rocco came back and told her he'd had breakfast with Scott after all, she was going to kill him, and no jury would find her guilty. Homicide was entirely justifiable for the abhorrent crime of starving a woman to death. She'd give him another ten minutes, and if there was still no sign of him, she was going to make a start on her taste-of-heaven pancake recipe.

Saturday was definitely a yoga pants kind of day. She liked yoga pants—she liked them even more when Rocco peeled them off of her. Showered and dressed, she prepped the ingredients for her breakfast of choice, and in the interests of giving Rocco a fair chance—because her pancakes truly were the eighth wonder of the world and the only thing she could cook to perfection—she was going to call him to see if he was hungry.

He answered immediately. "Hey. You've woken up then?"

Desire skimmed through her body at the warm amusement in his voice. It wasn't just his accent—there was a suggestive roughness to it that made all her lady bits snap to attention. "Of course, and I'm just about to make breakfast—pancakes. Want to join me?"

"Can you give me ten? I need to clean up, and I'm only just at the atrium now."

Sasha sprinted for the door. If she timed this right, she could intercept him on his way past her apartment.

"You look just fine to me."

Rocco slowed his pace as soon as he realized he wasn't hearing her via his cell, and came to a halt right in front of her. As she drank in his appearance, Sasha's hunger turned from food to sex. Would she ever not be starving for this man? Not when he looked so damn sexy in black sweats and a black tank. A casual jacket, also black, was slung carelessly over his shoulder. His hair was slicked to his forehead, evidence of physical exertion. When he looked her up and down, he didn't even try to hide his appreciation. "You look incredible."

The husky compliment almost vaporized every shred of clothing she wore, and she didn't need to look to know her beading nipples were now outlined by the figure-hugging top she'd chosen to wear. "Thank you. So, can I tempt you to those pancakes?"

The look in his eyes spoke of temptation of a different kind. "Give me time for a quick shower and a change of clothes, and I'll be right back."

"You could always clean up here." She was sure he wouldn't mind an audience—she could watch him for hours.

His shoulders lifted in a helpless shrug. "No clothes."

"Who says you need them? If you feel awkward eating naked, I don't mind joining you." Sasha took the neckline of her top between her finger and thumb to make it clear she had absolutely no objection to sharing a naked breakfast with him.

Rocco took a step closer and brushed his mouth across hers. "If you do that, we may never get around to eating. Food, that is. And I still have work to do."

The verbal equivalent of a splash of icy water curbed her libido. "Cruel man. Sure I can't distract you a little?"

"I wouldn't discount the possibility. As a matter of fact, I was going to ask you for some help anyway."

"Oh. And if I… render this assistance, you'll be through earlier than you thought?"

"There's a strong possibility. What do you suggest we do after that?"

Sasha's eyes narrowed. The man was impossible. He was deliberately teasing her. She'd show him. "Ever played strip poker?"

He leaned his elbow on the door frame at head height—his head, not hers—and leaned in a little closer. "Ever lost at strip poker?"

Sasha stood on tiptoe and gave him a chaste peck on the cheek. "Never," she whispered in his ear.

A cool, confident smile appeared on Rocco's face. "Challenge accepted."

"And I'm sure you'll—" she paused, glanced pointedly down at his groin, and adopted a sweet and innocent smile "—rise to it."

This time he roared with laughter. "You can count on it. Let me clean up, and while we eat, I'll ask you those questions. Is that okay?"

"Sure. I'll go make a start on the batter."

With a satisfied sigh, she watched him cover the distance to his apartment. Crazy though it was, she felt a lightness inside that had been missing for a long time. She was setting herself up for a colossal fall when he eventually left, but she couldn't help it. Until he went, she was going to grab every chance that came her way to spend time with him, and go wherever the wild ride took her.

~

When Rocco had asked Sasha about the on-site firing range over breakfast, the last thing he'd expected was for her to retrieve a SIG Sauer from a safe in her bedroom, take him to the facility, and challenge him to a shooting match.

She was an amazing woman—and not only because of her ability with the handgun. Combine that with the pancakes with which she'd seduced him, and he was a goner. While Geri's breakfast treats were obviously created by a consummate professional, Sasha's had a homemade quality that made him think of the closeness of shared mornings and intimate glances that made words unnecessary.

The kind of details that characterized long-term relationships, not brief flings that sprang to life out of convenience.

Standing by the bench behind the shooting stalls, he watched Sasha stow the handgun in its case. Her hands moved with an economic familiarity and confidence he found enthralling. She closed the lid, spun the combination locks, and turned to face him.

"Rocco, now that you know what I was before I came to work for Linzi, and I've proved I can handle a gun, will you let me take a more active role in Linzi's protection at the awards next week?"

Merda. She had to ask. Somehow, he'd known it was coming. "Sasha, you left the Agency for a reason. You told me you had no intention of going back."

"I did, and the fact that I want to do this is a million miles from me wanting to go back. It means I want to use my skills to help out—to help *you*. You need people you can trust—you know you can trust me, right?"

She'd just scored a direct hit on his Achilles heel—Scott was the only member of the security team he felt comfortable with bringing into a trusted inner circle, and other candidates in the immediate vicinity were rarer than rocking horse shit.

Apart from her.

Bringing Sasha in went against every protective instinct he possessed, but the fact was, he needed her. This being Texas, her carrying a gun wouldn't be unusual. He doubted she'd ever broadcast her past to anyone—only Gerry Brookes knew, and Linzi's manager had yet to show up for the first time since Rocco had arrived. "I do trust you."

"And you don't need me to spell out how many times I've been in far more hazardous situations. Do you?"

Now he was forced to think about it, and even though she'd have been trained thoroughly for her role in the Agency, Rocco's blood ran cold at the thought of her being in danger. "No, I don't."

"Then why not let me help?"

"Did I say I *wasn't* going to let you help?"

From her smile, she'd clearly drawn an accurate conclusion from what he'd implied. "Good. It's settled. And while we're down here, I can help you with something else as well."

"And what would that be?"

"You said you wanted to take a look at the waterfront. We have a couple of golf carts in the next building—we could go down there now, while I'm right here to answer any questions you might have."

Now what did he do? Admit he'd been outmaneuvered, that was what. He held up his hands in mock surrender. "Okay, I give in."

It was worth it when her face lit up with a triumphant smile. "Good choice." She picked up the gun case and started toward the exit. "Are you going to stay there for the rest of the day, or are you going to haul ass?"

Trying not to laugh, Rocco pinched his lips together and stared at the concrete floor. "I guess I'm hauling ass, ma'am."

Although, on balance, he'd rather haul Sasha's ass—onto his lap, so he could kiss her—because her ass did look spectacular in yoga pants. He consoled himself with the thought that later on, he would have the privilege of separating her from them, and getting up close and very—*very*—personal with the gift beneath that sleek wrapping.

It made sense to let Sasha drive—she knew the quickest way, and he could maintain surveillance on their surroundings without distraction. Apart from the distraction sitting beside him, of course, but he could handle that.

"So, what do you think?" Sasha asked when they arrived at the four-berth dock that dominated the waterfront.

"Could be worse," he admitted. "Plenty of cameras, with some redundancy regarding coverage, so if one goes down, the area's still covered. Assuming the guard in the control room monitoring the cameras is alert, not on the take, and doesn't take a break at the precise moment some lunatic mounts an assault from this location."

"Frank's supposed to have two guards on duty watching the cameras at all times," Sasha informed him. "I make random inspections of the schedules—they've checked out, in so far as he's always got two guys rostered overnight, but..."

"But?"

"I'm not sure I trust what I'm seeing. I've been thinking I should start going for random nighttime walks that take me past the security block."

"Maybe we could do that together," Rocco suggested. "Trust but verify?"

"Something like that. This time of year, we'd freeze our butts off, though."

"And we aren't now?"

Sasha arched an eyebrow at him. "I thought you special forces guys could operate in any conditions."

"We can. We're also very good at assessing situations. Do

you want to stay out here when I know I've seen enough?" he countered.

"Hell, no. What I want right now is a cup of coffee." She pulled her jacket more tightly around her body to emphasize the point.

"Good idea."

They returned to the cart, and as they returned to the garage, Sasha broke the easy silence that had accompanied them on the drive back.

"Do you really have to work today?"

Rocco almost groaned. He did not need that kind of encouragement to play hooky. "You know while I'm on assignment, technically I'm working or on call twenty-four seven."

"Oh, so you were working last night when we were doing this?"

Sasha parked the cart in its space, turned to him, curled her fingers into his jacket and pulled him in for a kiss. When she let him up for air, he rested his forehead against hers.

"Not making this any easier, Morgan," he murmured.

Her lips curved up in a satisfied smile. "Good. That's precisely what I was aiming for."

Rocco was about to retaliate when a cell phone rang—not his, but Sasha's, and unless he missed his guess, the tune was the one she'd assigned uniquely to her employer.

"Hi, Linzi. What can I do for you?"

And then Sasha was silent for a long, long time.

Rocco couldn't hear what was being said on the other side of the call, but he did see Sasha try to speak several times. Eventually, Linzi must have paused for breath long enough for her to break in.

"Linzi, it's all right. Text me the details and I will see to it. Give me a couple hours and I will let you know. 'kay? It'll be fine. I promise. Linzi, I promise. Let me get started and I'll let you know as soon as I have something."

When the call ended, Rocco glanced from the phone to Sasha, and with what he hoped was an innocent expression, said, "You were saying? About my job?"

From the glare she leveled at him, he had a feeling she'd have kneed him in the nuts if they hadn't still been sitting in the cart.

"I have an idea," she said. "I need a couple of hours to resolve this issue for Linzi—"

"Which is? Anything I can do to help?"

Sasha sighed. "How's your knowledge of fashion? Yeah, that's what I thought. I need to make some calls and plead with the couturiers to see if they can make some house calls between now and next weekend."

"That's going to take a couple of hours?" It sounded fairly simple to Rocco, but on the other hand, what did he know about the fashion industry?

"We're talking fragile egos in competition with one another—it's not so much the calls as the scheduling. First of all, they have to agree to drop in with suitable gowns and models, and then I have to arrange the visits so the ones who hate each other don't get to see each other."

Now it made sense. Rocco didn't envy her. He'd dealt with some very delicate egos during his career, and they were invariably a nightmare. "How are your diplomatic skills?"

"A little rusty. It's been a while. Seriously, though, it's not an issue—I need time to work out the logistics is all."

"If it has to be done by next weekend, is this all about what she's wearing for the awards?"

Sasha nodded. "She decided what she was wearing more than a month ago, but she's binge-watching awards shows and MTV, and it's given her some ideas. I need to contact the right stores."

Now that he had a better grasp of the issues, Rocco understood the scale of the task. It reminded him only too well of his own experience. "I see what you mean. Look, I'll grab my laptop from the office and take it to my quarters, so I can leave you in peace to do what you need to do. When you're done, let me know and I'll take you to lunch."

"That sounds wonderful—lunch, I mean, and thanks for understanding. All the talking would probably annoy you anyhow. The sooner we start, the sooner we can eat —let's go."

They returned to the house, and after he collected his laptop, Rocco reluctantly headed back to his quarters, where he made himself comfortable at the kitchen counter.

Instead of doing what he'd originally intended to do, Rocco made a start on planning for the event. Sasha had already emailed him a bunch of logistics information, including the running order. A quick glance down the list confirmed that Linzi was closing the show, so once she came off stage, it should be a relatively easy matter to spirit her away via the service entrance.

For the next hour or so, Rocco immersed himself in his work. The venue left a lot to be desired. Identifying potential threats would have been a lot easier if the Diamond ACE Music Awards had been taking place in a conventional theater setting. Nice, orderly rows made unexpected and potentially threatening movements a lot easier to spot and track. Large, circular tables, with ten people seated at each, acting as if they were out to dinner with friends, did not. At best, they were an obstruction—at worst, they could cost lives.

Rocco's plan to keep Linzi safe was relatively simple—the more complex a strategy was, the more potential points of failure there were, and he was not going to fail. Linzi would attend the awards, perform at the end of the evening, and they would then get her safely back to Casa Millefiori.

Mission accomplished.

Once he'd laid out the route, supported by two backup options, Rocco turned his attention to the more troublesome matter of personnel. He had one man he could rely on… and Sasha. If Spectrum had had more people available, he could have called on his boss for assistance, but Rocco himself accounted for fifty percent of their total current manpower. A call to Nick would be futile.

Or would it? Nick had mentioned some friends of his who might be able to lend a hand if needed. The way his boss had talked about them gave Rocco the feeling they might be or have been Tier 1 operators. Having a couple of them in attendance might be regarded as overkill, but then again, the latest social media threats were exhibiting further signs of escalation. The ones that threatened to kill Linzi if she didn't kill herself first were some of the least worrying.

Rocco pulled up some of the latest threats. If they were interpreted a certain way, he could see a connection to the awards ceremony. Then again, read them a different way, and they were the wild ravings of a lunatic.

Only a fool would ignore what his instincts were telling him. Those instincts were honed by training and years of experience, and they were telling him to be prepared for the worst.

His cell buzzed, alerting him to the arrival of a text.

Open the door.

. . .

The sender's name brought a smile to his lips. Rocco took a few seconds to stretch and ease the kinks out of his shoulders, and then went to the door in question. Already knowing who he'd find, he opened it and took a step back. "Two things—you were supposed to let me know so I could come for you, and you never need to ask permission to come in here. Just walk in."

Sasha did exactly that and stood on tiptoe to brush her lips across his cheek. "Thank you. It's great to see you, too. How's it going?"

"Making progress, although I'd be happier if I had more people I knew I could count on."

"There are no more Spectrum people over here?"

"Only one, and he's on assignment. Don't worry, I'll work it out. No problem is insurmountable. Did you manage to organize the dress thing?"

Sasha laughed. "The dress thing? Yes, I organized the dress thing. Every last one of them was only too happy to help out one of the biggest names on the current music scene. They know the media coverage will focus on her, and if she's wearing one of their designs, the value of that publicity for them is incalculable."

Not for the first time did the chasm between the haves and have-nots strike Rocco in a way that left a bad taste. Here was someone who had everything, and all she could do was fuss about what she was going to wear in front of some cameras for a couple of hours, when there were plenty of places in the world where people were starving to death. He'd seen more than his fair share of the latter while he'd been deployed.

"Hey. Earth to Rocco."

It was the gentle contact of her palm against his cheek as much as her soft words that brought Rocco out of his memories. He covered her hand with his and moved it so he could kiss her fingers. "Sorry. I was miles away."

Miles and years, when he should be focusing on the here and now. "Time to call it a day and get something to eat. Your place or mine?"

"Yours, and when we're done eating, I'm challenging you to a strip poker tournament. Get ready to kiss your shirt and everything else you're wearing goodbye."

He admired his woman's confidence. Pity it was so misplaced. "Don't count on it, sweetheart. Don't count on it."

Sasha was aware of Rocco's absence almost as soon as she opened her eyes. Without lifting her head from the pillow, she looked to the side of the bed he'd occupied. His pillow still bore the depression where his head had rested, and when she reached across the space, the heat of his body still warmed the sheets. Wherever he'd gone, he hadn't been gone long.

Then she heard it, the rumble of a masculine voice in the living room. Either someone was here, or Rocco was on the phone. For once, he'd left his watch on the nightstand. Sasha sprawled into his space and squinted at the dial.

Zero five-thirty. *Great.*

On a Sunday. *Even better.*

She yawned. In spite of spending a good portion of the last eighteen hours in bed, she was still sleepy. Hardly surprising, given that most of *that* time had been taken up with the best sex of her life and many, many losing hands of strip poker.

Sasha was about to turn over and burrow under the sheets when Rocco raised his voice. She still couldn't make out the words, but the agitated tone was unmistakable. She grabbed the nightgown she kept handy but never needed while she was with Rocco, and tiptoed over to the door that stood between the bedroom and the rest of the suite. Very carefully, she eased it open a crack, praying it wouldn't make a noise and betray her.

Rocco was deeply involved in an impassioned conversation in Italian on his cell. He might have told her they didn't talk, but she'd bet everything she possessed that his father was on the other end of the call. Something about Rocco's tone and demeanor suggested that this was a discussion that had taken place many times before.

Sasha was torn. Her heart wanted her to go and sit with him, to be his strength during what was clearly an emotional exchange, but her head counseled her somewhat differently, that he'd cut her off the one time she'd asked about his father, that this was none of her business, and he didn't need her to help him fight his battles. She closed the door as quietly as she'd opened it, stripped off her nightgown, and returned to their bed. She could at least be there if he needed her when the call finished.

A few minutes later, the bedroom door opened. Sasha leaned over to switch on the bedside lamp. As she resumed her position, Rocco was sliding into bed beside her. Without a word, he grasped the sheet and pulled it away from her. She gasped as his teeth closed on her nipple, and shivered as he began to suckle hard on the aching bud.

Without breaking contact, he bore her back to the pillows. Her head was swimming with the unrelenting attack of licks and nips, all doing a crazy jive with her flaring libido. She reached toward him, eyes widening when he grasped her wrist and pressed it to the bed.

Rocco raised his head. "I need this. I need you, Sasha."

She might not have known him long, but Sasha's instincts seemed to have little trouble tuning into this man and his moods. Something dark was riding him, and it had to be connected to his father. "You have me," she whispered. "I'm all yours."

That darkness made him a fierce lover. He rolled away from her, releasing her only long enough so he could remove his boxer briefs, then he closed in. As his mouth claimed hers, his cock—hot, long and hard—branded her thigh.

He took control of their loving in a way that was thrilling and exciting, and more than a little overwhelming. Then again, she was no shy virgin—she was the woman he needed, and she met his challenge kiss for kiss, caress for caress. And afterward, when he lay exhausted in her arms, she held him until he was ready to talk.

"I shouldn't let him get to me. It's been years."

Sasha needed no further explanation. "He's your father. No matter what's happened between you, you still love him. He still loves you."

"He still wants me to go home."

It wasn't so much Rocco's words that intrigued Sasha, as the tone with which he delivered them. There was doubt in them, where there had been cast-iron certainty when he'd told her he and his father were estranged. "Do you still feel the same way about that?"

"When I said we don't talk... All we talk about is me going back." Rocco's laugh was short and bitter. "He talks. I tell him no. The conversation ends. It's been that way for years. Going back would be... a dead end."

Except... he sounded less than convinced. With the luxury of objectivity, as Sasha saw it, if he'd been so adamantly opposed to cutting himself off from his father's side of the family, he could have changed his number years ago. However, family was family, and roots tended to run especially deep in the Italian communities she'd encountered over the years. Even the direst of circumstances wouldn't always be enough to sever family connections.

"Maybe it's not as dead as you think."

Though the words were her own, Sasha felt a frisson of loss as she uttered them. If Rocco was close to taking the first steps toward reconciling with Dario Equizi and returning to be with his remaining family, then she should be happy for him.

It was only then that she realized her subconscious had had taken a vague fantasy and woven it into a foolish pipe dream, of Rocco resigning his job with Spectrum and coming to work at Casa Millefiori, so they could be together and this idyll never had to end.

"Go back to sleep," she whispered. "It's Sunday—we can leave the real world outside for a little while longer."

CHAPTER 12

After a frank one-to-one with his boss, Rocco had to admit, his mood hadn't improved much on how he'd felt when he'd woken a few hours earlier, even though he'd spent the previous day and the whole night with Sasha.

The purpose of Nick's call had been to warn him the police would be visiting Casa Millefiori later that day. Having worked on the accounts all weekend—which probably hadn't gone down too well with his wife—the Spectrum CEO had uncovered incontrovertible evidence that Alilah Corday and Leah Bennett were colluding to steal thousands of dollars from their employer by passing very convincing but entirely phony invoices through the estate accounts. Nick had also informed Gerry Brookes, and only by the skin of his teeth managed to persuade Linzi's manager that there was no need to cut short his visit to New York and head back on the red-eye that night.

The call had also prompted Rocco to share his concerns about the fitness and reliability of the security staff available to escort Linzi to the awards ceremony. Nick's answer had almost been dismissive—he'd told Rocco to do whatever was necessary on site, and leave the rest to him. Unlike a magician with a top hat and an endless supply of rabbits, Nick couldn't produce additional Spectrum personnel out of thin air, which likely meant only one thing—he was going to contact the mysterious friends he'd mentioned.

At the end of the conversation, Rocco couldn't help but feel he was losing control in multiple areas of his life. His feelings towards his relationship with his father were changing and he had no idea why, his assignment wasn't as straightforward as he'd anticipated, and then there was Sasha, who meant far more to him than was wise, given the temporary nature of his presence in her life.

The last wasn't helped by a lack of willpower or desire on his part to turn away from her. She was too tempting and... he was too weak.

All in all, it was one massive shitshow, and he hated the resulting bedlam. Creating havoc wasn't in his job description—he was supposed to bring chaotic situations like this under control—yet, like a wildfire, mayhem was breaking out all around him.

Like the confrontation he'd had with Brian Schofield first thing that morning. Over the last few days, if looks could kill, Rocco would have been six feet under by now, because of Brian's habit of looking daggers at him whenever their paths crossed. Rocco had never risen to the bait, but it had all come to a head a few hours earlier, when, with no provocation whatsoever, the younger Schofield's passive aggression had mutated into the active variety. Rocco had been on his way back to the main house when Schofield had grabbed his arm as they passed one another, spinning him around.

"Equizi, I don't know who the hell you think you are, muscling in here, taking charge, fucking the secretary—"

With the speed of a striking cobra, Rocco had deflected the incoming blow before it could land, seized Brian's hand,

and forced the little finger back a fraction beyond its limit—enough to make him flinch and gasp, but not enough to break it.

"Schofield, I don't care what you say or think about me, but if you disrespect Ms. Morgan one more time like that, so help me, you'll answer for it."

Brian had tried to tug his hand away, but Rocco had only released him after he'd applied a fraction more pressure to the tortured digit. The man was half-crazy, and way too volatile to provide effective close protection. His father hadn't been too happy when Rocco had informed him just minutes before that he was standing Brian down from Linzi's security detail for the music awards. The older man would still be blustering now, had Rocco not walked out of his office as soon as he delivered the news. The altercation with Brian thoroughly vindicated Rocco's decision.

As he entered Sasha's office, she greeted him with a smile. "Frank called me a few minutes ago. You told him the bad news, then?"

It wasn't so much a question as a statement of fact. "I gather he's not too happy."

"He isn't, but I reminded him you were brought in as a highly experienced and respected security consultant, and what you say is final. My opinion, for what it's worth, is you made the right call."

Rocco nodded. "I didn't just go to the security block—I took a detour down to the main gate as well."

"Oh?"

Rocco closed the door behind him and went to perch on the edge of Sasha's desk. "Nick rang earlier, with an update on his investigation into the case of possible embezzlement. He found more proof over the weekend—enough to take to the police. They're on their way here to arrest the two suspects."

He was grateful her suddenly glacial expression wasn't directed at him. "I see. That didn't take long. Your boss sure works fast."

"I'm not even going to pretend I know what he was talking about, but long story short, they were starting to get too confident and were making mistakes. The discrepancies were more difficult to trace, the further back he went, but once he identified the patterns, he found dozens of fake invoices in the last six months alone, and some of them are quite high-value."

"I think it's time you told me who it is."

The woman who spoke the words wasn't the same one he'd woken up with that morning—this was the cool-in-any-crisis CIA agent she'd once been, and at this point, keeping the truth from her served no purpose. "Alilah Corday and Leah Bennett. I've just come from telling the guards on the gate to direct the police up here, and also to order them not to allow Alilah or Leah to leave the property under any circumstances."

Sasha gave a short, humorless laugh. "Those two. I should have guessed."

"Why? You said you didn't think they'd do anything that could put their roles here at risk."

"That was in the context of the social media attacks, and I still think that's true. When I said I should have guessed, I meant I should have guessed there was something else going on with them. I've had the same squirrelly feeling about them as I've had about Frank Schofield. I should have considered the possibility of an alternative explanation."

"Why? There's no reason why you should. Don't beat yourself up about it. It was an unknown unknown, and I only found it by accident. Even then, I wasn't sure."

Sasha's nod signaled reluctant agreement. "I don't suppose it really matters anyway. We need to concentrate on what's happening right now. Can you deal with the cops while I stop Linzi having a meltdown?"

Rocco didn't want to leave his woman to deal with Linzi alone, but with the law on the way, he had little choice. They'd probably have a few preliminary questions for him at the very least, with more to come later as the investigation progressed.

What interested him more was what he'd just learned from Sasha. If her instincts had told her Alilah and Leah weren't on the up and up, it lent credibility to her suspicions around Frank Schofield, which in turn, supported his own thoughts about the man, in spite of the fact that what Nick had uncovered about him had only confirmed what they already had on record.

And then there was Brian—how far had *that* apple fallen from the tree? He might be wrong, but Rocco had a feeling the answer was "not far enough".

For now, though, he had to park all thoughts of pursuing inquiries in that direction. Two alleged thieves were about to be arrested, and it wasn't going to be pretty.

The police left a good couple of hours after they arrived. They took with them their sobbing, handcuffed suspects, laptops sealed in official bags, the contents of two desks, and a mass of paper-based potential evidence. All Rocco had to do now was update Nick and send an email to Frank to keep him posted out of professional courtesy, and then he could take care of Sasha.

Rocco's conversation with his boss was short and to the point. Since he'd identified the fraudulent transactions, Nick would be the main point of contact for the investigation, for which Rocco was extremely grateful. No doubt forensic accountants would get involved, and at least Nick spoke the same language. Nick had ended the call with a cryptic message, warning Rocco to look out for a call from a phone number Nick was going to text to him. When Rocco had asked who it belonged to, all Nick had said was that it was a friend who could help if Rocco needed reliable assistance for the awards, and he should at least have an initial conversation with the man.

Sasha wasn't in her office when he came back from watching the police depart. She'd most likely returned to be with Linzi after her brief conversation with the detective in charge, so Rocco bypassed a visit to her apartment and headed straight to Linzi's wing of the mansion.

Her latest boyfriend, Ram, was in the sitting room. Engrossed in playing a game on his cell phone, he never even registered Rocco's arrival. Nor did he look up when Sasha emerged from one of the other rooms.

"How is she?" Rocco asked as he accompanied Sasha back the way she'd come.

"I'll let you see for yourself. I tried to explain it to her, but she brushed it off. Apparently it's my job to worry about 'crap like that', so she doesn't have to. I'll concede she has a point, but if someone were stealing thousands of dollars from me, I think I'd want to know about it."

Rocco would too, but he remained silent as Sasha led the way to what turned out to be Linzi's bedroom—without doubt, the most grand of all the bedrooms in all the properties on the estate, if a person happened to be impressed by glitz and glamor. Rocco much preferred the other two bedrooms he'd seen, but even then, he had a favorite—it was whichever one had Sasha in it.

When he saw Linzi dancing along to whatever she was listening to through her state-of-the-art wireless headphones, Rocco had to concur with Sasha's evaluation. With her eyes closed, Linzi appeared not to have a care in the world. One of her gyrations left her facing Rocco and Sasha, at which point she happened to open her eyes and notice Rocco was there.

"Oh. Hi. What are you doing here?"

The fact that she immediately closed her eyes and carried on pirouetting around the room without waiting for his answer spoke volumes about how much she cared about the answer. Having delivered the news, Rocco glanced at Sasha. She responded with a resigned shrug and a tilt of her head in the direction of the door, clearly sharing his opinion that they weren't going to make much more progress by talking to her employer. They passed Linzi's boyfriend—still gaming on his cell phone—and reconvened in the hall.

"I see what you mean." Rocco considered the options. "Given that she has nothing to do with keeping financial records, do you think we can avoid a situation where she has to testify?"

"It depends. Alilah and Leah may be offered a deal, so the case never goes to trial. It's too early to say right now."

He'd thought as much. "I know we've already discussed this, but are you sure there's no chance of them being behind the threats as well?"

"I suppose it's always possible, but neither of them's into technology in any way that I know of, so I doubt they have the technical expertise to hide their tracks the way we've assumed has happened so far."

Even before he'd asked the question, Rocco had had a feeling that would be the answer, because life was seldom that easy. However, it did leave Sasha with two significant vacancies to fill.

"I'll get some temporary help in," Sasha said as they made their way back to her office. "There's an agency we've used before—their people are reliable and good at what they do. And honest."

"That's a start. What will you do for the long-term?"

"Look into recruiting permanent replacements—there's not a lot else I can do."

"I know you'll have a handle on that, but if there is anything I can do to help, don't hesitate."

Much though he ached to fix things for her, Rocco knew Sasha wouldn't appreciate the intrusion—she was strong, independent, and in control. And more than capable of resolving the issue without interference from him.

"Thanks, but I think it'll be okay. Apart from anything else, this might drag on."

Until after you leave. Rocco heard the words even though she hadn't given voice to them.

"You know something?" Sasha continued. "It's almost the end of the day. I have a couple things to finish up, and then I'm going to take a swim. Care to join me?"

"For the skinny-dip we missed?" he suggested, half-joking.

"Sure. Why not?"

Rocco blinked. She hadn't missed a beat. He shot her a look, expecting to see an expression that confirmed she was winding him up, but it appeared she was deadly serious. "What time did you have in mind?"

"After dark. If we use the smaller pool, we can set the privacy glass so no one on the outside will be able to see anything."

There were few aspects of technology that appealed to Rocco, but he was more than happy to add switchable privacy glass to the list. He hadn't given the matter much thought last time a nude swimming session had been on the cards. "What time would be good for you?"

"Say, an hour or two to finish up a few things, then thirty minutes back at the apartment would be great."

Rocco checked his watch. "Cool. I'm looking forward to it."

Sasha stopped and halted him in his tracks with a hand on his forearm. He turned, and she timed it perfectly, a graceful lift onto her toes and a sweet, soft kiss on his lips.

"So am I."

Before the time she'd mentioned to Rocco was up, Sasha had two temporary replacement staff booked to start the following week, and had headed off another irate phone call from Frank Schofield, protesting about the way Rocco had handled the alleged embezzlement without reading him into the situation. She'd managed to soothe his blustering ego, although she wasn't sure how long the peace would last.

With time to spare, she'd retreated to the quietness of her apartment. It seemed empty without her man. Had she not made plans to go swimming, she'd have chosen beer instead of grabbing an ice-cold bottle of sparkling water to keep her company as she sat curled upon the couch.

Her thoughts gravitated towards the arrangements for the awards. She was as concerned as Rocco about the security personnel who would accompany Linzi and her party. Rocco. Scott. Herself. If something went down—depending on when it went down—the odds were not on their side, whichever way she sliced and diced it.

Years of training and experience were screaming for backup, and she knew exactly who she'd prefer to ask. He'd do it if he was available, maybe even bring some of his team with him, but there was no guarantee. The last she'd heard—

from his lovely and pregnant wife—was that he was incommunicado but not out of the country.

The question was, could she go behind Rocco's back? If she did, she'd be sending him the message that she didn't think he could do his job, something she wanted to avoid at all costs.

Sasha closed her eyes and sighed. There was no point in borrowing trouble—not until she had to, anyway. Her friend was expected back in a day or two, and a conversation with him then might turn up an alternative solution. Even sleeping on it tonight might help—today had not been a good day, and given the way she'd reacted to it, Sasha realized she was becoming way too accustomed to a civilian lifestyle.

She smiled to herself. Wasn't that exactly what she was supposed to be doing?

The sound of the door opening and closing behind her broadened her smile. She didn't hear any footsteps, but she didn't need the hand on her shoulder or the kiss to the crown of her head to know Rocco was standing behind her.

"Hey. You okay?" He came around the end of the couch and sat beside her.

She was so tempted to cuddle against him. As if he could read her mind, he slipped an arm around her and pulled her to him, while with his other hand, he relieved her of the half-empty water bottle and took a swig, before setting it down on the table. "I guess so. I used to be way more adaptable than this."

"You were blindsided in a place where it was the last thing you expected. Don't let it get to you, *cara*."

She loved it when his Sicilian side came to the fore—it gave her the warm fuzzies. "I won't. By the way, Frank called me about your email—thanks for copying me in, by the way."

"You're welcome. What did he have to say?"

"If I said 'The lady doth protest too much'—except we're not talking about a lady—would that give you an idea?"

Rocco raised his eyebrows. "I wish I could say I'm surprised. Sasha, I just came from checking Linzi's latest social media feeds."

"Any particular reason?"

"Not really. It's been quiet for the last few days. I wondered if there was anything new, and there was." Rocco pulled out his cell, swiped the screen a few times, and offered it to her. "Earlier today—after I spoke to Frank about Brian."

Sasha leaned closer. The images were of messages, posted earlier that day, and the text was horrifying. "Read those a certain way, and I'd swear they were referencing the awards. You think there's a connection between pulling Brian from the team on Sunday and this?"

"That, or coincidence, Santa Claus and the Easter Bunny are real. There's been nothing from the stalker for a while, so why escalate now?"

Sasha slowly shook her head. "I don't know. Maybe because the awards are only days away and they want to scare her more?" Even as she said it, she wasn't convinced. "Okay—if they intend to use the awards to harm Linzi in some way, why would they warn us? The logical reaction to that would be for us to increase the level of protection, but wouldn't that defeat their objective?"

Rocco remained silent, prompting her to wonder why. "What are you thinking?"

"Their objective—what is it?"

Sasha wasn't sure why he was asking such an obvious question, but she'd go with it. "Getting to Linzi—isn't it?"

"Yes, ultimately they want that, but what do they need in order to achieve it? The right people—or person—in the right place at the right time."

That added up, but she still wasn't sure where Rocco was going with it. "Okay..."

"Brian's the only one on the entire security team who has close protection experience. When I removed him from duty at the awards, maybe I also removed one of the key chess pieces. What better way to get him reinstated than by escalating the threats?"

"You're saying Brian's behind this? But why?"

Rocco shook his head. "Not Brian. At least, not on his own—he's a blunt weapon, not the brains. If I'm right, I think he's working with someone."

"His father." For Sasha, it was a light-bulb moment and a vindication of the uneasy feeling the head of security had given her for months.

"Keep it in the family. That would make sense." Rocco swiped through the images again. "You know what doesn't make sense, though?"

"What?"

"Look at the messages. The word play. Do you think either Frank or Brian is smart enough to come up with something so subtle?"

Sasha looked at the text again. "You're right. Someone else must be creating them. Do you think it's the person uploading them? The one with the technical know-how?"

"I think there's a very good chance, but I've no idea who it can be. Frank and Brian are next-of-kin for each other in the personnel records, and I can't recall seeing any other family members mentioned."

Sasha couldn't remember offhand, but she had no doubt Rocco was right in his assertion. "What can we do? We don't have enough to take this to the police."

Rocco's mouth settled in a grim line. "That's true, so we do the only thing we can—increase her security detail, of course."

Another light bulb flashed. This could be the opening she needed. "Are you going to bring someone in from the outside to help out?"

"If I did, would it bother you?"

The way he asked the question was encouraging. "You do what you need to do. Keeping Linzi safe is the only thing that matters."

"Agreed, which is why two things are going to happen. We're going to bring in that extra help… and I'm going to reinstate Brian, just like I'm supposed to."

"Is that wise? If we're right—"

"If we're right, we'll have him exactly where we can keep an eye on him. If he doesn't come with us, their plan is shot to pieces, which means they'll likely improvise. If they go off plan, that's when they'll be at their most dangerous."

There was an awful logic to what he'd said, so awful that Sasha didn't really want to believe it. As a former member of the intelligence community, however, she had to. "Are you sure about all of this?"

"No, but it's all we've got. It could be coincidence, my taking Brian off the op and the threats ramping up again, but like I said, I don't believe in coincidence. Do I have your blessing?"

"Only if you can bring in help you can trust." The last thing she wanted was for them—for Rocco—to have to fight on two fronts.

"I can." He leaned toward her for another brief kiss. "If I'm right, it'll be the kind of help we can rely on one hundred and ten percent."

Relieved, Sasha nodded. She was off the hook. Rocco need never know what she'd considered doing. "Do whatever you have to. Linzi has plenty of faults, but she doesn't deserve whatever they have planned for her."

And if the messages were any indication, the mind they

came from was truly vile and twisted. Sasha had seen plenty of sickening sights during her CIA career, but seeing evil such as this aimed at someone she knew personally was something else.

Rocco wrapped his arms around her and pulled her close. Gentle pressure at her temple was a fleeting kiss. "Everything will be okay, Sasha. I promise. I'm here to keep Linzi safe, and I will. Now," he added, his tone lighter, "I don't know about you, but I'm ready for that swim."

Sasha wanted to talk some more, but at the same time, she realized there was little more they could do until the extra help was confirmed. There was no point in putting a plan together if they didn't have the resources to support it. And maybe some downtime would help both of them.

"So am I." Just the thought of unwinding in the warm water was enough to ease some of the tension from her shoulders. "How do you feel about spending some time in the Jacuzzi as well?"

Rocco chuckled. "What makes you think you need bubbles to get you off in water?"

The man was incorrigible. "And here I was, thinking we'd have a relaxing swim together."

"We will. Then I plan to make love to you until you're exhausted enough to fall asleep while I hold you."

She could get on board with that. "Come on." She rose to her feet and held out her hand. "Everything we need is in the pool area."

Of all the swimming facilities on the property, the small indoor pool was Sasha's favorite. It was also the most private. The white-and-turquoise color scheme gave it a tropical beach feel, aided by the abundance of palms and other large potted plants. White lounge chairs surrounded the pool itself, all of them thankfully vacant—there was no sign of anyone else in the space.

Sasha went to the control panel on the wall, and with a couple of swipes and taps on the touch-sensitive pad, the glass wall at the far end darkened and the wall-mounted lights came on at a subdued and very intimate level. She turned to Rocco. "There. Is this okay for you?"

"Perfect."

The way he was looking at her left her in no doubt that he wasn't only talking about their surroundings.

Sasha held out her hand. "The Jacuzzi's at the other end, where the steps are. Why don't we change down there, so we can use it if we want to?"

"Towels?"

"In the cabinets, along with robes. We have everything we need."

She led Rocco around the pool to a cluster of chairs. As she kicked off her shoes and started on her shirt buttons, she became aware that Rocco, rather than emulating her, had made himself comfortable on one of the chairs.

She folded her arms and cocked a hip. "What are you doing, Equizi?"

"Isn't it obvious?" He grinned. "I'm watching you."

She shook her head. "That is so not fair. Don't I get to watch you?"

"If you want to, but I get to watch you first."

Sasha blessed him with a long-suffering look. She stalked over to him and pushed his shoulder until he sprawled a tad inelegantly on the almost fully reclined chair. "You want a show, mister, you can have a show."

She spun around and, with a provocative sway to her hips, strolled away from him until she was well out of touching distance. This would work better with music—Sasha had never imagined she'd be grateful for Linzi's insistence on having the sophisticated sound system installed, or the time she herself had spent on putting together a play list for it. As the first song filled the space around them, she took a hair tie from the pocket of her slacks, put her hair up in a ponytail, and resumed her place in front of Rocco.

With any other man, this slow striptease would have been a source of embarrassment, but doing it for Rocco was a different matter entirely. She didn't feel in the least bit foolish. The heat in his gaze burned her up, and when she dropped the final garment on the nearest lounge chair and turned to him, he was already on his feet. He covered the distance between them with a couple of long strides, and then his mouth crashed into hers.

"You're wearing too many clothes," she murmured. "Again."

"I know. Give me a minute."

He didn't need a minute. She'd never seen a man get naked so fast, his clothes ended up scattered far and wide. Before he could do anything else, though, Sasha turned and dived into the pool.

She was a proficient swimmer but Rocco was better. Barely a splash as he entered the water, and he must have only taken a few strokes to draw level with her. He emerged beside her and shook his head like a bedraggled dog. Sasha shrieked.

His response was to laugh, and at the totally carefree sound, something inside her tipped and settled into place, as if a space she'd never been aware of was suddenly filled. His hands cupped her face, and when he kissed her this time, feelings she'd kept locked up her whole life suddenly soared into the air, flying free at last.

"Sasha? Are you all right?"

She wanted to tell him, more than she'd ever wanted to tell anyone anything in her life. The words waited impatiently to be released, but at the same time, she was so painfully aware that liberating them could ruin everything. She tried for nonchalance instead. "Er, yeah… I guess."

To her surprise his brow creased, his concerned gaze darting over her face as if searching for something. "Maybe this wasn't such a good idea after all."

That brought her back down to earth. "Oh no, you're not short-changing me on this."

"Not even if I can make you a better offer?"

She grinned, ducked away from him, and swam for the far end of the pool. He came with her, matching his stroke to hers. The sensation of the water flowing over her body without the obstruction of a swimsuit was blissfully relaxing, but at the same time, she was supremely conscious of the lithe beauty and efficient grace of Rocco's form as he cut through the water beside her.

They swam a few laps, and when they reached the end of the pool after their last, Sasha held onto the edge and trod water, while Rocco leaned his forearms on the edge and gave her a wonderful view of his biceps and deltoid muscles. The man would have made an incredible model for a life drawing class. If she only had the talent…

"Hey. Earth to Sasha. Race you back to the Jacuzzi?"

He'd beat her without breaking a sweat. "Only if you give me a head start."

He glanced won the length of the pool. "I'll give you ten seconds—no more."

And he'd still win. "What's the prize?"

"Depends who wins. If you win, we get to sit in the Jacuzzi until we turn into prunes."

Somehow, he managed to make it sound far less attractive than it was. "And if you win?"

He smiled the smile of a man who knew he was onto a sure thing. "If I win, we get the hell out of this wet stuff, dry off, go back to your place or mine, and fuck like rabbits."

Sasha blinked. "You said that without missing a beat."

He shrugged. "I figured we could use an alternative way of burning off some energy. Sex is as good a way as any."

And better than most. "I've got an idea."

"Go on."

"We swim back, dry off, get dressed, go back to my place and have wild monkey sex. Then I feed you dinner, and we have even wilder monkey sex."

He raised an eyebrow. "Your suggestion is not without merit, Ms. Morgan. Let's go."

They were on their way back to Sasha's apartment when Rocco's phone rang. He checked the caller ID, only for his frivolous mood to evaporate as he answered. "Nick. Everything okay? Of course, put her on."

He remained serious as the conversation progressed. Sasha wished she could have heard the other end of the conversation as well, but all she could do was listen to Rocco with a mounting sense of trepidation. When the call ended, he looked at her with a chillingly grim expression.

"Nick's wife, Charity. She's pulled in a few favors with a cyber analyst who specializes in the psychology of online threats. While she and Tex have been trying to trace the source, this specialist has been looking at the content—they even caught today's examples, which confirmed their conclusions. The escalation is real, and there's every chance it'll come to a head at the awards."

CHAPTER 13

Two days later, Rocco's phone buzzed with the call he'd been waiting for. Nick hadn't said anything directly when Rocco had asked him if there was any chance his friend could contact them earlier, but he had alluded to the man being incommunicado, in a way that led Rocco to only one conclusion—that Nick's friend was a member of a special forces unit. If true, then having someone of that caliber on the team would give them a strategic advantage.

"Rocco Equizi. Who am I talking to, please?"

"Keane Bryson, but you can call me Ghost. Nick told you to expect my call?"

The voice at the other end of the phone was both confident and the very definition of laid-back. Then again, if Rocco's suspicions were correct, he wouldn't expect anything else. "He did."

"I hear you've got a problem and could use some assistance. Fill me in."

Rocco was glad the call had come through while he was in his quarters. Sasha might not be there, but neither was anyone else. He gave Ghost a rundown of everything that had happened to date, including Charity's news about the escalation of the threats. "According to the analyst who's been working with Charity and this expert—"

"Tex."

That came as a surprise. Rocco hadn't considered there might be a connection. "That's the guy. You know him?"

"Tex and me, we go back a long way—so do the guys in my team. You were saying?"

"They think whoever's behind this is getting ready to bring it into the real world, and with Linzi attending the awards on Sunday, there's a very good chance they'll choose that event to do it."

"I wouldn't disagree with that. Look, I've got a couple things I can't get out of tomorrow, but I can be in your area Friday—want to meet up then?"

"Can you come out to the compound?"

"Sure. Text me the time and location, and I'll be there."

At the end of the conversation, Rocco needed time to think, and he thought best in the kitchen. He was making dinner for Sasha anyway, and it was about time he treated her to fresh pasta the way Nonna made it, along with her recipe for the best sauce in Sicily. All he needed was a well-stocked refrigerator and store cupboards to match. Was it really less than two weeks since he'd arrived here and been surprised to find there was even a pasta maker stashed in the kitchen?

Was it really even less time since he'd unknowingly started down the path to feeling about Sasha the way he'd never felt about another woman before?

However long it was, it didn't matter. His immediate priority was feeding his woman, and Sasha was due to walk through the door any moment now. She'd been working late to accommodate the couturier who was providing Linzi's outfit for the awards ceremony, and who had returned for a final fitting, complete with shoes and other accessories. Sasha had laughed and sworn Rocco's eyes glazed over when she started to explain the reason for the visit.

He liked it when she laughed. If he could make her laugh every day for the rest of their lives, he'd die a happy man.

Rocco pushed the longing to one side, along with the sour taste of all the reasons why it wasn't going to happen. Instead of brooding about it, he concentrated on finishing off the sauce, and as he heard the door to the apartment open, the latest taste test confirmed it was almost ready. One final touch and it would be perfect.

Arms snaked around his waist. "That smells delicious. Your nonna's recipe?"

He lifted an arm so she could snuggle in beside him more comfortably. "Would you like to try it?"

"I want to say no, I'll wait until we eat, but I don't have enough willpower."

Rocco selected a clean spoon, loaded it with a good sample of the meaty sauce, and offered it to Sasha. "Blow on it, it's hot."

She did, then took the spoon from him and tasted the spicy Italian deliciousness. "Mm, I think I've gone to heaven." She peered into the bubbling saucepan. "What have you put in there?"

"I can't tell you—if I do, I'll have to kill you," he deadpanned. "And if I don't, Nonna will."

"I'd love to meet her one day."

The innocent comment slammed into him and formed an instant bond with his earlier musing. He couldn't help but wonder what would happen if he took Sasha with him on a visit back home. Nonna would be over the moon and planning their wedding, but his father... Dario would be more difficult to deal with. He'd try again to convince Rocco to stay, but if Rocco were to take Sasha with him, she would be the very reason why he could never do that. She'd never want to spend the rest of her life with him at the winery, surrounded by his somewhat overbearing extended family, with Nonna just waiting for the day Sasha and he announced they were having a baby…

Grief at the loss of something he'd never had and never would have brought him emotionally to his knees.

"I'm sorry, did I say something wrong?"

Sasha's uncertain question banished the shattered fragments of the impossible daydream. "No, not at all. Why don't you grab a couple of beers, then we can eat? And you can tell me how the fashion thing went."

Her body shook with laughter. "Really? You want me to go through the minutiae of matching heels and a clutch to an evening gown?"

"Hmm, let me think—maybe skip the tiny details and go for the big picture?" Doubtless there would be tiny details, lots of them, and he wouldn't have a clue what ninety-nine percent of the conversation was about.

Sasha wrinkled her nose at him before ducking out from under his arm to get the beers. "Party pooper. I had to sit through it, I don't see why you should get out of it, but for once, I'll take pity on you. Long story short, she's finally happy that the label she's wearing will make all the front pages the day after. What are you doing?"

Rocco drizzled a little more of the pasta cooking water into the sauce from the ladle. "What? You don't trust me? I'm half-Italian, you think I can't cook pasta?"

He checked the sauce and tried another taste—*perfetto.* He dumped the water from the ladle, drained the pasta and added it to the sauce, stirring it in so it was all coated.

"You sure don't cook it the way I do."

"Then you are in for a treat. Sit down."

He'd already laid the place settings on opposite sides of

the counter. A rustic meal like this suited less formal surroundings, and he wanted to see Sasha's face when she took her first proper bite of Nonna's signature sauce—or a close approximation, at any rate. He served up a healthy portion in both bowls, topped each with the perfect amount of freshly grated parmesan, and carried them to where she was waiting.

In an effort not to look like a nervous schoolboy, he twirled his fork in the pasta ribbons, ensuring they were coated in the right amount of sauce. Sasha was doing the same thing, but where he paused before eating, she went straight for it.

He wasn't expecting the squeal or the way her eyes widened. Then she closed her eyes and made a noise that almost sounded like a purr. Her food orgasm scored a direct hit on his dick. He shoved his own forkful of food into his mouth and chewed.

"That is amazing, I've never knew pasta could taste so good." She twirled her fork again and took a second mouthful, with much the same reaction.

If she carried on like that, he was going to die of blue balls over a meal.

"You like it, then."

"Like? 'Like' doesn't even begin to do this justice. I thought the sauce on its own was delicious, but with the pasta, it's unbelievable."

Rocco reined in the urge to fist-pump. All those cooking lessons with his mother and Nonna had been leading up to this moment—he offered them his silent thanks for their patience and persistence. "I'll take that as a yes."

At the end of her meal, Sasha sat back and gave a deep sigh of contentment. "I am going to have to run twice as far tomorrow, but it will be worth it. That was incredible. Thank you." She leaned over and kissed him. "Am I supposed to feel like I need a nap now?"

"Maybe that has more to do with the length of your working day than Nonna's pasta." Rocco gathered up the used crockery. "You go and sit down. I'll be right behind you, and then I can bore you to sleep with my day."

"Can I use you as a pillow?"

"Any time."

Rocco stacked the dishes in the dishwasher, for once not bothered about leaving them until the morning. If Sasha needed to nap, he didn't want the noise keeping her awake. She hadn't taken her half-full beer bottle with her, so he picked it up along with his, and went to join her on the couch.

How he came to be lying full-length on it with Sasha lying mostly on top of him, Rocco wasn't sure, but he wasn't complaining—although he might if she wriggled like that again.

"Are you comfortable enough now?"

"Uh-huh. So tell me about your day."

Her hand was resting on his chest. Rocco covered it with his. "Nick's friend called. He's coming over on Friday."

"Do you know anything about him? Like his name, what he does for a living?"

People who were fading fast tended to mumble like that. Maybe he should have suggested the bed instead. "His name's Keane Bryson, and I'm pretty sure he's a Tier 1 operator."

A gentle snore came from the left side of his chest. She probably hadn't even heard him, but it didn't matter—she'd know soon enough. With slow, cautious movements, he pushed the cushion to a better position under his head and, resigned to the fact he wasn't going to be able to move for a while, settled in for the duration. He could always carry her to bed later.

~

For the first time ever, Linzi had almost succeeded in reducing Sasha to tears.

No, not tears. More like justifiable homicide, even though this was her job and she was paid handsomely to do it.

To be fair, it probably wasn't all Linzi's fault. A sizable part of Sasha's irritation was probably connected with the way she'd fallen asleep on top of Rocco on the couch last night and woken up in his bed—or more to the point, overslept in his bed. His side had been cold as well as vacant, and he hadn't been in her office when she'd finally gotten her ass in gear. Her last chance of seeing him before lunch evaporated when Linzi summoned her for a spontaneous mid-morning meeting.

There was no point in denying it any longer—she was addicted to Rocco Equizi, and she was in a lousy mood because she hadn't yet had her fix for the day. There was also the little matter of how she felt about him, whether she should tell him or not, or even if it was worth telling him, given what they shared didn't have any kind of future.

And now she had to deal with Linzi having yet another meltdown about her outfit for the awards—the same outfit that had been 'perfect' just twenty-four hours earlier.

"Linzi, you look fantastic in the gown. It fits perfectly, and the designer is at the top of his game. Everyone wants to wear him, but he told you he's only dressing you for Sunday night, remember? He wouldn't lie about that—it would destroy his reputation."

"But look!" Linzi screeched and pointed at her tablet. She jumped to her feet and stomped across the dining room.

Sasha slid the tablet over to her side of the table. The first thing she saw was the headline bearing the name of one of Linzi's greatest rivals. The second was the dress she was wearing—a completely different color from the one destined for Linzi, in a vastly different style. Whatever Linzi was freaking out about, Sasha couldn't see it.

This wasn't the first time she'd wondered about her suitability for the role of personal assistant to a temperamental star, and she doubted it would be the last. She was thinking more and more about what else she might do, once her CIA experience was no longer relevant because Linzi was out of danger. The frequency of those thoughts might or might not have been connected with Rocco Equizi.

"Linzi, please. Come and sit down. Tell me what's upset you, and then we can fix it."

Linzi folded her arms and spouted. "It's too late."

"Not necessarily. Come and talk to me—please."

Placating a diva having a tantrum was a lot like quieting a wild animal, and the best way to do both, as Sasha had learned from experience, was to maintain a calm demeanor and an even calmer tone.

Linzi returned to the table and sat down again. She was still frowning, and her lips were pinched together. "It's not the dress in the picture that's the problem. It's the name of the designer she's got. Third paragraph. He's bigger than mine will ever be."

The significance of the comment escaped Sasha, and it must have shown on her face, judging by Linzi's next comment.

"You don't follow fashion, do you?"

As comments went, it was relatively innocuous—the scathing, judgmental look that scraped over her from head to toe could have cut to the quick if Sasha had allowed it to. Instead, she pasted on a rigid smile. "I don't have to. People aren't interested in me like they are you. If I attend an event like this with you, it's my job to look invisible."

Linzi rolled her eyes. “Whatever. I want him to design something for me.”

Which wouldn’t change anything with the big show being only three days away. The situation was not without hope, however, provided she could convince Linzi to compromise. “I have an idea. The Oscars are a month away—that’s a much bigger event, with a global audience. Media representatives from all over the world will be there, to see who’s on the red carpet. I’ll make a few calls and see what I can do to get this guy on board for that. How does that sound?”

Sasha wasn’t hopeful, but it was the best compromise she could think of on the spur of the moment. It seemed to satisfy Linzi, though.

“Okay. Can you get me something to eat? I’m starving.”

And that was Linzi being Linzi. Her mood could turn on a dime, and whatever she was complaining about could be dismissed as quickly. “Lunch is a while off yet—why don’t I get you a light snack?”

Sasha didn’t really expect a reply. Linzi had returned to scrolling and tapping her way through the celebrity news feed on her tablet, so Sasha might as well have dematerialized.

On her way to the kitchen, Sasha stopped off at her office—still no sign of Rocco. With Sunday evening fast approaching, she wondered if he’d stepped up his sessions with Scott Monroe. As far as she knew, Rocco still needed to speak to Frank about reinstating Brian to Linzi’s entourage on Sunday. She wasn’t sure why he hadn’t, but she figured he had a good reason. She’d have felt better about the whole thing if she could have gotten in touch with her friend, but he was still unavailable.

To her surprise, Geri was still in the kitchen when Sasha arrived in search of snacks. “Shouldn’t you have gone by now?”

"Just on my way. Chef asked me to take an inventory and put together a list of everything we need, and I wanted to get it done early. What can I do for you?"

There was no way Sasha was going to delay the other woman any longer. "It's okay. You go. I can put a fruit platter together for Linzi."

Geri laughed. "You think? Do you have any idea how picky she is about fruit? You better let me do it. You can sit and watch, and tell me all about you and Rocco, because I'm telling you, if I preferred boys to girls, I'd be giving you some serious competition."

For someone who was way past the age of blushing when the subject of relationships arose, Sasha didn't expect fire to blaze in her cheeks. "If I said there was nothing to tell, would you believe me?" She could hope.

"Not a chance. Every time I've seen you two together, I've been expecting you to self-combust." Geri retrieved a selection of fruit from the refrigerator. "Is he as good in the sack as he looks?"

Sasha almost choked as she perched on one of the tall stools by the counter, where she'd had breakfast with Rocco the first morning. "I'm pleading the Fifth."

Geri looked up from her cutting board to give a jubilant whoop. "He is! You go, girl! About time you got yourself some action."

Sasha's eyes widened. "I had no idea my social life was subject to such close scrutiny."

"Only by me. I've been waiting to see who'd be good enough for you." She winked. "You made a great choice."

Sasha couldn't help smiling. "I'm not sure choosing had anything to do with it."

"Ah-ha! I knew it. But sometimes it's like that. The heart knows what it wants, and if you're lucky, if it crosses your path, it's life-changing in the best way imaginable. Here."

Geri pushed the platter laden with delicate slices of various fruits toward Sasha. "That should take her through to lunch. Any idea what she might like, then I can leave Chef a note?"

"I'd recommend one of her favorites. She's had… an upsetting morning."

Geri raised her eyebrows and huffed. "Don't tell me—she didn't like the color of the sky when she finally got up, and was upset because you couldn't spray-paint it the right shade of blue to suit her highness."

Sasha sighed. "Something like that."

Geri folded her arms and aimed a stern glare at Sasha. "So, don't you think it's about time you told me?"

"Told you what?"

"Who is the real Sasha Morgan? Why are you working for the brat who signs our paychecks?"

Sasha felt like a bug under a microscope. She couldn't tell Geri the truth. "There was—is—a job that needed doing here, and I have some relevant experience." She shrugged and picked up the platter. "That's it. Nothing weird or special."

Without saying a word, Geri continued to study her. "Okay, I'll let it go for now, but I still think there's more to it than that. I've got to get going now, but… if there's ever anything you need, or you need to talk about stuff, I'm here, okay?"

"Okay. You get out of here. I have this to deliver." Sasha glanced down at the delectable selection of fresh fruit. The exquisite presentation would be lost on Linzi.

"I have an idea." Geri pulled on her jacket and took the platter from Sasha. "I'll take this to Linzi on my way out, you go find your man. Where is she?"

"The small dining room. With what she was doing, I doubt she'll have moved. Thanks—I owe you one."

Sasha watched the young woman leave. With a deep sigh, she let out all the tension that had built up while she was talking to Linzi. Geri's words were still echoing in her mind. *The heart knows what it wants.* Her heart was speaking more loudly than ever about what it wanted—it wanted Rocco, and it wasn't ready to take no for an answer. She didn't want it to take no for an answer.

Sasha needed to run. Doing it outside wasn't really an option, but there was an energy inside her that she needed to get out of her system. The true problem, though, was her lingering indecision over revealing how she felt to Rocco, and the quiet, desperate hope he might have feelings for her.

In the opposite corner, however, was the fear that he didn't, and all he'd do was laugh at her… or worse, pity her.

By the time she'd changed into her running gear and arrived in the gym, Sasha had made her decision—it was better that she say nothing to Rocco about her feelings for him. Linzi's safety at the awards had to be their priority, and pointless declarations would only cause unnecessary complications.

"Thanks for coming."

Rocco held out his hand to greet the friend Nick Blackmore had sent to provide some assistance. Although they'd only just met, he had a good feeling about Keane Bryson. While he'd been in the SAS, Rocco had been on more than enough joint ops with his US counterparts to recognize one in civilian clothing. Delta Force was his guess.

"My pleasure. You want to bring me up to speed?"

Rocco gave him a brief summary of what he'd discussed with Sasha, that the escalation was aimed at getting Brian back on the team. "I have a meeting with Frank later on this afternoon to tell him."

"I don't envy you. Who else did you discuss this with?"

"Linzi's assistant. She hasn't always been in this line of work, but I'll leave it up to her if she wants you to know anything more. I'll introduce you now, then I think it might be a good idea if we go down to the firing range to discuss details. It's unlikely we'll be overheard there."

"Copy that."

Rocco led the way to Sasha's office. She was standing behind her desk when he opened the door and ushered Ghost in ahead of him. He was about to perform the introductions when Sasha looked up from rummaging in her desk drawer, and it was instantly apparent that introductions weren't necessary.

"Ghost, what the hell are you doing here? I've been trying to contact you. Rayne told me you were out of town. How is she?" She came around the desk and straight into Ghost's arms for a hug.

For a second or two, Rocco entertained the idea of punching Bryson into the middle of the next millennium, but then the green-eyed monster retreated in the face of Ghost's laughter and the realization that the hug could only ever be described as brotherly. "You two know each other?"

"Sure do," Ghost replied as he released Sasha and stepped back. "We hauled her ass out of some trouble in Colombia a while back."

Sasha fired a mock-indignant glare back at him. "My ass could have gotten out of there perfectly well without your help, Captain Bryson."

"Whatever you say, Special Agent Morgan. And Rayne's doing fine, by the way."

"I'm glad to hear it. And that's Former Special Agent Morgan to you."

Ghost shot her a searching look. "You not a spook anymore?"

Sasha shook her head. "Gave it up a couple of years ago

now."

Ghost nodded. "I heard what happened to Jack. I'm sorry."

"Thanks, but… not your fault. Not anyone's fault. Just damn bad luck."

A solemn silence settled between the two of them. From too much experience, Rocco recognized the moment of shared grief for a fallen colleague. "I hate to break up the family reunion, but we have a job to do."

"That's what I'm here for. We gonna take that walk to the firing range now? I came prepared." Ghost lifted back his jacket to reveal a shoulder holster complete with weapon.

"Sounds good to me, gentlemen. Let's go." Sasha bent and retrieved her gun case from under her desk. "I was going to practice this afternoon anyway."

They made their way on foot to the range. Sasha and Ghost were reminiscing about their shared past, which gave Rocco a useful and fascinating insight into both of them—Sasha in particular. He'd already created an image in his mind of the kind of operative she might have been, but from what he was now hearing, she was so much more.

When they arrived at the firing range, Rocco waited until Ghost and Sasha had chosen their stalls, then took the vacant one next to Ghost. Although he would have preferred to take the one on the other side of his woman, the need to gauge Ghost's ability took precedence. If Rocco's assessment was right, there would be little to worry about. Also, he had no doubt that Ghost would want to get the measure of him, too.

His assumption about Ghost's pedigree was confirmed with their first round of shots. All three of them achieved a perfect placement to take down the enemy. While they were reloading, Ghost had some questions of his own.

"So… you from the same outfit as Nick?" Ghost looked down the sights of his handgun before sliding the magazine into place.

"Nope."

Ghost's hand stilled. He looked Rocco up and down. "Uh-huh. Gotcha. I think you and I speak the same language… Trooper?"

At that, Rocco's attention swung from his firearm to the man beside him. "Delta Force?"

"You got it," Ghost confirmed.

"And the last I heard, which was a while ago," Sasha said, "he was in line for a promotion to captain."

"You heard right." Ghost grinned. "You okay with that, Rocco?"

"I'm okay with that." Rocco glanced down at the human-shaped targets with their clusters of bullet holes. "And yes… we do speak the same language, Captain." He didn't usually make a point of revealing his former regiment, but it was necessary now, as it had been when he'd told Sasha. "SAS until a couple of years ago."

Ghost nodded. "I'd have been more surprised if you hadn't said that."

"Gentlemen," Sasha said, "now that we all know what we really are or were, and we've proved we can all handle firearms, why don't we grab a cup of coffee, find a quiet place to talk, and work out what we need to do to keep Linzi safe at the awards?"

Rocco strode down the corridor in the direction of Frank Schofield's office. Although he'd already informed the security chief out of courtesy that he wanted a word, his present mood was anything but civil.

After a call to Tex, Ghost had agreed with their assessment of the high probability that the Schofields were involved in the campaign to terrorize Linzi. Their motive was still a mystery, as were the means by which they were delivering the threats—neither of them possessed computer skills advanced enough to cover their tracks so thoroughly. Everyone agreed something crucial was missing.

Rocco knocked on Schofield's door and was already through it before the other man invited him in. After their previous one-to-one encounter, he was expecting a somewhat less than friendly reception, but that was all right—he was in no mood to observe more than the minimum niceties.

"Equizi. To what do I owe this honor? You here to fire some more of my men?"

Schofield almost spat the last word as he stood to greet Rocco—although "greet" was perhaps too friendly a word to describe his attitude, so different from the fake sociable front he'd deployed the first time Rocco had come to his office.

Rocco didn't let the inaccuracy of the question rile him, or the open aggression in the other man's stance. "I haven't fired anyone, *Mr.* Schofield. Although maybe you should take appropriate action to fill in the gaps in their training—specifically in close protection. Your son is the only one with relevant training and experience."

"Which is why I assigned him to accompany Miss Suto on Sunday. I'm not the one responsible for removing the only man with experience from her entourage."

The self-righteous vibe made Rocco bristle, as did the condescending attitude. "Then you'll be glad to know I'm reinstating him."

"You're what?"

"You heard. He's on duty on Sunday evening. I trust you'll inform him to that effect."

Rocco didn't even wait to hear Schofield's response. If they were right about the Schofields, he'd just told Frank what he most wanted to hear, and one of their primary suspects was back in play.

CHAPTER 14

Rocco gave an irritated grunt and yanked the bow tie free of his collar for the third time. The damn thing was going to strangle him before the evening even started.

The fourth attempt worked, however, in spite of the fact that this time, he was concentrating more on the arrangements for the evening than what was going on around his neck. He'd already run through them several times, and even though he could list them backwards, there was never an occasion when "one more time" was a bad idea.

With his bow tie now in place, Rocco grabbed the tux jacket from the back of a chair and pulled it on. He patted the right hand pocket, checking for the comms pack he'd dropped in it earlier, and then left his quarters. Given there was still plenty of time before they had to set off, his destination was Sasha's suite. With so many members of the domestic staff still milling around, he took the precaution of knocking on the door instead of walking right in.

"Who is it?"

He frowned. She sounded a little… odd. "Rocco. Everything okay?"

"Come in."

He opened the door just wide enough to slip inside. The sitting room was empty, and so was the kitchen area. His gaze slid automatically to the bedroom, and there she was, leaning against the door frame, clad in nothing more than the lace and thin straps of a black garter belt.

Rocco's hungry gaze took in the glorious, golden length of her legs, her smooth mound, flat belly and high breasts. He blew out a deep breath. "Don't you think you're a little over-dressed for this evening?"

Sasha gave a casual shrug and examined her nails. "You're a little out of touch with the latest fashion trends. Don't you know this is *the* outfit to be seen in on the red carpet this season?"

As long as he was the only one lined up to see her in it, Rocco was fine with that. "So what are you wearing?"

She sighed. "You want to help me choose something? I spent so much time dealing with Linzi's outfit that I haven't yet made a final decision about my own."

Rocco doubted that was entirely true. "You know I'm no fashion expert." Like a lot of men, which probably explained the invention of the tux. It was difficult to go wrong with black and white.

"Irrelevant. I need another pair of eyes. You're it."

As missions went, he'd had worse.

Sasha had pulled a number of gowns out of her walk-in closet and hung them up around her bedroom. Several pairs of elegant footwear were arranged along one wall. Even Rocco could identify which ones went with which outfit. His eyes, however, were mainly on Sasha. He could never get enough of her. Even with her back to him, she was the most beautiful woman he'd ever seen in his entire misbegotten life. He wanted nothing more than to stand right behind her and pull her back against him, so she'd be in no doubt about how she affected him. Then he'd take her to bed and make love to her until all she could do was fall asleep in his arms. He loved watching over her then, knowing she'd found peace with him.

Knowing she was his to protect, in a way that had nothing to do with his work.

All he had to figure out was how to tell her… and how to deal with the consequences.

Instead of doing any of that, he took a deep breath and cleared his throat in an effort to get his concentration back where it should be. "You go to a lot of these events?"

"Only when Linzi's invited, and even then, only when the invitation includes sufficient numbers. Truth is, I'd much prefer to stay back here and spend the night with a good book."

Rocco raised an eyebrow. "A book?"

"Did I say book?" Sasha gave him a sultry look over her shoulder. "I meant to say, I'd much rather stay back here and spend the night having a really good f—"

"Ms. Morgan, do you talk to your mother with that mouth?" Rocco folded his arms and gave her a stern look. Her smile might have been innocent, but the thoughts behind it matched his, sin for sin.

She feigned a dramatic sigh. "Oh, well. I suppose I'll just have to keep on getting ready, then."

And everything would have been fine, but for the saucy wiggle of her hips that tipped Rocco over the edge of frustration. He strode forward, spun her around to face him, and framed her face with his palms. Her gaze flared with the same desire that was riding him, and with no thought for the consequences, he moved into the perfect position to deliver a soul-deep kiss.

"My lipstick."

Her husky whisper sent another surge of blood to his dick. "Don't worry—the color suits me."

It was a totally asinine comment but it served the purpose of dialing back the lust that was in danger of making them late. Sasha's silent laughter made her whole body shake.

"You idiot," she scolded without a hint of ill humor. "Now I have to do my makeup again."

"You look fine to me—more than fine."

Sasha rolled her eyes. "Only a man would say that. While I repair the damage, you look at those dresses and see which is the most suitable for tonight."

"Still not a fashion expert!" he called after her as she disappeared toward the bathroom. He'd give anything to follow her, drag her under the shower, and… Yeah, washing her back didn't figure highly on the list of what he'd like to do then.

Rocco turned his attention to the dresses. Five of them. Different styles and different colors. The only thing they had in common was the length—which did not earn his approval. Legs like Sasha's deserved to be shown off.

Or maybe not. He was absolutely not in favor of any man leering at her—something he'd probably better keep to himself if he wanted to hold on to his balls. Going all out caveman on that gorgeous, spirited woman, no matter how much he wanted to, would not earn him any brownie points.

So… Dresses. Each of them would be amazing on her, but that wasn't why she was asking for his input. He removed the comms pack from his jacket pocket and set it to one side. His own rig had been easy to put on, but female fashion brought its own complications to the game.

Rocco was still considering the gowns when Sasha emerged from the bathroom, laid her arm on his shoulder as a rest for her chin, and blew on his ear before kissing it. "So, which one?"

"You'll look incredible in any of them. Not as good as you look right now, though."

"Typical man."

He could almost hear her rolling her eyes. "I'll take that as a compliment. Okay, decision time. You know what we're aiming for. This one will make it easier to conceal the mic wire." He draped an elegant sleeve over his palm. It belonged to the short jacket that matched the sparkling, black sleeveless gown.

"I kind of knew it would be, but just for a while, it was nice to think I might wear something different." She sighed. "Practicality always wins."

"Not always." Rocco kissed her hand. "If it's any consolation, I'd have loved to see you in the red one. You'd outshine everyone there."

"Thank you." She gave him a peck on the cheek, and in the next moment, she was rubbing her thumb over the same place.

"More lipstick?"

"Uh-huh. All gone now." A triumphant smile lit up her face.

"I'll end up wearing more of that than you before we get out of here," he grumbled.

"That'll teach you to say the color suits you. Will you help me with the wire?"

"Of course."

"Great. There's something else I need first, now that I know what I'm wearing." She vanished into the walk-in closet again.

Unable to help himself, Rocco watched, drinking in everything about her. She opened one of the drawers beneath the mirror in the walk-in closet and withdrew a slim package. *Stockings.* Rocco drew in a deep breath. His imagination was running riot with how they'd look on those amazing legs. "Need any help with those?"

She glanced in the direction of his hands. "Only if you can do it without putting a run in them."

"Is that a challenge I hear, Ms. Morgan?"

"I believe it may be, Mr. Equizi."

Rocco lifted his arms, pushed his sleeves up, and waggled his fingers as if he were about to perform a feat of magic. "You see these hands, Ms. Morgan? These hands have been known to defuse the odd bomb in their time. Challenge accepted. Hand them over."

The branding on the pack screamed quality. While he knew next to nothing about the finer points of lingerie—his expertise lay more in the field of parting a woman from hers—he did recognize the name of the fashion house. Sasha's taste was impeccable. "Okay, then. Take a seat." He gestured toward the bed.

The black stockings were gossamer-fine and more dangerously delicate than any explosive device Rocco had ever encountered. One false move, and they'd be ruined. Then again, hadn't the British Army invested millions in his training, so he could confront any enemy, conquer any obstacle, achieve any objective? Adapt and overcome. He could handle this.

He draped the nylons carefully on the bed beside Sasha and dropped to his knees in front of her. "You look wonderful."

Her lips—pink and luscious with their fresh application of lipstick—curved in a small, wry smile. "I look almost naked."

Rocco shrugged. "Details. Besides, it's a look that suits you."

She was leaning back, her palms flat on the bed behind

her for support, all legs for miles and utter perfection. With great care, he cupped her heel and lifted her foot to rest on his thigh. He liked that she didn't paint her toenails—they didn't need the enhancement.

Now came one of the most perilous phases of the op. Defusing a bomb with a trembler device would be easier than handling these babies. Rocco very carefully rolled up the first of the stockings. As he did so, for the first time in his life, he wished he'd been an accountant or a lawyer—soft hands would make the task of applying the damn thing much less risky. Still, he managed to get her toes in, then the rest of her foot and her ankle followed.

"Would you mind standing, please?"

And now that gorgeous limb was right in front of him, in all its golden, sun-kissed glory. It was criminal to cover it up, but on the other hand, with the side split in that dress, Rocco's inner Neanderthal was celebrating the fact that she wouldn't be totally nude beneath the gown. He drew the stocking up slowly, pausing to stroke her calf before covering it, then her knee and her thigh, and finally to phase two—fastening the delicate nylon to the garter straps.

His special ops training might not have encompassed this precise activity, but it had taught him to assess a situation and come up with an appropriate course of action. With that in mind, within a second or two—maybe three, given the distraction of her mound just inches from his mouth—he had the tricky little clasp fastened. "Turn, please."

Again, Sasha complied without a word—and Rocco was in serious trouble. His body was reacting the only way it could to the sight of her sweet ass right in front of him, mere inches from his nose. The fact that he had to put clothes on his woman instead of removing them was downright criminal.

"You okay, Rocco?"

Sasha's question and the way she looked over her shoulder at him slammed home how domestic this scene was. The way he thought about her—repeatedly and more frequently—reminded him how much he was starting to hate the prospect of leaving her for his next assignment. "Sure, everything's fine. Almost done."

He fastened the second garter clip and stood, pausing briefly to kiss the peach-like curve of her ass. When she pivoted to face him, she was smiling.

"Thank you. Want to help me with the other one?"

"My pleasure."

This time around, Rocco blatantly stole the occasional glance as he carried out his task. Sasha was watching him with that sultry, smoky gaze that usually preceded a stolen kiss in her office. No time for another of those at the moment, but there was a way he could help her get through the evening. "Come with me." He offered her his hand.

Her face lit up with an eager, intrigued smile. "What are you up to?"

He grinned back. "Nothing. Come with me."

Her fingers were warm between his. He led her over to the full-length mirror and stood her in front of him, so they were both looking at her reflection.

"See her?" he murmured close to her ear. "She's the most beautiful woman I've ever met."

"She's still half-naked."

An assessment he couldn't dispute. Rocco stroked her waist, gradually moving his hand to her lower belly.

"Part your legs for me."

He expected her to question him, but to his surprise, she obeyed. He lowered his head and kissed her shoulder. As he did so, he slipped his hand between her thighs and parted her labia. Her clit was as taut as her nipples, and she was already wet.

"What are you doing?"

The words might have been a protest, but her languorous tone contradicted their meaning. "Giving you something to remember if you get bored out of your mind tonight."

"You think I'll have time to be bored when we're on a mission?"

She had a point. So did he. "You might, if nothing happens. However, it is advisable to have a plan for every eventuality, which gives me a very good reason to do this." He swiped his finger across her clit again—enough for her knees to buckle. "It's all right—I've got you."

"You sure have."

The scorching undercurrent of double meaning in her murmur had to be a figment of his imagination, his feelings for her imbuing her words with reciprocated emotion that simply couldn't exist.

Even though he didn't have as much time as he would have liked, Rocco wasn't about to cancel this side op. With his free arm wrapped around Sasha to steady her, he continued the lazy stroke of her slick folds.

Every quiver, every tortured gasp was a reward in itself, and when she came, her orgasm was so intense and powerful, she'd have collapsed in a drained, trembling heap if he hadn't been there for her.

He kissed the side of her neck. "At this point, I'd prefer to carry you to the bed, but I don't think your stockings would survive," he whispered. "We have a few minutes yet. Are you okay?"

Her soft, replete sigh was his answer.

When Sasha had recovered enough to stand on her own, he helped her with the comms equipment and her gown. The bolero jacket was the final touch, and along with her long hair, helped to conceal the various wires.

"I'll get your shoes. Is there anything else you need?"

"Earrings—they're on the vanity. With my purse, I'm good to go."

Rocco scanned the room, locating the items she'd mentioned. "No problem. Your purse—is it large enough for you to carry?"

"This is Texas, babe." She kissed his cheek. "It's large enough to accommodate a compact weapon. You never know when you might run into a psycho security guard and need to defend yourself."

For Rocco, it was a double-edged sword. "Don't get me wrong—I'm glad you've got it, but if anything happens, you get to Linzi and run." He shot a blistering look at the ankle-busting heels. "Can you actually run in those?"

She retaliated with an excoriating expression of her own. "Ginger did everything Fred did, backwards and in high heels. There's a technique—it can be done."

Rocco figured he'd take her word for it. On balance, he'd rather take on a bunch of pissed-off insurgents than run in heels, whether there was a technique to it or not. "Okay, then, but if you have to run for it, I'll make sure Scott's with you. Get out as quickly as you can, head for the Hummer, and come back here. I'll take care of everything else, and then I'll contact you."

Sasha nodded. "Copy that. Please… be careful."

He had more reason than ever, now. The urge to tell her how he felt was overpowering, but this was neither the time nor the place. "I will. I think there's something else we both forgot, though."

"What's that?"

He leaned in close, so his lips were close to her ear. "Your panties. They're the devil's work, and as soon as we get back here, I'm getting you right back out of them."

By the time she reached the atrium of the main house, Sasha was confident no one would ever guess what she'd been doing with Rocco barely fifteen minutes earlier. What that man did with those hands of his was nothing short of sorcery, and what he'd promised her for later would make sure the evening wasn't a drag.

Because hopefully it would be a drag—the alternative would mean they were right and they had serious trouble on their hands.

Rocco had gone to escort Linzi and her boyfriend from her suite. The rest of her entourage and her security detail was waiting here, and once Linzi and Ram joined them, they'd be on their way to attend the Diamond ACE Music Awards.

A loud whoop drew Sasha's attention to the top of the main staircase. Linzi was already in celebratory mood, and so was her boyfriend. Rocco was right behind the couple as they descended the stairs, his expression the epitome of stoic professionalism, and a million miles away from the lover who had gifted her an orgasm so explosive, she could still feel the echoes of it now.

No doubt the rumor that Linzi was up for an award was the reason for her riotous behavior—she thrived on being the center of attention. Even if she didn't win, she'd still be on the receiving end of plenty, especially when she gave the closing performance of the evening, which was why four more of her backup dancers were also joining them. At least there'd be plenty of room for all of them in the stretch Hummer.

Even without alcohol, spirits were high between Linzi and her dancers. However, while they hadn't consumed any alcohol—yet—Gerry Brookes had already gulped his way through almost a full bottle of champagne. Linzi's manager had returned from New York a day or two earlier, and given his level of intoxication right now, Sasha was glad they'd decided to keep him in the dark about the possibility of a threat against Linzi being carried out that evening. He couldn't shoot his drunken mouth off about what he didn't know.

And then there was Linzi's producer. Trent Birling was so engrossed in his cell phone, Sasha doubted anything short of nuclear Armageddon would get through to him.

Linzi's security detail was a different matter. Rocco was the consummate professional, of course, and Scott was quiet and focused, standing straight as his gaze swept dispassionately over the gathering.

Then there was Brian. To an outsider, he might appear as cool and collected as his colleague, but to Sasha, there were plenty of red flags to tell her he was as taut as a bowstring. Hardly proof positive of intent to do harm, but why would a supposedly experienced bodyguard radiate that kind of negative energy on what should have been a virtually risk-free endeavor? She was more relieved than ever that Ghost and his team were providing backup.

"May I have your attention, please?"

Rocco's voice rang around the atrium. Oh, that sexy accent. It had done crazy things to Sasha right from the first moment she'd heard it, and the command it carried now underscored its impact on her.

"This is the first time Linzi's been out in public for a while. We have reason to believe there'll be a significant turn-out of her fans at the venue, wanting to catch a glimpse of her. Some of them may be a little too enthusiastic. I've also had a report from the guard on the gate here that there's been an unusual increase in traffic in this area—it may not be connected, but on the other hand, I don't believe in coincidence. Brian, Scott—I want you both to be alert to possible threats as soon as we leave the compound. Linzi?"

Sasha watched as Rocco addressed her employer—and waited. It was going to be one of those evenings. Sasha stepped forward to where Linzi was still laughing with her boyfriend. "Linzi, Rocco needs to tell you something. It's important."

At least Linzi didn't roll her eyes, but the look she bestowed on Rocco was little better—classic Linzi. Sasha doubted she'd remember a word of what Rocco was saying, and judging by the subtle changes in his expression, Rocco likely shared her opinion. He'd barely finished when Linzi went back to draping herself over Ram.

"Scott. Brian. A word."

Rocco beckoned the two men over to a corner of the atrium. Sasha wandered over in the general direction, feigning interest in a flower arrangement to cover her eavesdropping.

"You know your assignments for this evening," Rocco continued. "Comms check now."

Sasha turned her attention to the two guards. Scott was fully focused on what Rocco was saying, but Brian was a case study in crackling tension. His jaw was rigid, and his dark, resentful glare was directed straight at Rocco, barely changing as he completed the check. His hostile demeanor continued as Rocco confirmed again that each man was clear about what he was expected to do.

"Okay, that's all in order. Any questions?"

Sasha held her breath—was this the moment when Brian would lash out? She waited, but both men merely confirmed they were good to go. Scott moved away first, and it was then that Brian struck.

"Equizi, you might think you're in charge here—"

Before Brian could even finish his sentence, Rocco had twisted his arm up his back and bundled him face first into the nearest wall with minimal disturbance to the people around them. "You listen to me, Schofield. If anyone—*anyone* —in this party comes to any harm tonight because of you, I'll kill you myself. Understood?"

Schofield's expression was a picture of snarling hostility. He shook Rocco off, but only because Rocco allowed it. "Understood... *sir*."

With a final, venomous glare, Schofield followed Scott to the center of the atrium. When he was out of earshot, Sasha closed the distance between herself and Rocco. Though she longed to ask him if he was all right, she couldn't undermine his authority. "Have you heard from Ghost?"

"While I was waiting for Linzi. His team are all in place. Beatle and Truck have been outside Frank's place since mid-afternoon—they've seen him moving around, but he hasn't left the property. Ghost and Hollywood are at the venue. They're going to meet us in the lobby."

A little of Sasha's tension eased. "They're good men—they know what they're doing."

"They're Delta Force. I should bloody well hope they know what they're doing."

Sasha had been around enough service personnel to recognize friendly rivalry when she heard it, and saw it in Rocco's wink and half-smile. "Is Scott okay with driving the Hummer?"

The half-smile became a fully-fledged grin. "He's looking forward to it. Says he hasn't driven anything that big since he left the army. He can handle it. Why? Were you going to volunteer?"

Sasha's eyes narrowed. "You think I can't, mister?"

Rocco raised his hands in an expression of surrender. "Not arguing that one, *cara*."

A commotion near the main door interrupted their conversation. Scott and Brian were herding everyone out to their transport for the evening, and from the way they were now behaving, the party had started in earnest. Sasha and Rocco were about to join them when Sasha heard a low buzz. It wasn't her cell, so it had to be Rocco's. "I think that's you."

Rocco acknowledged her as he pulled his cell from his pocket. His expression, when the called ended, sent an arctic chill of alarm down her spine. "Who was it?"

"Nick. They've identified the source of the threats." His voice was low and urgent. "She's a cyber expert on the east coast—name's Sandra Schofield Powell. She's Frank Schofield's daughter. She's covered all their tracks really well, but everyone makes mistakes. They found an email—just one —but she sent it, and the content confirmed Frank and Brian are in on this. There was no direct link to what's happening tonight, but from what else was said in this email, it's almost certain they have something planned."

So, they were right after all, but that didn't help. "I swear… In all the time Frank's been here, he's never mentioned having a daughter, and Brian's never said anything about a sister. Why? What's their motive? The kind of threats they've made… Their viciousness points more to revenge than anything else, but if that's true, revenge for what?"

"They don't know the story behind it yet, but Charity and Tex are still working on it," Rocco said. "There's no point in worrying about that right now. We have to assume they have something planned for tonight. We'd better get moving, otherwise our diva's going to be late." He nodded in the direction of the main door, where Linzi was dancing her way to the Hummer with her boyfriend. "Not to mention we don't want Brian to suspect we're onto them."

"Are we still going ahead as planned?"

"I think we have to. Dropping Brian again at this stage could still make them panic. I think it's better to let them believe their plan's still on track." Rocco's mouth settled into a grim line. "We need to draw them out and get this finished."

"I agree." She held out her hand. "Let's go. We have a job to do."

CHAPTER 15

As Rocco had anticipated, chaos reigned outside the venue—one of the many reasons he generally preferred working with VIPs rather than celebrities.

With VIPs, experience had taught him that the potential threats were more likely to come from business competitors, political adversaries, or individuals with an ax to grind, and tended to be more cold-blooded and pragmatic.

Celebrities, on the other hand, attracted devoted admirers whose fanatical adoration could transcend the norms of regular human emotion, to the point where it translated into a dangerous, possessive obsession. And the more popular a celebrity was, the greater the number of followers and the higher the risk that one of them would take their enthusiasm to the ultimate extreme.

Normally, Rocco would have ridden shotgun with Scott, but like the riddle about the farmer transporting a fox, a goose and a bag of beans across a river in a boat that could only hold the farmer and one item, there was no way he'd leave Brian alone with either their chauffeur or his charges.

Scott steered the black beast to the end of the line of similar vehicles waiting to deposit their passengers at the main entrance. So far, Rocco had been impressed by the security guard, especially by the authority he'd demonstrated when Brian—in spite of Rocco's orders to the contrary—had objected to his being assigned as driver for the evening. Monroe had shut Schofield down with a handful of quiet but forceful and well-chosen words. Although Schofield had made no further protest, his demeanor had, however, become even more ill-tempered.

As the Hummer drew to a halt in line with the red carpet, Rocco exited the vehicle before it fully stopped and was at the door where Linzi would emerge to greet her fans, ready to open it. Even though he was convinced the threat to her safety was within her entourage, it didn't mean the screaming crowds couldn't harbor further unpredictable danger.

The noise was almost deafening, and combined with the constant flashing from paparazzi cameras and waving cell phones, provided plenty of cover for a potential attack. Rocco filtered out the light and noise, concentrating instead on the behavior of the crowds, and with quiet urgency, ushered Linzi and her boyfriend into the building as quickly as possible, walking a fine line between assuring her safety and not disappointing her fans.

Each time he carried out a visual sweep, he checked Sasha's location, and each time, he caught a glimpse of the agent she'd once been. He might be biased, but in his opinion the CIA had lost one hell of an asset when she left. Brian was shepherding the remaining members of Linzi's entourage behind them, while Scott drove off to park their transport—hopefully not too far away. Rocco had planned ahead as much as he could, but on the night, there was no guarantee all the pieces would fall into place exactly as he would prefer.

Even the best-laid plans could be thrown out by the smallest of unexpected variables.

Conditions were little better once they entered the building—the lobby was teeming with the great and the good who'd been invited to attend. Not just a multitude of stars from the music world, but a whole host of other individuals who were in the public eye, and all of them were enjoying the hospitality offered by the servers with their laden silver salvers. Laughter and conversation added to the background music, but Rocco wasn't interested in any of it. He was looking for one person in particular. His gaze roved over the crowd, finally alighting on a tall, tuxedo-clad male shouldering his way through the throng. His greeting was a silent chin-lift.

"You get the message from Nick?" Ghost asked without ceremony.

Rocco nodded. "Your team's aware?"

"I briefed them as soon as Nick contacted me. Beatle and Truck reported in ten minutes ago—Schofield Senior hasn't left the house all afternoon, but I have a feeling at some point that's going to change. Hollywood's checking out backstage." Ghost's keen gaze carried out another sweep of the area.

Rocco didn't need to be a mind-reader to know the other man was as unhappy with their surroundings as he was. There were too many people—too much cover for the Schofields, too many prospective victims if everything went sideways. Rocco didn't like it one bit.

A disturbance in the milling crowd drew their attention to one side. Instantly on high alert, both Rocco and Ghost moved closer to Linzi.

"Ms. Suto, it's wonderful to see you. Welcome to the Diamond ACE Music Awards."

The exuberantly enthusiastic greeting came from another walking tux, this one inhabited by the well-known TV chat show host who was the compère for the evening. Rocco tuned his incessant chatter out and returned to concentrating on their surroundings and more importantly, Brian Schofield. He was maintaining a position at the rear of the party, potentially putting himself in an ideal position to slip quietly away and carry out whatever he might have planned.

Still jabbering away about timing and dressing rooms to Linzi, even though only Sasha was paying attention, the tux-in-charge was now leading the singer and her entourage to the ballroom where the awards were to take place. The space was only one area among many in the vast building, so for Rocco, the location was one unholy mass of potential trouble.

Since Linzi's party was one of the first to be escorted into the ballroom where the main event was taking place, Rocco took the opportunity to have a look around before it became too busy. There was nothing obviously wrong, but he couldn't shake the suspicion that something wasn't right. His inspection was interrupted when Scott ran up to him. Rocco took him to one side.

"I found a neat place to park—not too obvious and not too far, just a couple streets away."

Rocco made a mental note of the address, at the same time wondering where the monster of a vehicle would be "not too obvious". Then he remembered—this was Texas, where everything was oversized.

"Good work, Scott. Remember, if there's an attack, or anyone tries to get to Linzi, you get her out of there—that's your primary objective. Take Sasha, too, if you can, and anyone else from our group who's close by, but don't wait for anyone. Head for the service yard. I'll take care of any stragglers."

"Copy that, boss."

Rocco looked at the man standing beside him. It wasn't

the first time he'd called Rocco that, but Rocco had decided it was no longer worth reminding Scott that he wasn't his boss. Although after tonight, there was a high probability his real boss would no longer be his boss, either. "You just stick close to Linzi, okay?"

"Got it."

Scott executed a sharp about turn and walked briskly in the direction of the table around which Linzi's party was already seated. Sasha glanced up as he approached, then her gaze switched to Rocco. To anyone else, she'd appear relaxed and ready to enjoy the evening, but there was an aura of vigilance around her. Even so, his protective instincts strained at the leash to get her out of there and to some place safe.

Then again... Sasha was a trained, experienced professional, with more resolve and backbone than most of the people around her put together and multiplied tenfold. She wouldn't thank him if he tried to coddle her.

The space, vast though it was, soon filled up as all the guests made their way there from the lobby. Gradually, they took their seats, and the waitstaff swapped their trays of drinks for trays of food. Rocco declined his meal, as did both Scott and Brian—eating would only divert his attention from where it was supposed to be focused.

Once the tables were cleared, the host who'd greeted Linzi when they arrived took his place on the stage. Rocco did not take that as his cue to relax. As the event proper got underway, he continued his surveillance of the room, noting the discreet presence of Ghost and Hollywood as they moved around the space, creating as little disturbance as possible while announcements and presentations were made. Rocco offered up a silent prayer of thanks that acceptance speeches were not required.

The first sign of something abnormal was when Ghost reacted very subtly to something coming in on his comms.

He ducked away to a quiet corner of the room, and as soon as he reappeared a few seconds later, Rocco's cell phone vibrated.

As silent as the wraith he'd been trained to be, Rocco stood and retreated a few feet from the table, so as not to disturb the flow of proceedings. "What have you got?"

"I just heard from Truck and Beatle—Senior is on the move, and they're following. And get this—he's wearing a tux. You thinking what I'm thinking?"

It could be a coincidence, but Rocco doubted it as much as Ghost apparently did. "He's on his way here. Whatever they're doing, it's going down here, tonight. Alert everyone. Now."

They were running out of time.

With twenty minutes to go until Linzi's performance and the scheduled end of the event, the stage manager had come to their table to request Linzi's presence backstage, to prepare for her set. Ram and her other backing dancers had gone with her, and so had Scott, following Rocco's orders to stay close.

As Rocco expected, Brian had protested about Scott accompanying Linzi, but his protest had lacked conviction, and he'd backed down too easily for Rocco's peace of mind. Consequently, Brian was still at the table. Outwardly, he appeared the cool, calm bodyguard focused on doing his job, but the way he regularly checked his watch was telling. Sasha had noticed too, and when her gaze meshed with Rocco's, she rested a hand on her purse, signaling she was armed and ready to help.

From his position at the circular table, a couple of seats away from Brian, Rocco had a good view of everything he needed to watch. That didn't include what was going on up on the stage, but that wasn't his primary focus.

Movement to his right caught his eye—Brian, ready to leave the table. Rocco caught hold of his arm as he was going to pass behind him.

"What? I have to ask permission to go to the john now?" Brian snarled. "You wanna come hold my hand while I take a piss?"

What Rocco really wanted to do was punch his lights out. He released the other man's arm. "You're here to do a job, remember?"

Schofield stalked off and disappeared from view. Sasha watched him too, then turned back to Rocco. "Do you want me to follow him?"

"No, I'd rather you stay here. I'll ask Ghost."

Unfortunately, neither Ghost nor Hollywood were conveniently placed to follow Schofield. Rocco was left with no choice but to go himself, but before he reached the doorway, Schofield was on his way back. He walked straight past Rocco, muttering as he did so, "Checking up on me… *boss*?"

The taunting question was no doubt intended to provoke. Rocco waited until Schofield had resumed his seat, then returned to Sasha, crouching down on her left to put some extra distance between him and Schofield.

"I'm going to go backstage. Ghost's on his way there now, but I've got a bad feeling about this."

"I'll come with you—"

"No, I need you to stay here. Keep an eye on Brookes and Birling. If anything happens, I want to know where you are, unless…"

"Unless it happens right here. Look, just go. Do what you have to do, and… if necessary, you can find me afterward."

He knew that. He'd find her if the world was ending.

Moments later, it seemed as though it was.

Three blasts, seconds apart, rocked the building. The first threw Rocco across the floor, with the second and third coming right behind. The explosions came from different directions, adding to the cacophony of panic that swept through the room like a whirlwind. Alarms screeched and wailed, fighting for dominance with the screams of the people around him.

He staggered to his feet. His ears felt as if they'd been stuffed with cotton, his head was buzzing, and his brain was being spun in a centrifuge at high speed. In spite of all that, he zeroed in on the stage, to see only the staggering, stumbling forms of Linzi's backing dancers as they struggled to their feet—of Linzi, there was no sign.

Rocco prayed it was because Scott had done his job. Prayer was all he had—comms were a hiss of useless static, and when he dragged his cell phone from his pocket, there was no signal. Damn it, everything was fucked.

He turned automatically to the table, to see the remainder of their party sprawled every which way.

Apart from one—Brian Schofield was nowhere to be seen.

Professional priorities clashed violently with personal ones. His job demanded he do everything to confirm Scott had gotten Linzi to safety, but his instincts as a man in love were in direct conflict. The latter prevailed.

He reached Sasha as she was picking herself up from the floor. "Are you all right?" he yelled, trying to make himself heard above the ringing in his ears. "Sasha. Are you hurt?"

She shook her head—slowly. "I'm okay—I will be. Where's Brian?"

Rocco looked around, widening his search to the whole room. "Gone. Stay here, *cara*. I'm going to—"

"You all okay?" Ghost emerged from the smoke and chaos, Hollywood right behind him.

"More or less. You?" Rocco doubted what had happened would even put a dent in the two Deltas. Like him, for them this would be a quiet day at the office.

"We're okay. Where's Schofield?"

"Disappeared. We've lost him. This must be his handiwork."

"A diversion. At least Monroe got Linzi and her boyfriend to safety. I saw them heading for the service tunnels."

"What about Frank? Have you heard from Truck and Beatle?"

"They checked in just before the explosions," Hollywood replied. "They said he was heading in this general direction, but was still several minutes away. This is going to cause gridlock while the fire department and EMTs attend."

Wherever Scott had parked the Hummer, Rocco hoped it was on the right side of any police cordon and he, Linzi and Ram were already on their way home.

Ghost nodded in agreement. "With luck, this'll keep Schofield away, and Truck and Beatle will deal with him."

"What about Brian? He's in the wind," Sasha said. "We have to—"

"My job." Rocco cut across what he knew would be Sasha's insistence on going with him. He couldn't allow that. He looked around, taking in the terror and alarm. This was his error to put right, not hers, and there was no way he would allow Sasha to put herself in the line of fire. He had to go after Brian alone.

A sudden eruption of sound drowned out the cacophony of fear and panic around them. The service doors had crashed open. Rocco and Ghost pivoted on the spot, weapons raised, to see Scott stumble through and collapse on the floor, one hand clutching the back of his head. As his knees hit the carpet, his hand came away, revealing bloody fingers.

Having holstered their sidearms, Rocco and Ghost lifted Scott and sat him on the nearest chair. He was still conscious but groggy, and clearly needed medical attention.

"I'm sorry, boss," he groaned. "I grabbed Linzi, like you said. She was screaming for her boyfriend—wouldn't move until she could get a hold of him. I got them both to the entrance of the service tunnels, and Brian was right behind us. He shot Ram and was going to shoot me but his gun jammed. Linzi was freaking out behind me. I managed to get off a couple of rounds but he was flying at me and I only winged him. I remember him raising his hand… I turned to push Linzi out of the way, but the back of my head exploded. I think I was only out for a minute, maybe two, and when I came to, I saw Ram still lying there. I checked his vitals, but he was gone."

"Linzi and Schofield?" Rocco prompted, sparing a glance at Ghost. A minute or two might as well have been an eternity. With all the pieces in place, if Frank had made it in time, they could even be miles away by now, in any direction. On the other hand, if Frank hadn't arrived, there was an outside chance Brian had gone to ground somewhere in the labyrinth to wait for him.

"No sign," Scott said. "They're gone, boss—it's all my fault. I'm sorry."

"It's not your fault," Rocco ground out. "My op, my responsibility. Ghost, I'm going down to the tunnels. I'll get her back."

Ghost responded without hesitation. "You'll need backup."

As if to emphasize the point, Hollywood joined his captain in drawing his weapon. However, the last thing Rocco wanted was for Ghost and his team to get into serious trouble for what they'd done. "No. You guys aren't supposed to be here. The police will arrive any time to start asking questions, and I don't want you around here when they do. Go. You've done plenty and I'm grateful for that, but you're wasting time."

Ghost glanced at Hollywood, who nodded in acknowledgement of whatever silent communication had passed between the two Delta Force operators, then turned back to Rocco. "Good luck."

The two men disappeared back into the mayhem. Rocco turned to Sasha, who was pressing a napkin to the back of Monroe's head. Anguish in her eyes, she turned her gaze on him, looking for answers, yet at the same time, offering hope.

He needed to give her something to do—before she insisted on coming with him. "Sasha, I need you to do something for me. Get the dancers, keep everyone together, and keep them safe."

"Let me come with you. I can watch your six."

His fierce woman. He'd have given anything to keep her with him, so he'd know exactly where she was. "I can't. Please—do this for me. You're important to me, and… it's the only way I can protect you."

Her internal struggle was written all over her face, but in the end, she caved. "Go get Linzi—bring her back safely. I'll take care of things here." She glanced at Linzi's manager and producer, dazed but unharmed, sitting a few feet away from her.

He wanted to go, he had to go, but there was one more thing to do before his feet would cooperate by moving in the desired direction. He framed Sasha's face with both hands and pressed a fast, hard kiss to her lips. It was all or nothing. "I love you."

Her hand clamped around his wrist as he started to leave,

stopping him in his tracks. "I love you too. Now go get her back."

Leaving Sasha in the midst of all the mayhem surrounding them was the hardest thing he'd ever done. He'd blurted the words out in desperation, never expecting her to return them. There was so much they needed to talk about, but there simply wasn't time. He made his pledge in the kiss he placed on her palm. Her gaze clung to his as unspoken questions flew between them, but then he had to let her go.

"Go. We can talk when you come back."

Rocco couldn't hear her say the words against all the background noise, but he saw her soft lips form them. He also saw proof of her feelings for him in her eyes and her expression, and took that memory with him as he barged through the doors leading to access to the maintenance tunnels.

Though he'd been expecting it, it was still a bitter blow when he encountered Ram's lifeless body in a pool of blood —another death on his conscience. He stopped briefly to confirm Monroe's assessment, then set off again.

The maze of tunnels was lined with pipes and cabling, and seemed to bear little resemblance to the plans Rocco had been able to examine only a couple of days ago. As he made his way through them, he found himself wishing for a loud, hysterical scream from Linzi. Even factoring in the echoes, it would at least let him know he was on the right track.

And that she was still alive.

The hollow silence around him, the haunting echo of his own rapid footsteps, did not bode well, although Rocco couldn't see Brian killing the golden goose. Not yet, at any rate, and not ever, if Rocco had any say in the matter.

He ran on, slowing on the approach to each junction, so he could check the next stretch for any threats. He should have been getting closer to the exit to the service yard and the loading docks now, with a greater risk of running into innocent bystanders… or Brian and Linzi, and maybe Frank as well, if luck wasn't on Rocco's side. He glanced at his weapon and, satisfied that it was ready to fire, peered cautiously around the next corner.

A voice rang out.

"Hey. You look like a man who's looking for something…"

CHAPTER 16

He recognized that voice. Knowing there was no point in taking cover behind the wall, Rocco stepped into the open. At the end of the tunnel, against the backdrop of the brightly lit service yard were the outlines of five figures. Two were kneeling, hands clasped behind their heads—one of them favoring an arm, as if protecting a gunshot wound—with a third person behind them, clearly holding a weapon on them. The fourth was on the ground, slumped against the wall, with the fifth crouched at their side.

Had Rocco not recognized that voice, this would have been a trap, and there was no way he'd be walking into it like this. As he approached and details resolved themselves, his assumption was confirmed. Frank and Brian Schofield—the two men on their knees—radiated seething anger in the face of utter defeat. Ghost stood to one side behind them—still wearing his tux, but with the added accessory of a black bandana covering the lower half of his face, a combination mirrored by Hollywood, who was kneeling beside an apparently semi-conscious Linzi. Head moving restlessly from side to side, she moaned softly.

Rocco picked up his pace to join them. "Is she all right?"

"He used chloroform—I can smell it," Hollywood said. "Only a light dose, just enough to subdue her. She's coming out of it now, but she should be checked out by the EMTs."

"On their way," Ghost said. He turned his attention to the two men with their hands behind their heads. "So are the cops."

Mention of law enforcement reminded Rocco of what he'd said only a few minutes earlier. "I thought I told you to go."

Rocco might not have been able to see the man's mouth, but he could see the grin in his eyes. "Cell signal came back online. I heard this one," Ghost gestured toward Frank, "was only a couple minutes away, figured you might need a little assistance."

"And your source for this information? Safe?" Rocco knew it came from the two members of Ghost's team who'd followed Frank to the venue, but he wanted confirmation that they weren't in danger of being apprehended.

"Watching our six but not about to get themselves caught. They'll warn us when the cops are about to arrive."

Hollywood pulled his cell from his pocket to check a message. "Consider us warned. We've got about thirty seconds."

"Think you can take care of these guys for that long, trooper?"

His handgun aimed unwaveringly at the Schofields, Rocco took the question the way it was intended. "Watch and learn, my friend… watch and learn. But I suggest you do it from a distance."

At the sound of running footsteps in the tunnels behind him, Rocco tightened his grip on his weapon, but then realized almost immediately that the sound wasn't being made by heavy, booted feet. The lack of reaction from Ghost confirmed there was no threat bearing down on them. A presence halted at his side, and a familiar scent of wildflowers instantly calmed him.

As did the sound of the slide being racked on the handgun that appeared in his peripheral vision.

"We can take care of them," Sasha confirmed with quiet confidence. "Ram's dead and a lot of people are hurt because of them. I don't need much of an excuse to take care of them *permanently*. Now get out of here."

"On our way, ma'am," Ghost responded. "We'll be in touch."

Rocco had one more thing to say to the Deltas before they left. "Thanks for everything. I'd say I owe you one, but I think it's more like several. Any time I can help…"

"Understood. It was our pleasure." Ghost offered a chin lift. "Sunday nights are always too damn quiet."

The two operators disappeared in the direction of the service yard. Sasha circled around the back of Rocco and went to Linzi, who was showing more signs of regaining consciousness. She crouched beside the young woman and took hold of her hand to comfort her. "It's okay, Linzi, it's all over now. The EMTs are on their way."

Rocco moved, putting himself squarely in front of the Schofields, with the women behind him. "We know Sandra's involved in this now—you needed her technical expertise to plant the cyber threats. Why? Were you intending to demand a ransom?"

An evil smile appeared on Brian's face before an equally evil laugh rang out. "Ransom? You think we planned all this just for a few million bucks? That would have been the icing on the cake, smart ass."

"Shut the fuck up, son," his father snarled.

Rocco's face remained expressionless, but his mind was busy processing what had just been revealed. If cash was an added extra, then what had been the real motive for the attempted kidnapping? If their purpose wasn't financial gain and they'd let Linzi see their faces, that could only mean one thing—their main objective must have ultimately been to kill her, but why?

Before he could ask more questions, though, Rocco heard the sound of running behind him once more. Heavier footsteps this time, which meant only one thing—the police were about to find them. He took up a position behind the father and son, and motioned to them to move over to the side, away from Sasha and Linzi.

Between him and the police, there was nowhere for the Schofields to go, so Rocco made his gun safe, set it on the ground—well away from the two men in front of him—and raised his hands. Sasha followed suit, nudging her weapon well to one side with her foot as she rose, hands in the air. After everything they'd been through, the last thing they needed was for the police to assume they were on the wrong side...

Sasha returned to Casa Millefiori with the rest of Linzi's entourage. They'd been allowed to leave on the understanding they'd make themselves available for interview over the following days, so they'd all taken refuge in the stretch Hummer, and Sasha had driven them home. All of them were now occupying guest accommodation, and trying to come to terms with what had happened.

That was, all of them except Rocco and Scott. She could still feel Rocco's arms around her as he'd explained that he was going to the nearest ER with Scott, to make sure the other man was taken care of. Sasha had been torn between wanting to stay with him and making sure everyone made it home safely, but when he'd held her, the emotional connection between them gave her the strength to do what he needed her to do.

He'd been right, of course. Apart from anything else, no one else had been capable of driving, or even in a legal position to do it. Linzi was in no state to be left alone, so Sasha had remained with the sobbing young woman until her parents had arrived at the compound—thankfully, a major traffic holdup had delayed their arrival at the venue, so they hadn't been caught up in the carnage. They'd relieved Sasha of the necessity to stay with Linzi, which meant Sasha was now at a loose end and free to worry about Rocco.

However, before she went to his suite—the best place to wait for him—she made a quick stop at her office. There was something she needed to check, and she had to do it before she saw Rocco. The task took only a few minutes to complete, and the results, thankfully, were what she'd hoped for. She hadn't realized how much she was hoping until she nearly dropped to her knees in relief.

Time dragged by. Sasha suspected her frequent checks for any new messages on her cell were contributing to the perception. The last one she'd received had been from Rocco, to let her know the doctor was still with Scott. The initial signs were that his injuries were relatively superficial, with no lasting damage, for which Sasha was extremely grateful.

Unable to rest, she brought a blanket from the bedroom and made a nest on the couch. With the lights low, it was all too easy brood about what had happened that evening, events replaying over and over in her mind in a series of images that brought back other memories, too. What she remembered most clearly of all were Rocco's last words to her before she'd left him behind.

We have to talk. Go home and wait for me there. Promise you'll wait.

She'd promised, and now her mood swung from hope to dread and back again. She had no doubt it was connected with the declaration she'd blurted out before he'd left her to look for Linzi—and the words he'd returned. Did he intend to tell her he hadn't meant it, after all?

Sasha picked up her tablet from the low table in front of her. Reading the latest novel by her favorite author might help. She swiped and tapped her way to the book and stared at it, but the words on the screen refused to make sense. They were fighting a losing battle for her attention against a formidable enemy—her worries about Rocco and Scott. So absorbed in those concerns was she, that she barely registered the door opening behind her.

"Rocco!" Sasha flung the blanket away and ran at him full tilt, flying into his arms. Playing it cool with him wasn't even on her radar, not any more. "How did you get here? You should have called me—I'd have come for you."

With one arm wrapped around her, Rocco stroked her hair away from the side of her face. "Ghost showed up at the hospital and gave me a ride back. I thought you'd be asleep, and I didn't want to disturb you."

The way his worried gaze roamed over her face almost broke her heart. "How could I sleep without you? Is Scott all right?" She needed to know.

"He's fine. They're keeping him overnight for observation, just to make sure. How are you doing?"

"I'm okay." Sasha could barely get the words out. "I'm glad you're back, though. Is there anything you need?"

"Only you," Rocco murmured, his breath moving her hair as he spoke. "I'd like to hold you for a while, if that's okay with you?"

As if he needed to ask. She stepped away from him, took his hand, and led him around the couch to where she'd abandoned the blanket. "Would you mind if we stayed here? It's just—"

"Wherever you like," he agreed readily. "You don't have to explain."

Rocco removed his jacket and toed off his shoes. His bow tie had disappeared at some point, but Sasha guessed he cared as little as she did. She coaxed him into lying full-length on the sofa, then nestled close and pulled the blanket over both of them.

"The police will be here tomorrow afternoon to start taking statements," Rocco said at length. "They'll need to speak to everyone in turn. Especially you and me. Thanks for being there tonight."

"Where else would I be?"

Rocco seemed not to hear her. He was staring into the distance, consumed by whatever dark thoughts were taking him away from her. No matter what he'd seen and done in the past, he was still a human being—what he said next bore that out.

"Sasha, it was a fucking disaster. I should have pulled the plug on her appearance. If I'd known they had explosives, that Ram would... just for being her boyfriend—"

"Shh." Sasha laid a gentle finger over his lips. She'd almost been expecting this. "Listen to yourself. *If you'd known*. Yes, you would have done things differently, but you *didn't* know. You didn't know Linzi would be so stubborn about taking Ram with her when Scott tried to get her to safety—you *couldn't* know it, either. And the Schofields—there was nothing in their records to suggest they'd go as far as this. I know, because as soon as I could, I checked. You checked too, remember? Neither of them has any history of experience with explosives in their résumé, and that's all we could go on. Okay, for all we know, they could have experience, but all it takes is a simple search on the internet to find out how to build a bomb. We couldn't know how far they were willing to go, and *you* are not responsible."

Rocco's expression didn't alter, but she wasn't surprised. It was going to take more than a few words from her to relieve him of this burden of guilt, no matter how mistaken it might be. Several people had been injured in the explosions and the ensuing panic, but thankfully, there were no life-changing injuries and no additional fatalities. It could have been a lot worse, but Rocco, being the man he was, could only see what he viewed as his failure. For now, Sasha would let it slide, but not for ever.

Rocco shifted beside her and pulled her more closely to him. "There's something else we need to talk about."

And here it came. Sasha braced herself, hoping that the way he was holding onto her meant something good, something positive would come out of this, selfish of her though it might be.

"I meant what I said, Sasha. I'm in love with you."

Her heart soared skyward and then plunged back down to earth. Emotionally overwhelmed, she turned her face into his chest and let the tears flow. Her whole body quaked with the force of the feelings she was trying to control.

"Hey. I didn't think it would be quite such bad news."

"It isn't." The arm she'd draped across him held him more tightly than ever. "I meant what I said, too. I was so scared I was going to lose you tonight."

His chest jerked under the force of a humorless bark of silent laughter. "It takes more than a couple of deranged lunatics to see me off, *cara*. And Ghost and his team were there."

Hopefully she'd soon have an opportunity to thank her friends properly. Without them, the evening might have ended very differently.

Without them, Ram might not have been the only fatality,

and Linzi might have been in the hands of kidnappers, maybe even dead by now.

Without them, Rocco might have been wounded or even killed.

"It's all right, Sasha. It's over."

It was only when he held her even more tightly to him that the trembling stopped. "What are we going to do, Rocco?"

He tilted her chin up so he could kiss her forehead. "Don't worry about it tonight," he urged softly. "It'll be all right. Everything will be all right. Rest now."

CHAPTER 17

During the investigation that took place over the following weeks, the full story behind the attempted kidnapping of Linzi Suto emerged piece by piece.

The whole Schofield family was involved—what remained of it. While the story was heart-breaking, it in no way justified the revenge they had planned.

Frank Schofield, rather than being divorced as he'd claimed, had been widowed in tragic circumstances. His wife had lost her life in an automobile accident a year or so before he'd been hired to work for Linzi, leaving not only him mourning his partner of almost three decades but her twin adult children—Brian and Sandra—grieving for their mother.

The accident had involved only one other vehicle—a powerful convertible driven by one Thane Murdoch, who had also been killed on impact. The tox screen carried out during the autopsy had revealed Murdoch been driving under the influence of both alcohol and illegal drugs. However, he'd been more than a drunk and an addict—he was Linzi's elder sibling, her half-brother by her mother's first husband. The different surnames had concealed the relationship, adding an unanticipated layer of complexity to Tex and Charity's investigations.

Frank's grief had torn him apart, quickly transforming into a cold, deadly rage that had also infected his children. That rage had led directly to a dark lust for revenge. The opportunity to take that revenge had come when a cyber-stalker, not content with polluting Linzi's social media accounts with all manner of disgusting suggestions, had progressed to sending her anonymous "gifts" of roadkill. Gerry Brookes had deemed that his star client needed a head of security, and so Frank Schofield had been recruited into the position.

What no one had known was that Sandra Schofield Powell had created the stalker, and her father had been responsible for sending the packages. Sandra's skill and talent with IT had then played a major part in Frank's appointment as the security chief, after she'd hacked into the computer system used by the specialist consultant handling the recruitment process. Thanks to her manipulation of the applications, Frank had been the last candidate standing, so Gerry had had no choice but to offer him the job. After that, Frank had simply bided his time, waiting for the right moment to bring his son onto the team.

Once the two of them were in place, it had simply become a case of building up a solid, unblemished reputation until it was time to strike. Sandra had played her part again, using her technical expertise to create the cyber threats once more, to hack into various computer systems to corrupt information relating to the family, and to cover her tracks—until Charity and Tex had collaborated in tracking her down and identifying her, courtesy of one simple mistake.

The threats, bullying and intimidation had been intended to drive Linzi into committing suicide, but with Sasha running interference—unknown to Frank—that plan had failed. They had then switched their strategy to kidnapping the singer and demanding an astronomical ransom for her safe return.

Except… there wouldn't have been a safe return. The official investigation had uncovered incontrovertible proof that Frank had wanted to do to Linzi's family what a member of her family had done to his. And as if the documents and emails found on the computers owned by all three Schofields hadn't been enough, Frank had shown not one iota of remorse as he'd described to the police how he planned to put a gun to Linzi's head, tell her exactly why she was going to die, and then put a bullet in her brain, before he and his family fled to a country where there was no extradition treaty with the US.

The Diamond ACE Music Awards were supposed to have provided the perfect opportunity for the final phase of their plan. Brian had planted the bombs twenty-four hours earlier, and on receiving the go-ahead via text from his son, Frank had triggered them with a burner phone while on the way to pick up his son and their target. The purpose of the bombs had not been to cause serious material damage, but to create confusion and act as a diversion while they carried out the kidnapping.

During his time in the military, Rocco had fought and killed for the greater good—and not always at a distance—but the cold-blooded intent behind the Schofields' planned abduction and murder of Linzi Suto, not to mention the ruthless execution of her boyfriend, had chilled even him to the bone. Theirs was a different kind of evil, and with their confessions now a matter of record—and a total lack of remorse for what they'd done and for the lives they'd ended—the death penalty was almost guaranteed.

The atmosphere at Casa Millefiori remained as volatile as

an ocean storm. Continuing distress and turmoil rolled through the place at every level. While his job there might have come to an end, Rocco was of the opinion that he shouldn't leave yet. For him, there was a sense of unfinished business, and it wasn't all connected with Sasha, or even his recommendations for upgrades to the estate's security operations once the new head of security was confirmed.

No, in his quieter moments, what weighed so heavily on his mind was the disintegration of the Schofield family. The loss they'd suffered reminded him keenly of how his own family had lost one another.

Or rather, how he'd lost them—his father, Nonna, his cousins and their families—by turning his back on them. What he'd once viewed as shackles that would enslave him to a life he'd rejected, he now saw as the loving support of a close-knit family. What had happened to the Schofields—the loss of a wife and mother, taken in isolation from what had followed—had cracked the walls of denial he'd built around his own heart, and what he felt for Sasha was widening that breach every day.

Futile though it was, a part of him wished he could go back to those summers in Sicily, when Nonna had tried to teach a teenaged Rocco how to make pasta from scratch and he'd gorged himself on her cannoli, flavored with lemons from the groves on a neighboring farm. He found himself growing to hate the distance between him and his father—not just geographical but emotional, too. Dario wasn't getting any younger, and neither was Nonna. One day they'd both be gone, and what then?

When all was said and done, what else was there but family?

A few weeks later, after winter had given way to spring and bluebonnets bathed the Hill Country in color, Rocco knew he was running out of time. The fragments of his life swirled around him in total confusion. Awake in the early hours, with little else to do but think, all he could see was the unending conflict between all the things he wanted in his life but were mutually exclusive. On the one hand, he wanted his family back, but on the other, he wanted Sasha, for now and forever. Whichever way he looked at it, though, he couldn't have both. One would have to be sacrificed for the other, and he would have to make that decision.

A deep sigh welled up from the overwhelming pit of misery inside him. A small movement beside him drew him out of his thoughts and reminded him he wasn't alone in bed. He hadn't spent a night alone since he'd told Sasha he loved her.

The woman he couldn't stop thinking about moved again, and he found himself gazing into her eyes. The way she was looking at him tore him apart. She was lying on her stomach, partly on him, and her hand lay over his heart. The symbolism didn't escape him. He'd delivered his heart into her hands weeks earlier.

"There's something about this time of day that encourages the type of conversation you shy away from in daylight." She kissed his chest. "When it feels as if the whole world is asleep, apart from us, and we can share the things we don't want the world to hear. Our most secret hopes… or our most horrifying fears. Whatever we talk about, when the light's just like this, it stays here, suspended in time… where it can be forgotten, if that's the way it has to be."

The quiet undercurrent of vulnerability in her soft voice broke his heart wide open. She was asking him to talk to her. Perhaps it was time. He shifted position so he could enfold her in his arms and hold her close. She draped her leg over his so her thigh was nudging his cock and balls.

"How am I supposed to think when you do that?" he grumbled without rancor. "I'm only a man."

"Not *only* a man—and not to me. I love you, and I can't stand to see you like this. Please let me help."

Rocco shifted so he could tuck her more closely into the protection of his body. The irony struck deep. What she needed protection from most was him. "Can we just stay like this for a while?"

His gruff request earned him a kiss, and a fresh burst of pain flooded through him. Everything he wanted and couldn't have was in that soft, sweet contact.

"For as long as you want." She wrapped her arm around his torso.

He wanted to say "How does forever sound?" but forever in her arms couldn't be his. Whatever happened, his long-term future wasn't in this country, and so he had to level with her. He owed her the truth about the worthless promise he'd made, that everything would be all right.

Because, not only would it not be all right—he was going to end it himself.

"Sasha, first of all, I'm sorry I haven't been open and honest with you."

Be careful what you wish for.

The words reverberated around her mind, taunting her with what might yet prove to be her own stupidity. If Rocco was going to open up, as she'd longed for him to do, then she could probably kiss goodbye to her fantasy about him accepting the role of Linzi's head of security, so they could stay together. "Does that mean you're going to be open and honest now?" She tried to keep her tone light and free of her inner anguish.

"I have to be. You deserve the truth... the whole story. Before I came here, I'd just finished my latest assignment. For personal reasons, I was considering resigning, thought it was time to move on. Ros Northwood, my boss back home, offered me the chance to come here instead. It wasn't only for a change of scenery—it was to put some distance between me and my father."

She'd known this would come eventually. "Go on."

"I should warn you—it's a long story."

She didn't care. She'd willingly listen to him for the rest of her life. "We have all the time in the world."

He hugged her more closely to his side. Sasha rested her head against his shoulder and laid her palm flat on his abdomen. The ridges of muscle, hard beneath her fingertips, helped to ground her, even though she was cold and shivering inside. She'd never felt so emotionally vulnerable before, not even when Jack had been dying in front of her.

"My mother—Claire—met my father when she went to Sicily for a holiday with some friends, a final fling before they all went their different ways to university. She wandered off on her own, got lost, and my father was a member of the search party that went looking for her—or so the story goes. You probably think I'm going to tell you it was love at first sight, but I think there was rather more lust than love."

Sasha smiled to herself. "Isn't that usually the case, though—when you meet someone new, exciting, and attractive? Especially when he's saved your life."

She felt Rocco shrug. "I suppose so," he said without emotion. "She wanted to stay behind when it was time for them to go home, but her friends talked her out of it. Apparently, they complained loud and long about not seeing much of her after she met Dario."

"How old were they? When they met."

"She was nineteen, I think. He would have been twenty-three."

"That obviously wasn't the end of it, though."

His chest vibrated with a brief chuckle. "Obviously. At the end of her first year of university, she decided to go back to Sicily, but this time, she went on a working holiday."

"And Dario was waiting to meet her off the plane?" It was a ridiculously romantic notion, but Sasha couldn't stop herself asking the question.

"Not at all—he didn't know she was going. Although they'd spent all that time together, she had no idea where to find him, because he'd always gone to the hostel to meet her. She assumed he must have lived close to the area where she'd vacationed a year earlier, and she hoped—somehow—their paths would cross."

"Wasn't that risky? Going all that way alone?"

"She didn't think so, until my father found her in the bar where she was working. When she told him what she'd done and why, he put her over his knee and spanked her until she couldn't sit down… right there, in front of all the customers."

Sasha opened her mouth to speak, but for a few eternal seconds, nothing came out, until her stunned brain finally rediscovered its ability to think. "What happened next?"

"He kissed her. Then he told the bar owner she was no longer working there, and eventually he took her home to meet my grandparents."

"Isn't that a bit Neanderthal? And *eventually*? What does that mean?"

"It was a lot Neanderthal, and that was exactly what she told him as soon as they left the bar. And eventually he took her home, because everyone came out of the bar to enjoy the spectacle of Dario's sweet English rose giving him hell. They all knew he'd been totally besotted with her since their initial meeting, because he'd done nothing but talk about her for the whole damn year."

If she hadn't known what kind of man Rocco was, she'd almost have thought he was making it up. "So, did she spend the summer there, or…?"

A shadow of sadness fell over Rocco's expression. "That summer, and the next decade. They were married as soon as it could be arranged. The Gramps gave her hell for it."

"The who?" Sasha could guess who he meant, but confirmation wouldn't hurt.

"The Gramps—a collective noun for my maternal grandparents. As they saw it, she'd cheated them out of the big white wedding they'd always wanted for her. There was more to it than that, though—she'd also deprived them of a socially acceptable son-in-law. They bore that grudge right up until the day they died. Not being able to reconcile with them hit my mother hard."

"Did they refuse to see you, too?"

"Not at all. In spite of my… heritage, I was the grandchild they'd always wanted. When my parents' marriage broke down, my mother took me back to England, and even though her parents wouldn't see her, she sent me to see them every Sunday until I was old enough to recognize the atmosphere between them for what it was."

Sasha's heart contracted with aching sadness for what the young Rocco had gone through. "What happened then?"

"I was almost fifteen by that time, and when I finally understood what their attitude was doing to my mother, I refused to go again."

"What about your father? What happened to him?"

"He never got over losing her. He tried all ways to get her to go back to him, and when she died, he started on me, telling me I needed to go back to Sicily permanently, for the sake of my birthright."

As she listened to the delicious tones of his accent, Sasha realized that what he'd told her was only the tip of an intensely private iceberg. She had so many burning questions, but she had no right to ask them.

"Sasha, I can hear you thinking. What do you want to know?"

His hand stroked her back in a soothing motion that gave her the reassurance she needed. "How old were you when your mother took you back to England?"

"Almost ten. I know you're doing the maths, but yes, they had me in the first year of their marriage, and that may have been part of the problem—they didn't have enough time together before I came along."

"Even if that's true—which I doubt—there must have been more to the split than that, surely?"

"There was. Although she learned to speak Italian fluently, my mother still felt isolated. She tried so hard to fit in, but it was a lot to ask of anyone, even with the love they had for each other. She went from living a very comfortable, very middle-class life in a British suburb, to trying to raise a family and make her marriage succeed on her husband's family home in rural Sicily. She did it, too, for over ten years... until she couldn't."

And he was so proud of her for doing it—Sasha could hear the love and admiration and respect in the words, and her heart broke for him. "Did you ever go back to Sicily?"

"Every year. My mother sent me back for the summer holidays. She wanted to give me a chance to get to know... the other half of me, I guess. I went back every year until I was sixteen. She wanted... she hoped I'd have some sort of relationship with my father. Every year, Dario did his best to convince me my future was with him, but I wouldn't have it. The thing is, Dario never gave up—still hasn't."

Sasha wasn't sure how she knew it, but those last two words were central to what he was telling her... why their relationship was over. She waited, silently willing him to find his way back to her.

"The vineyard's been in my family for generations. Ownership has always passed to the first-born son. I know—a load of macho, sexist bullshit, and I have been trying to get Dario to understand that for years. It hasn't stopped him telling me at every opportunity that it's my birthright, and I owe it to the family to go home, learn the business, and..."

Rocco's chest rose and fell beneath Sasha's hand as if he were struggling to breathe. Whatever he'd been planning to divulge next was clearly causing him even more emotional conflict. Families could totally screw a person up, and when that person was the man she loved, Sasha was ready to go toe-to-toe with the source on his behalf. If she ever ran into Dario Equizi...

"And get married to a nice Sicilian girl, so she can have lots of children and ensure the line continues."

Sasha's heart lurched, at the tension and overpowering unhappiness in Rocco's voice and the implication of his words. The devil of insecurity started whispering in her ear. Even if there was a chance for them, if Rocco wanted those children, time was running out for him to have them with her. She might be able to fight Dario Equizi, but she couldn't fight time. No one could do that.

"The fights really started after my mother died, a week after my seventeenth birthday. The next time Dario called, he didn't pull his punches, and I can't say I blame him—after all, I told him in no uncertain terms he wasn't welcome at the funeral. It was for me to say goodbye to my mother, not for him to ease a guilty conscience. That was how that immature kid… how *I* saw it.

"But he laid into me—I no longer had a reason to stay in the UK, no family there, it made perfect sense for me to go to him and start my real life in Sicily. As if my life before I lost my mother meant nothing. He didn't know that I'd been making plans."

As if he knew he'd have to find a direction for himself when she was gone, which led to another question—how had Claire died? *Patience, Sasha. Patience.*

"That was when you enlisted?"

"As soon as I could, six weeks after the funeral. When she found out she had a particularly aggressive cancer and it was terminal, my mother didn't keep it from me, because she knew I'd need a purpose for… afterwards. We talked a lot. When she couldn't sleep because of the pain, I stayed up with her. She told me more about her side of my family, the generations that had served the country, and I knew that was the direction I needed to take. Training before I signed up was how I coped with losing her."

The missing pieces of Rocco Equizi were falling like raindrops in a cloudburst, filling in the blanks of the man who had captured her heart. Sasha's eyes filled with tears for the boy who'd had to become a man too soon.

The questions finally burst free. "When did you tell Dario you were joining the army? *Did* you tell him?"

"Yes, I told him—the day before I left for basic training. He still didn't get the message—never has."

"Wait—he was still in touch with you while you were serving? How?"

Rocco's short bark of laughter spoke volumes. "You'd think it'd be easy to cut off all communication. I've thought about doing it more times than I can count, but… something holds me back each time."

Because he still cared. In spite of everything, he still cared about his father, because his father had never stopped loving his wife and son, and never stopped wanting his son to be a family again. Rocco's parents had never stopped loving one another—they'd been separated by circumstances beyond their control. Sasha's heart broke for the three of them, all caught up in relationships that had the odds stacked against them.

"Claire never dated anyone else, did she, when she took you back to England?"

"Never. And Dario's never seen himself as anything other than married to her, even though he's been a widower for years."

Another overwhelming wave of sadness washed over Sasha, for the family that had fractured but never fully broken. "I can understand why you came here now, for that extra distance between you and Dario."

"Palermo is less than twelve hundred miles from London, and three hours on a cheap flight. Over here, I'm nearly five thousand miles further away. I needed time to think."

About what? For Sasha, a different kind of alarm bell started to ring. Rocco was working up to something, and her gut was twisting with the fear that, if she did nothing, she was about to lose him forever.

"Sasha? I need to ask you something."

And here it comes. She braced herself for the worst, that he was going to go back to the UK after all and she'd never see him again. That it would be the first step in reconciling with his father and starting a new life in Sicily, and the end of her pipedream that they could build a life together here. She would get through this without begging him to reconsider… to stay. No one would ever be able to accuse her of applying emotional blackmail. "Sure. What is it?"

"I came straight into this job from my last one, so Nick's

given me a generous amount of extra leave. I know I'm asking a lot, but will you come to Sicily with me? It's time I made my peace with Da—with my father."

There was only one answer she could give him. Resolutely ignoring the myriad questions for which common sense demanded an answer, she propped herself up on her elbow to look the man she loved in the eye as she gave him her decision.

"Rocco, I'll go anywhere with you. Tell me when, and give me thirty minutes to pack."

EPILOGUE

The weather was amazing, and perfect for a glass of Dario Equizi's best vintage. It was a pity it wouldn't be passing over her lips again any time soon. Sasha took another sip of mineral water, before setting the glass down on the low table beside her. She settled more comfortably on the oversized lounge chair and scooped up her book again. With the latest Susan Stoker paperback to shield the lower half of her face and her sunglasses concealing her eyes, she could drink her fill of a shirtless Rocco working at his father's side. Just watching him as he helped to roll casks into the winery's barrel room made her insides writhe with impatient, unfulfilled need.

With Nick Blackmore's ready agreement, Rocco had deferred his vacation for a few weeks, so they could travel when the weather was warmer. They'd made the journey to Sicily almost three weeks ago now, although it hardly seemed possible. Time had flown by—more so, once Rocco and his father had had the heart-to-heart conversation they needed. A couple of nights into their vacation, sensing something important was in the wind, she'd left the two men here on the terrace.

Hours later, Rocco had returned to their room, quiet and subdued to an extent that had her fearing the worst. He'd joined her in bed, taken her in his arms, and she'd waited until he was ready to talk. Eventually, in the small hours of a Sicilian late-spring morning, he'd told her his feud with Dario was finally over. She didn't ask for details—if he wanted to talk about it, he would when he was ready—but from the way he and his father had greeted one another over breakfast the next day, the air was well and truly cleared between them. Since then, on a daily basis, she'd witnessed the two of them gradually growing closer once more.

Watching them together, Sasha was overcome by a profound sense of family, the feeling enhanced by her own parents' welcoming reaction to Rocco when they'd visited her family home before leaving for Europe. Having reconciled with Dario, Rocco seemed so at home here now—so very different from the cool, distant, focused killing machine she'd first met.

He glanced in her direction, his smile becoming even broader as his gaze meshed with hers. The quick wink teased her lips into an answering smile, but it was the play of his muscles as he resumed rolling the latest cask that did crazy stuff to her lady parts.

Baby-making crazy stuff, and she already had proof of how well it had worked, in the three sticks she'd peed on that morning, and which were currently stashed in a dark corner of their bathroom. Rocco had left her alone in their bed to make a start on helping his father, unknowingly giving her plenty of privacy to try one of the pregnancy tests she'd impulsively and sneakily bought from a small pharmacy during a trip to the nearest town. When it gave a positive result, she'd assumed it was a fluke and tried a second. It had taken the third to convince her fully, and in a happy daze, she'd hugged Rocco's pillow and daydreamed about the previous evening, the riotous dinner with all his extended family, and how relaxed and carefree Rocco had been in the company of his cousins and their families, and his beloved and formidable Nonna.

Rocco had looked so natural with Raffaela in his arms. The little girl was the daughter of one of his many cousins, and as he'd danced around the courtyard with her, she'd giggled wildly, and Sasha had fallen in love with him all over again. Laughter had been the last thing on her mind when he'd been inside her later that night. She'd wished for what should have been impossible, little knowing it had already happened.

Just once without protection, and Rocco's little swimmers had scored a direct hit.

Still, at least her job wouldn't get in the way of anything now. Since she no longer had a reason to watch over Linzi, Sasha had resigned before she and Rocco had left for Europe—the handover to her rigorously interviewed and thoroughly vetted replacement had gone well, and Sasha hadn't received any hysterical phone calls from either her or Linzi.

In addition, the loose ends had all been tidied up. As she'd explained to Linzi's godfather, Scott Monroe was now in place as her head of security, and one of the first items on his agenda had been the overhaul of Linzi's security arrangements, with Rocco acting as a consultant until the job was done. Alilah Corday and Leah Bennett were awaiting trial—their permanent replacements were now in post, having gone through the same process as Sasha's successor. The extent of their dishonesty and theft had been staggering, and with the evidence initially uncovered by Nick Blackmore plus what had come to light in the ensuing official investigation, their fate had been inevitable.

As for the Schofields, due process had taken care of them, and they'd never again be a threat to Linzi or her family. Even after all Sasha had witnessed during her career with the agency, a biting chill still swept through every cell in her body when she thought about what could have happened.

A kiss to her forehead broke the hold of the recent past. Rocco was standing before her, a towel draped around his neck as he used one end to wipe the sweat from his face. The concern in his dark eyes preempted his opening question.

"The sun is shining, we're on vacation, and we don't have a care in the world, so I can't help but wonder why you look so preoccupied, *amore*."

She was definitely slipping. There was a time when her expression would have revealed nothing of what was going through her mind. Still, it was an opening, although she wasn't sure the timing was quite right.

If not now, when?

"Hey, soldier! Come and sit beside me." She glanced at the vacant half of the lounge chair.

Rocco lifted his arm and sniffed. "I stink. Let me take a quick shower—"

"I've told you before—I don't care. Come here." She patted the space.

He shrugged but once he'd removed his dusty work boots, he stretched out beside her, legs crossed at the ankles. Sasha rolled onto her side and slipped neatly into her place beneath his raised arm. He was wrong—he smelled delicious, all Sicilian sun and good, honest work. The first time he'd come to her like this, she hadn't expected the overwhelming sense of calm that had wrapped itself around her, but was now as essential to her soul as breathing was to her body.

"So, what's all this about?" Rocco asked.

There was a forced lightness in his words she didn't like. Almost as if he were troubled by something and trying to keep it from her. Sasha laid her palm on his abdomen, hoping it would be enough to reassure him. She was trying to reassure herself too, because she wasn't sure how best to tell him her news.

We lost the coin-toss that time when we couldn't wait for you to suit up, and now I'm pregnant.

I hope you meant it when you told me you like babies, because a few months from now...

His arm tightened around her. "Whatever it is, you can tell me."

"Rocco, I..."

Anguish was tearing her apart. Why couldn't she find the words to tell him?

His chest lifted on a silent sigh. "Are you ready to go home?"

Anyone else would have thought his tone neutral, but to Sasha, it held sadness and maybe even a tinge of regret. She reached up to lay her palm against his cheek, her gaze locked with his. "That's the last thing on my mind. I still feel as if we've only just arrived. It's awesome here. I love your father, and Nonna, and meeting all your family's been amazing. I don't want to go home."

"Yet."

So much resignation and acceptance in one word, but at the same time, it had the effect of clarifying her mental dilemma. "I don't want to go home... period."

Rocco's eyes narrowed beneath a puzzled frown. "Sasha?"

She took a deep breath. In the course of her career, she'd faced some of the worst criminals and terrorists in the world, but baring her soul to the man she loved was suddenly infinitely more terrifying. "I know we haven't really talked about the future, but what we have is something I don't want to let go—ever. I've been hoping you might feel the same way. And if you do, I was wondering how you might feel about moving back here."

Rocco went still, almost frighteningly so. "If we were to stay, what about your parents? We'd be thousands of miles away from them."

His thoughtfulness made her heart ache. She had to lighten his mood somehow. "There are these things called planes, you know. You may recall we came here on one. These days, they even fly in both directions."

Her attempt at humor seemed to work. He gave a gentle laugh. "How about that. You learn something new every day."

"Then here's tomorrow's teachable moment a day early. When Mom was showing you those awful photos of me as a teenager, Dad took me into the garden and told me that, although I didn't need his blessing, if I wanted to spend the rest of my life with you, I had it."

Rocco nodded. "That's good to know."

"You okay with that?" she asked cautiously.

"Why wouldn't I be?"

Sasha took a deep breath. The next part, though, had the potential for disaster. "That's fine, but… it gets worse."

"Worse? Wait—let me guess. It was when your dad was entertaining me with a glass of his favorite bourbon and stories about you skinning your knees, while you were in the kitchen with your mom?"

Sasha clamped her lower lip between her teeth. "First of all, she approves."

"Good. That's always a bonus. And…?"

"And she also said she was looking forward to us producing some beautiful grandbabies for her to show off to her friends when we go visit. She's quite taken with your eyes and hopes you'll pass them on to our kids."

It sounded amusing now, but at the time, it had been an excruciating conversation. Sasha had even tried to point out to her mom that she and Rocco had known each other for mere weeks, only to have her argument dismissed as a minor detail.

Rocco shook again, this time with laughter. "You were right, you can never accuse her of being subtle." Then he frowned and added, "Although… that's not a bad idea. And if your parents fancied a European vacation, we could always fly them over here."

He lapsed into silent contemplation. With each passing second, Sasha felt more and more apprehensive. Why had she brought this up now? They could have had this conversation back in Texas, where she could have sloped off and licked her wounds once he decided she was asking too much. She was so wrapped up in her thoughts, she barely noticed him shift slightly.

Rocco ended his silence suddenly and decisively. "This isn't exactly how I planned to do this. I was thinking dinner at the best restaurant in town, a bottle of champagne, roses, the works, but sometimes, an opportunity presents itself, and when it does, you have to run with it."

He detached himself from both her and the chair. She watched him walk around to her side, and as he drew level with her, he dropped to one knee and brought up the hand he'd been careful to keep out of her sight. He opened the small jeweler's box and presented it to her. The flash and sparkle of a diamond solitaire set in a yellow gold band—elegant and classic—caught her eye, but her focus was on Rocco, gazing at her with those deep, dark eyes she loved so much.

"*Ti amo,* Sasha. *Vuoi sposarmi?* Will you marry me?"

Sasha didn't need a translation. She swung her legs off the lounger, framed his face with her palms, and kissed him, hoping her improving Italian would be up to the job. *"Sì,"* she whispered. *"Mille volte, sì. Ti amo anch'io."*

The ring wasn't a perfect fit but that didn't matter—what it represented was a million times more important. She kissed him over and over, scarcely aware of sliding off the lounger and into his arms. She'd never known happiness could soar like this. Her eyes stung—it was the stupidest thing ever, but she didn't care.

Rocco carried her into the house. They passed Dario on the way, and when Rocco informed his father they were going to get married, the elder Equizi whooped and hollered as if he'd won the lottery, before hurrying away to find Nonna. Sasha blushed and buried her face in her fiancé's neck—embarrassed, but at the same time… not.

"Where are you doing, Rocco?"

"Where do you think? As a newly-engaged man, I'd be failing in my duty if I didn't make love to my fiancée for the rest of the day—and the night."

As Rocco shouldered his way into their room, Sasha threw back her head and laughed for the sheer joy if it. The conversation she wanted to have with her man was no longer such a daunting prospect, and as he lay beside her on the bed, images of building a life with him here, of making a home with him and filling it with children, set her imagination ablaze with a future full of wonderful possibilities.

Much later, when she lay sated and drowsy in his arms, she decided that, rather than wait any longer, this was the perfect time to share the secret she'd cherished since early that morning.

"Rocco, there's something I have to tell you…"

At the end of the Skype call, Nick sat back and sighed. He couldn't say he was particularly surprised by the content of the conversation—apart from the news about Sasha—but it did give him an organizational headache. Still, that was his problem and hardly a showstopper.

"Is everything okay?"

Nick looked up to see his wife sticking her head around the door to his office. He held out his hand. "Come here, sweetheart."

She slipped her hand into his and took his favorite seat for her, on his lap. She was exactly what he needed right now.

"Want to tell me what's happened, hon?" she prompted.

"Conference call." He nuzzled her neck and kissed her cheek. "Rocco Equizi and Ros Northwood. It seems that Rocco's not coming back after his vacation."

Charity frowned. "That doesn't make sense. He left a bunch of his belongings in the cabin."

"He'll be coming back to collect everything at some point, but he's not returning to Spectrum. He's resigning so he can stay in Sicily. It seems he and Sasha are in love—she's pregnant, by the way—he's reconciled with his father, and is now making plans to settle there permanently with her. He's going into the family business with his father, with a view to taking over the whole operation when Dario retires."

"That's wonderful. Didn't you say one of the reasons he came here was because of his relationship with his father?"

"I did, and it is wonderful," Nick agreed. "It's also a prize pain in the ass for us, because we're a man down now, and I had another job lined up for him. Just as well our recruitment drive has been so successful. I can't blame him, though. He's found his peace with Sasha, and I know how priceless that is."

Nick's gaze met his wife's. She was the reason why he understood Rocco's decision so well, because she had gifted him the peace Rocco had found with the love of his life.

"So what are you going to do about it?"

"The only thing I can do—accept his resignation gracefully, wish them both all the best, and assign someone else in his place."

"Then you'd better get to work." Charity gave him a tease of a kiss and slid off his lap. "You have some calls to make."

Nick kept his eyes on his wife's perfect ass as she sashayed out of his office. He was one lucky, lucky man.

And yes, he had some calls to make, to see which member of his now-substantial team was ready for another close protection assignment, but they could wait until the next day. Right now, he had a much more important conversation on his agenda. Their turn to host the barbecue had come around again, and it was time to make the arrangements, starting with the invitations. His call was answered almost immediately.

"Thanks, I'm fine. So's Charity. You and Rayne? Great. Ghost, it's about time you and your team brought your families over here again and we all grabbed some time to catch up. Saturday okay for all of you? Understood. Okay, we'll see you then."

With the caveat that they might be called on to go wheels up with virtually no notice, Ghost had been happy to accept the invitation on behalf of his team. Now all Nick had to do was break the good news to his wife.

Piece of cake.

Nick reached for the top folder on the stack of personnel files. At least Lucas Brand was sticking around. He'd arrived shortly after Rocco, and with a number of successful investigations under his belt, was currently enjoying a well-earned period of leave.

Which gave Nick pause for thought—he hadn't heard from Brand for a few days now. The man might be enjoying his vacation on a tour of different parts of the state, but he'd agreed to check in regularly on grounds of personal safety.

For a man whose definition of "late" was being less than ten minutes early, the interval since Nick had last heard from him was troubling—especially since Brand had talked about something coming up that needed his attention.

Nick cursed himself for not demanding more of an explanation at the time. He picked up his cell again, swiped to Brand's entry, and made the call. The fingers of his free hand drummed a rapid tattoo on his desk while he waited for it to be answered.

And waited. Something was wrong. The former Royal Military Police officer always picked up more promptly than this. Nick was about to hang up when the calling tone stopped, but all he could hear at the other end were indistinct fumbling sounds—not the voice he was expecting. His feelings of disquiet multiplied exponentially.

"Brand, are you... Who am I talking to? Where's Lucas Brand?"

ABOUT THE AUTHOR

When Christie Adams, author of contemporary steamy romance, isn't completely absorbed in the writing process, she's probably thinking about it - either the book she's currently working on, or one of the dozen other stories she'll have percolating away at the back of her mind.

In addition to writing, she also loves investing time in reading a good book, or browsing the internet in search of cute videos of dogs and puppies, a pastime that often helps with writer's block - or so she claims. On those rare occasions when she can tear herself away from the computer, she has a weakness for James Bond movies and romantic comedies - she's watched "Notting Hill" more times than she can remember.

Good chocolate is also one of her passions in life, often accompanied by a glass of her favourite tipple, English sparkling wine. And if she can be persuaded to abandon her writing for a while, she finds that chocolate, wine and a good movie on TV is an excellent way to pass an evening.

www.christieadamsauthor.com
christie@christieadamsauthor.com

facebook.com/christie.adams.author

There are many more books in this fan fiction world than listed here, for an up-to-date list go to www.AcesPress.com

You can also visit our Amazon page at: http://www.amazon.com/author/operationalpha

Special Forces: Operation Alpha World

Christie Adams: Charity's Heart
Denise Agnew: Dangerous to Hold
Shauna Allen: Awakening Aubrey
Brynne Asher: Blackburn
Linzi Baxter: Unlocking Dreams
Jennifer Becker: Hiding Catherine
Alice Bello: Shadowing Milly
Heather Blair: Rescue Me
Anna Blakely: Rescuing Gracelynn
Julia Bright: Saving Lorelei
Cara Carnes: Protecting Mari
Kendra Mei Chailyn: Beast
Melissa Kay Clarke: Rescuing Annabeth
Samantha A. Cole: Handling Haven
Sue Coletta: Hacked
Melissa Combs: Gallant
Lorelei Confer: Protecting Sara
Anne Conley: Redemption for Misty
KaLyn Cooper: Rescuing Melina
Janie Crouch: Storm
Liz Crowe: Marking Mariah
Sarah Curtis: Securing the Odds
Jordan Dane: Redemption for Avery
Tarina Deaton: Found in the Lost
Aspen Drake, Intense
KL Donn: Unraveling Love

Riley Edwards: Protecting Olivia
PJ Fiala: Defending Sophie
Nicole Flockton: Protecting Maria
Alexa Gregory: Backdraft
Michele Gwynn: Rescuing Emma
Casey Hagen: Shielding Nebraska
Desiree Holt: Protecting Maddie
Kathy Ivan: Saving Sarah
Kris Jacen, Be With Me
Jesse Jacobson: Protecting Honor
Silver James: Rescue Moon
Becca Jameson: Saving Sofia
Kate Kinsley: Protecting Ava
Rayne Lewis: Justice for Mary
Heather Long: Securing Arizona
Gennita Low: No Protection
Kirsten Lynn: Joining Forces for Jesse
Margaret Madigan: Bang for the Buck
Trish McCallan: Hero Under Fire
Kimberly McGath: The Predecessor
Rachel McNeely: The SEAL's Surprise Baby
KD Michaels: Saving Laura
Lynn Michaels: Rescuing Kyle
Olivia Michaels: Protecting Harper
Wren Michaels: The Fox & The Hound
Annie Miller: Securing Willow
Kat Mizera: Protecting Bobbi
Keira Montclair, Wolf and the Wild Scots
Mary B Moore: Force Protection
LeTeisha Newton: Protecting Butterfly
Angela Nicole: Protecting the Donna
MJ Nightingale: Protecting Beauty
Sarah O'Rourke: Saving Liberty
Victoria Paige: Reclaiming Izabel

Anne L. Parks: Mason
Debra Parmley: Protecting Pippa
Lainey Reese: Protecting New York
KeKe Renée: Protecting Bria
TL Reeve and Michele Ryan: Extracting Mateo
Elena M. Reyes: Keeping Ava
Deanna L. Rowley: Saving Veronica
Angela Rush: Charlotte
Rose Smith: Saving Satin
Jenika Snow: Protecting Lily
Lynne St. James: SEAL's Spitfire
Dee Stewart: Conner
Harley Stone: Rescuing Mercy
Sarah Stone: Shielding Grace
Jen Talty: Burning Desire
Reina Torres, Rescuing Hi'ilani
Savvi V: Loving Lex
Megan Vernon: Protecting Us
LJ Vickery: Circus Comes to Town
Rachel Young: Because of Marissa
R. C. Wynne: Shadows Renewed

Delta Team Three Series

Lori Ryan: Nori's Delta
Becca Jameson: Destiny's Delta
Lynne St James, Gwen's Delta
Elle James: Ivy's Delta
Riley Edwards: Hope's Delta

Police and Fire: Operation Alpha World

Freya Barker: Burning for Autumn
B.P. Beth: Scott
Jane Blythe: Salvaging Marigold
Julia Bright, Justice for Amber

Anna Brooks, Guarding Georgia
KaLyn Cooper: Justice for Gwen
Aspen Drake: Sheltering Emma
Emily Gray: Shelter for Allegra
Alexa Gregory: Backdraft
Deanndra Hall: Shelter for Sharla
Barb Han: Kace
EM Hayes: Gambling for Ashleigh
India Kells: Shadow Killer
CM Steele: Guarding Hope
Reina Torres: Justice for Sloane
Aubree Valentine, Justice for Danielle
Maddie Wade: Finding English
Stacey Wilk: Stage Fright
Laine Vess: Justice for Lauren

Tarpley VFD Series

Silver James, Fighting for Elena
Deanndra Hall, Fighting for Carly
Haven Rose, Fighting for Calliope
MJ Nightingale, Fighting for Jemma
TL Reeve, Fighting for Brittney
Nicole Flockton, Fighting for Nadia

As you know, this book included at least one character from Susan Stoker's books. To check out more, see below.

SEAL Team Hawaii Series

Finding Elodie
Finding Lexie (Aug 2021)
Finding Kenna (Oct 2021)
Finding Monica (TBA)
Finding Carly (TBA)
Finding Ashlyn (TBA)
Finding Jodelle (TBA)

Eagle Point Search & Rescue

Searching for Lilly (Mar 2022)
Searching for Bristol (Jun 2022)
Searching for Elsie (Nov 2022)
Searching for Caryn (TBA)
Searching for Finley (TBA)
Searching for Heather (TBA)
Searching for Khloe (TBA)

Delta Team Two Series

Shielding Gillian
Shielding Kinley
Shielding Aspen
Shielding Jayme (novella)
Shielding Riley
Shielding Devyn
Shielding Ember (Sept 2021)
Shielding Sierra (Jan 2022)

SEAL of Protection: Legacy Series

Securing Caite (FREE!)

Securing Brenae (novella)
Securing Sidney
Securing Piper
Securing Zoey
Securing Avery
Securing Kalee
Securing Jane

Delta Force Heroes Series

Rescuing Rayne (FREE!)
Rescuing Aimee (novella)
Rescuing Emily
Rescuing Harley
Marrying Emily (novella)
Rescuing Kassie
Rescuing Bryn
Rescuing Casey
Rescuing Sadie (novella)
Rescuing Wendy
Rescuing Mary
Rescuing Macie (novella)
Rescuing Annie (Feb 2022)

Badge of Honor: Texas Heroes Series

Justice for Mackenzie (FREE!)
Justice for Mickie
Justice for Corrie
Justice for Laine (novella)
Shelter for Elizabeth
Justice for Boone
Shelter for Adeline
Shelter for Sophie
Justice for Erin
Justice for Milena

Shelter for Blythe
Justice for Hope
Shelter for Quinn
Shelter for Koren
Shelter for Penelope

SEAL of Protection Series
Protecting Caroline (FREE!)
Protecting Alabama
Protecting Fiona
Marrying Caroline (novella)
Protecting Summer
Protecting Cheyenne
Protecting Jessyka
Protecting Julie (novella)
Protecting Melody
Protecting the Future
Protecting Kiera (novella)
Protecting Alabama's Kids (novella)
Protecting Dakota

New York Times, USA Today and *Wall Street Journal* Bestselling Author Susan Stoker has a heart as big as the state of Tennessee where she lives, but this all American girl has also spent the last fourteen years living in Missouri, California, Colorado, Indiana, and Texas. She's married to a retired Army man who now gets to follow *her* around the country.

www.stokeraces.com
www.AcesPress.com
susan@stokeraces.com

Made in the USA
Monee, IL
03 January 2024